Murder in the House of Usher

Craig padded down the hall in his bare feet, grumbling all the way, and we followed.

Mike Holberg was precisely where I had left him. The flame in the hearth burned low.

Craig hit the light switch and snorted. "Very funny, Mike. I get it. Payback for my little joke."

"Uh, Craig." Seeing Mike in this light, along with the way he hadn't moved at all at the sound of our coming or the light blinking on, made me look at him more closely.

The handle of the knife looked familiar. It matched the carving knife that had been used with the roast beef. I recalled it lying on the silver platter on the table. This was the very same knife, or one from a matching set.

I was beginning to think this was not a fake rubber knife handle that Mike Holberg had glued to his chest.

"What is it, Amy?" Kim pressed up against my back.

Mike's shirt was loosened, and he was in stockinged feet. His shoes were upside down at the edge of the love seat.

Craig stepped to the love seat. I intercepted him. "Mike?" I placed my hand on the side of his neck. "His skin feels cool."

Craig shoved me aside. "He's not sick, is he?"

"I wish he was." I felt the other side of Mike's neck and glanced nervously at his chest. "He's dead, Craig..."

Books by J.R. Ripley

DIE, DIE BIRDIE

TOWHEE GET YOUR GUN

THE WOODPECKER ALWAYS PECKS TWICE

TO KILL A HUMMINGBIRD

CHICKADEE CHCKADEE BANG BANG

HOW THE FINCH STOLE CHRISTMAS

FOWL OF THE HOUSE OF USHER

Published by Kensington Publishing Corporation

Fowl of the House of Usher

J.R. Ripley

LYRICAL UNDERGROUND
Kensington Publishing Corp.
www.kensingtonbooks.com

To the extent that the image or images on the cover of this book depict a person or persons, such person or persons are merely models, and are not intended to portray any character or characters featured in the book.

LYRICAL UNDERGROUND BOOKS are published by

Kensington Publishing Corp.
119 West 40th Street
New York, NY 10018

All Kensington titles, imprints, and distributed lines are available at special quantity discounts for bulk purchases for sales promotion, premiums, fund-raising, educational, or institutional use.

Special book excerpts or customized printings can also be created to fit specific needs. For details, write or phone the office of the Kensington Sales Manager: Kensington Publishing Corp., 119 West 40th Street, New York, NY 10018. Attn. Sales Department. Phone: 1-800-221-2647.

First Electronic Edition: May 2018
eISBN-13: 978-1-5161-0618-9
eISBN-10: 1-5161-0618-0

First Print Edition: May 2018
ISBN-13: 978-1-5161-0619-6
ISBN-10: 1-5161-0619-9

Printed in the United States of America

1

It all started innocently enough. Life is like that, at least mine is. I was rearranging boxes of merchandise in my storeroom to make space for an expected shipment later in the day, when I saw it.

There was a dead body in the middle of the floor.

A rat.

I yelped and dropped a case of squirrel-proof birdhouses on my feet—squirrel-proof because the clever feeders contained a mechanism that effectively shut the seed ports. That didn't stop the hungry squirrels from scooping up every morsel the birds dropped. And the birds seemed to drop as many seeds as they consumed.

My yelp turned to a curse that would have caused my mother to blush had she been present. Fortunately, she wasn't. Because she probably would have laughed, too.

I repeat: A RAT.

No, not an old boyfriend, ex-lover, or cheating husband. A real rat. Cash Calderon, he's my contractor, had warned me that once he starting ripping open walls—we were in the middle of some extensive renovations—we could expect to see some critters who were being driven from their residences deep within the nooks and crannies of my three-story Queen Anne Victorian–era house.

Those critters had, thus far, included rats, gray squirrels, a raccoon and two snakes.

Plus, the brown rats. I had a feeling some of those rats were direct descendants of the house's Founding Rat Fathers.

And I was alone in the store with the beastie.

Not a pleasant thing, alive or dead.

With the number of creatures popping out of the woodwork, I could have opened a pet shop rather than a store selling bird food, birdhouses, birding gear—everything for the bird lover.

In addition, a small section of the store was devoted to beekeeping. Depending on the season, we also carried a selection of plants specific to supporting local bird and bee populations.

I moved the fallen box out of my way and limped toward the ripe rodent remains.

This rat didn't look homeless. And it didn't look like it had succumbed to old age. This rat looked like it had been—I wrinkled my nose and bent down for a closer look—gnawed on.

"Esther," I muttered.

Esther Pilaster—or Esther the Pester, as I sometimes called her when she was out of sight but still in the forefront of my mind whenever she did something particularly irksome—had a cat.

She denied it, but I was sure of it. Each time I broached the subject of her hiding a cat, she stalwartly repudiated my claim. That did nothing to lessen my conviction that she did.

Now the evidence was right here in front of my eyes.

Maybe it was circumstantial, but under the circumstances, that was good enough for me.

"Let me see you get out of this, Pester," I grumbled to no one but the walls, and the walls had long ago stopped listening to me. If they had been listening, they would have done a better job of keeping out the rats.

And the cold.

Esther lived on the second floor. When I'd bought the building that would become my own home and the home to my planned business, Esther had been a tenant. One of the owner's conditions of the sale to me was that Esther's lease would be honored. I now had a second renter, Paul Anderson, also on the second floor. Mom and I lived on the third.

The rats had no floor preference. They apparently lived everywhere.

I retreated to the hall closet for the broom and dustpan. I'd scoop up the dead critter and give it the best burial I could, considering how frozen the ground was outside. I snatched my charcoal down jacket off the nail by the rear door and bundled up, popping a knit cap over my head and pulling gloves onto my hands.

It was winter. In western North Carolina, that meant temperatures dipped and we got our share of snow and ice. Nothing like the Northerners got, sure, but that was their fault for choosing to live in such climes.

I set the little dead guy down outside and went to the toolshed against the back of the building. I pulled out a garden shovel that probably hadn't been expecting to see duty again until nearer to spring.

I spied around for a nice spot to bury the rat and settled on a space near the holly bushes along the back fence that separated the shops on Lakeshore Drive from the single-family homes behind us.

The hard ground gave way slowly. Fortunately, rats don't take up much space. I laid the little guy inside a shallow hole and covered him up.

I returned the shovel to the shed and hurried back to the relatively warm interior of Birds & Bees. I removed my outerwear and walked to the front of the empty store. The original fireplace in what had been the house's living room had long ago given up the ghost. The chimney stack had been sealed shut with cement.

The simple stone fireplace had a narrow wood mantel and slate hearth. We now used the fireplace as a display space. Currently, that display was winter-themed and featured roost boxes, suet, and a couple of heated birdbaths.

Happily, somebody along the way had added a woodstove at the rear of the first floor, in the space that now held a small kitchenette and seating for customers to relax, enjoy a drink and a snack, and read from our small library of birding books and magazines.

As I approached the sales counter, Mrs. Gruber came in waving a photo of an owl. Her nose glowed red from the cold. As gelid as the tip of mine felt, it was probably glowing, too.

"Look!" Mrs. Gruber flapped the letter-sized paper in front of my face. "I shot a photograph of a barn owl in my backyard."

She set the picture on the counter and turned it around to face me. Mrs. Gruber was a mature woman and an enthusiastic backyard bird-watcher. She wore a knee-length, multicolored houndstooth wool coat, red gloves, and a red hat that covered the tops of her ears.

"It's a great shot," I replied. "But I'm afraid it's not a barn owl." I handed her back the photo of the mottled brown and white bird.

"It's not?" Mrs. Gruber's face fell.

"No. This is a *barred* owl." The medium-sized owl was perched on a branch up against the trunk of an oak. Its eyes were closed. "The barn owl is much more ghostly in appearance and has a heart-shaped face. Your owl has a rounded head. Did you hear it speak?"

Mrs. Gruber shook her head. "I believe it was sleeping. It never moved the whole time I watched." She studied the picture more closely. "Is it a male or a female?"

"I can't be sure. There isn't much difference in plumage or coloration between males and females of the species. If you see two of them together and one appears larger than the other, it's likely that the larger bird is the female."

"I'll keep that in mind. We get a lot of birds in our yard. We back up to a nature preserve."

"Lucky you." I lived in the middle of town. With my business also being my home, and that business relying on the presence of people, I needed to be someplace that the people frequented, not necessarily the birds. But if it hadn't been for the need to be where the action was, albeit small-town action in a place the size of Ruby Lake, North Carolina, I'd have chosen something more rural for myself, as well.

"If you see the bird again, they have a distinctive call. People say it sounds like 'Who cooks for you? Who cooks for you?'"

Mrs. Gruber laughed. "I do all the cooking in my house. The mister can barely toast bread."

I grinned. "I'm single, and nobody cooks for me, either." That wasn't strictly true. Mom lived with me and spoiled me with her home cooking.

Mrs. Gruber held the photograph up in front of her nose. "Now that you mention it, Amy, on occasion I've heard a sound like 'Who cooks for you' coming from the woods." She matched her eyes with mine. "During the daytime, however."

"That's not unheard of," I said. "Put the picture up on the bird board. The others will love to see it."

Mrs. Gruber's bird photo wasn't exactly headline material, but that particular bulletin board was for posting bird photos. I should know—I'd hung it there myself on the thick support beam in the center of the store. The board was an excellent way for myself, my staff, and our customers to let others know what birds they were seeing and when.

"I will."

"Good." I handed her a felt-tipped pen. "Don't forget to write down the location, date, and time of day of the sighting."

Mrs. Gruber filled in the data and tacked her photo proudly to the bulletin board.

"If I had a trained barn owl like that one in the store at night, I wouldn't have to worry about the rats," I quipped.

Mrs. Gruber pulled her purse closer to her chest as her eyes darted anxiously across the floor. "You have rats?"

"Huh? No, I was only joking," I assured her.

I wasn't sure Mrs. Gruber quite believed me, because she did the remainder of her shopping very quickly and beat a hasty retreat.

Esther came down to work at noon and would be staying until closing. She's a small, narrow-shouldered woman, with long, uneven teeth, a hawkish nose, sagging eyelids, and silver hair habitually worn in a sharp four-inch-long ponytail. Wispy white eyebrows sit atop her gray-blue eyes.

Esther had never married, at least so I thought. For a woman who didn't like to keep her opinions to herself, the septuagenarian was the keeper of a lot of secrets, including the cat.

Esther not only worked for me and rented from me, she was also now a partner in Birds & Bees. Truth be told, it was her recent investment in the business that was allowing us to move forward with the long-needed and heretofore unaffordable repairs to the property.

Esther once thought I was a killer. I once thought she was a pain in the patooty. In the months we had gotten to know one another, though, we had gotten past those initial first impressions.

Well, mostly.

Mom was out and I didn't feel like eating alone upstairs. It would only mean peanut butter and jelly or baloney sandwiches with a side of baby carrots and cheese puffs anyway. I'd been there, done that, a hundred times or more already since returning home to Ruby Lake.

"I'll be back in an hour or so, Esther." I was running next door for lunch at Brewer's Biergarten. "Can I bring you back anything?"

"No, thanks. I'll take my lunch upstairs when Kim gets here."

"Okay, see you soon." I grabbed my wool coat from the coatrack by the front door and wrapped a cashmere scarf around my neck.

This time of year, I kept a coat at both the front and the rear of the store. Not only did it facilitate going in and out more quickly, but I often helped customers to their vehicles with some of the heavier items, like bulk birdseed. "Please let Kim know I'll be back in an hour or so."

"You got it." Esther popped open the register and began counting the cash in the till. She was a stickler for knowing how much was in the register when she started each day.

The "Kim" in question was Kimberly Christy. Kim's a long-legged, blue-eyed blonde. My shoulder-length hair was the color of chestnuts roasting. My eyes were blue, but not as blue as Kim's. I had all the same parts that she had, but somehow those parts just seemed to look better on her.

While we rarely shared our wardrobes, we shared the same age: thirty-four.

Kim and I had grown up together. She was my best friend and proverbial partner in crime. She was a literal partner in Birds & Bees, too. She had started out as a small investor, helping me out when the store was nothing but a crazy idea in my head. Recently, she had quit her real estate gig and asked to work full-time with me at the store.

How could I say no?

How the store was going to manage the additional payroll, I, as yet, had no clear idea.

I opened the door and closed it quickly behind me. The air was cold and the wind was hard. My house is on Lake Shore Drive, one of Ruby Lake's main thoroughfares. Many of the town's businesses, like mine, occupied the road, especially those catering to tourists, because Lake Shore Drive was the road on which most of those tourists drove in and out of town.

Across the street to my left was our namesake, Ruby Lake, with a lovely park and marina. Directly across the street was the quaint Ruby's Diner.

I slogged my way down the brick path to the sidewalk, avoiding the icy patches that refused to disappear. I'd asked Cousin Riley over and over again to do something about them, but he hadn't gotten around to the job yet.

From Birds & Bees, it was only a matter of steps to the entrance of Brewer's. Brewer's used to be a garden supply store. Now it was a brewpub, and a thriving one at that. The space between Birds & Bees and the main portion of Brewer's Biergarten had been transformed from an outdoor plant sales area to an outdoor dining room.

I couldn't help but be a little jealous. I had opened Birds & Bees long before construction of Brewer's Biergarten had begun, but judging by the often-filled-to-capacity seating and the lines out the door most Friday and Saturday nights, their business was booming.

It seemed there was more money in beer than in birds. No matter. I loved my birds, and if I wanted a beer, I could buy one.

I approached the front door of the brewpub. A waiter at the door pushed it open and welcomed me. "Hi, Amy. Table for one?"

The cozy outdoor seating area was open except during the worst weather. In the winter, like now, large propane heaters generated plenty of warmth. Nonetheless, I opted to sit indoors. "Hello, Mitchell. Inside, please."

Mitchell took a quick look and escorted me to a small two-top in the middle of the dining room. There were plenty of seats at the bar, but I usually avoided sitting there alone. I had learned that being a woman alone at a bar was a man magnet.

I wasn't looking to attract any.

I had one. His name was Derek Harlan. My mother liked to tease me that I had come home to Ruby Lake and I found my own jewel.

She wasn't wrong.

We'd had a slight hiccup in our relationship before the holidays. I thought he had been keeping things from me. The truth was, he had only been doing his job. He'd had a client whom I'd thought might be involved in a murder. When I found out later that this person had been Derek's client and was innocent of any crime, I felt Derek should have told me so up front.

Of course, I was wrong.

And I might have gotten mad. And I might have stormed off. But I prefer to rewrite history and remember it as nothing more than a bump in the road, the growing pains of any relationship.

I had to get used to the fact that Derek, as an attorney, was sometimes privy to information that wasn't available for public consumption—even if that public was me and even if I really, really wanted the dirt.

I took a look at the lunch menu and ordered the Portobello melt and a diet lime soda. Behind me, a couple of men were throwing darts.

Halfway through my melt, a manicured hand gripped my shoulder from behind and squeezed. "Hey, hey, hey. Look who's here!"

I turned and spat out a mouthful of mushroom, lettuce, and brioche bun. "Craig?"

"Hi, Amy."

I jumped to my feet and took a step back to be sure I wasn't hallucinating. "Craig, what are you doing here?"

In front of me stood Public Enemy Number One. Well, Amy Simms's Enemy Number One—with a bullet.

Craig Bigelow was my ex-boyfriend. He and his cheating ways had played a big part in my decision to return to Ruby Lake.

It was bad enough that he and his partner, Paul Anderson, had opened Brewer's Biergarten in my hometown, but they did it right next door to me. And now Craig was standing right in front of me.

As was his custom, he was wearing black designer jeans and a black T-shirt, neatly tucked of course, and a black leather belt with a silver buckle. Up close, I caught a whiff of his cologne: Eau de Lying Scum.

A member of the biergarten's cleanup crew scooted between the two of us with a dustpan and a broom and swept up my mess.

"Sorry," I muttered to the industrious young man.

"Paul's on vacation. Didn't he tell you?" Craig was smirking in a major way. He took a step in my direction as if threatening me with a one-armed hug. His right hand held a foaming beer mug.

I pulled back further, almost getting clipped in the cheek by a passing dart that flew by like a missile or some exotic insect far from its Amazon rainforest home.

"Sorry, lady!" its thrower called.

"Yes, he told me." I planted my hands on my hips. I was even watching his black and tan hound dog, Princess, for him while he was away. "He also told me that he had somebody coming in to manage the business while he was gone."

"Gone" being a three-week trip to the Bahamas. And no, I wasn't jealous, I merely hated him for his good fortune.

"That's me." Craig thumped his chest with his thumb.

"Whatever." There was nothing I could do about it anyway. Except kill Paul for not warning me about Craig's arrival. The big chicken.

"Don't think for a minute that you are going to be staying in Paul's apartment, though." Like, I said, Paul rented an apartment on the second floor of my house. A few months back, I'd allowed Craig to share that space for a day or two, against my better judgment.

I wasn't about to repeat the mistake.

"Don't think for a minute that I intend to," Craig replied. "We rented a house."

"We?" I furrowed my brow.

"Hi!" A perky woman with perky breasts appeared from the doorway leading to the restrooms and oozed up alongside my ex-boyfriend. Dark jeans clung to perfect legs, and a white cashmere sweater lay across her chest like snow atop the peaks of the Alps.

I began to frown. It was the bimbo blonde, the latest long-legged, curvy cutie with whom Craig had cheated on me last before I caught him and dumped him.

Okay, so she was a redhead and had a master's degree in psychology. She was still a bimbo in my book. I mean, anybody with a master's in psychology ought to know better than to get involved with a lying, two-timing, two-faced, cheating piece of scum like Craig "The Gigolo" Bigelow.

Her name was Candy something.

Craig snaked his arm around her impossibly narrow waist. "You remember Cindy."

Cindy, Candy, the whole scene was as sickeningly sweet as the girl ten years younger than Craig and attached to him now at the hip.

"Hello, Cindy." I shook the hand she offered. It was younger, healthier, and better manicured than my own. While her nails were shiny and pink, mine had birdseed crud under them from rooting around in the seed bins earlier and the nails themselves looked like my manicure had been performed by a one-eyed grackle. "I hear you'll be staying in Ruby Lake a while."

Candy, or Cindy, bobbed her head excitedly. I noticed that the middle two fingers of each of her hands held shiny rings. If I wasn't mistaken, that one on the left with the big diamond was an engagement ring. Was Craig getting married?

"Isn't it great?" Cindy rubbed up against Craig. What was she, part cat?

Cindy's layered locks were parted down the middle. Her eyes were blue with a hint of silver-gray. Her nose was so pert that I'm sure a lesser ex-girlfriend than I would have wanted to take a poke at it.

Unlike Craig, her skin was fair; where he was of the tall, dark and, yes I admit it, handsome variety. Craig has deep brown hair, cut short and he has dimples, too, most evident when he smiles, which he likes to do. A lot.

"We rented a house and everything," Cindy explained. "It's up in the mountains and looks straight down on the town."

"Wow." I was impressed that Craig was willing to spend a few bucks for one of the higher-end vacation rentals. A house with a view like that could not have come cheap.

Then again, this was winter. It could have come dirt cheap. "Which house is it?"

"It's called the Usher House." Craig squeezed his main squeeze's hand.

I began to smile. "The *Usher* House?"

"That's right, Amy." Cindy drew a lock of long red hair across her face. "You should come visit sometime. Hey!" Her face brightened, and I squinted in the glare of all those big white teeth. "You could be our first dinner guest!" She turned to Craig. "Right, honey bear?"

"Sure." Craig cracked a smile. "We'd love to have you. Bring Kim, too."

"I'm sure she'd love that," I said with a soupçon of sarcasm. I'd caught him ogling Kim on more than one occasion the last time he'd slithered into town.

"Who is Kim?" Cindy asked.

"Amy's best friend," explained Craig. "In fact, bring that other guy, too. What was his name?" He snapped his fingers thrice. "Dirk?"

"His name is *Derek*, Craig. Derek Harlan."

"Right, him." He planted a kiss on Cindy's cheek. "I'll call you and we'll set something up."

"I'll be looking forward to it," I said with a pasted-on grin. "Honey bear."

Not.

"My lunch hour's up." It really wasn't, but my appetite was shot and I'd spit half my lunch on the floor. "I need to head next door."

Craig turned to Cindy. "Amy's got a little bird store."

"Ooh," Cindy exclaimed. "I love birds."

"That would explain your attraction to birdbrains," I replied.

"Excuse me?" Cindy blinked.

Craig squeezed Cindy's hand. "It was a joke, honey."

"Oh." Cindy grinned.

I threw some money on the table and left.

The joke was on Craig. Two jokes, actually. Because, number one, I was never in this lifetime going to accept that offer. And, number two, everybody in town knew that the Usher House was haunted.

2

I didn't know if it was the cold weather smacking me in the face or the cold reality of what I'd seen at lunch, but by the time I'd walked back to Birds & Bees, I was chilled to the bone.

"Where have you been?" Kim gaped at me from behind the counter as she handed Floyd a brown Birds & Bees–branded tote.

"Having lunch next door." I waved hello to Floyd. "Didn't Esther tell you?"

"You look more like you were out walking in a tundra," replied Kim, planting her hands on the counter and eyeballing me. "Doesn't she, Floyd?"

"You do look a mite frigid, Amy. You might want to go sit by the woodstove." Floyd Withers was dressed in rumpled corduroys and a brown coat over a thick gray sweater. Floyd was a retired banker with gray, thinning hair. His hair and mustache appeared freshly trimmed.

"Not a bad idea." I pulled off my gloves one finger at a time and rehung my jacket on the coat tree.

I looked around the shop. "Where is Esther, anyway?" I had a feeling that she and Floyd were sweet on one another, although, so far, they seemed to both be in denial. Floyd's wife had passed away a little over a year ago.

"She disappeared a few minutes ago." Kim walked with Floyd to the door.

"Thanks again, ladies. Tell Esther I said hello, won't you?"

We promised we would.

"Watch the ice!" I cautioned. When Cousin Riley showed up, I was going to insist that he clear the sidewalk first thing, because the last thing I needed was a customer slipping and breaking an arm or leg—or worse, a neck—on the property.

Fortunately, the day passed without any broken backs or bruised behinds. I spent most of it trying to forget about you know who next door.

* * * *

That night, Mom and I were washing the dinner dishes when there was a knock on our apartment door.

"Who could that be?" Mom turned toward the door.

I dried my hands on the dish towel and set it on the counter. "I'll get it. It's probably Esther." With Birds & Bees locked up for the night, the only people who could get in were those with a key.

Princess lifted her head from her paws. She had been snoozing on the dog bed under the front window. She rose, shook herself, and padded to the door with her nose lifted in expectation. I had tried to tell her that her master, Paul, wouldn't be home for weeks, but the fact did not seem to be sinking in.

I slipped the chain from the track on the door and pulled it open. "Craig?"

"Hi, Amy." My ex-boyfriend stamped his black-booted feet on the doormat. He slapped his hands over his charcoal-colored wool pea coat. "Cold out there. Mind if I come in?" He gave Princess a pat. "Hi there, girl. How've you been?"

Princess threw her front paws against Craig's thighs and licked his waiting hand. It appeared that Craig had one ally in the House of Simms.

"Who's at the door, dear?" Mom called.

"It's only a cockroach, Mom. Not to worry. I'll take care of it. Where's that can of bug spray?"

"Ha, ha. Very funny, Amy." Craig squeezed past me. "Hi, Barbara. Good seeing you again." He waved to my mother, then removed his leather gloves and unwrapped the gray cashmere scarf from around his neck.

Craig handed his things to me and I had no choice but to take them. I set them on the table near the door so he wouldn't have to waste time fetching them on his way out.

"Hello, Craig." My mother shot a puzzled look my way. "Amy didn't mention that you were in town."

"I was trying to forget it." My eyes smoldered in Craig's direction.

Mom pulled at the tie strings of her saffron-colored apron, then gave Craig a cordial hug. "How long are you staying?"

"I'm covering for Paul while he's on vacation. I have to say, Ruby Lake is a great little town. I can't thank you enough for recommending it, Amy."

"I didn't exactly recommend it." Craig and I had dated for six years, starting in college and continuing a couple of years past graduation.

In those years, we had visited my hometown together a few times. Plus, to be sure, I had mentioned Ruby Lake fondly over those years to him. That was why, much to my chagrin, when he and one of his business partners, Paul Anderson, had decided to start up a brewpub they'd chosen Ruby Lake.

Lucky Craig.

Not-so-lucky me.

"Well, whatever the case," my mother said, "I hope you enjoy your visit. Will you be staying in Paul's apartment?"

"No," I answered quickly. "Craig is renting the Usher House."

Mom's face twitched. "The Usher House? You don't say..."

"I do say." My eyes danced with delight.

"That's right. In fact," he said, throwing himself down into my dead father's favorite chair without waiting for an invitation, "that's why I'm here."

Princess curled up at his feet.

"What is it?" I said, taking a seat at the end of the sofa. "Don't tell me you are having trouble with ghosts over there already?"

Craig frowned and waved a hand at me. "Will you stop with the ghosts, Amy? The joke is getting stale."

"Would anybody care for some tea, or perhaps something stronger?" Mom hung her apron over the oven door handle.

Craig swiveled his head. "Have you got any Scotch?"

"I believe we do." Mom went for the bottle atop the refrigerator. "Will Tennessee whiskey do?"

"In a pinch," Craig answered.

"What about you, dear?"

I readily agreed. Craig went better with alcohol than without these days.

Mom brought us our drinks along with a cup of hot chamomile-lemon tea for herself. She sat down on the middle of the sofa and balanced the cup and saucer on her lap. "Tell us what's on your mind, Craig."

Craig took a small sip of whiskey and ran his tongue across his lips. "It's like this. That whole scene in the biergarten today has really got Cindy worked up."

"Cindy?" Mom interrupted.

"The girlfriend," I explained, taking no small sip of my own whiskey. "Why is she worked up, Craig?" I started to smile. "Don't tell me she's jealous of me? The ex-girlfriend?"

Craig snorted. "Nah. It's nothing like that."

I felt my face heat and wished I could sink under a sofa cushion. I focused on my tumbler.

"She's so excited about having you over for dinner that she wants to have a party tomorrow night." He shifted in the chair. "You're invited, too, Barbara."

"Tomorrow?" I gulped and coughed. "Why so soon?"

"You know Cindy. She gets an idea in her head and she can't get it out."

"Actually, I barely know the girl at all." A less kind woman might have said something to the effect that the fact that she had *any* idea in her head made it worth savoring.

Craig emptied his glass. "Then tomorrow you'll get your chance. You, too, Barbara. Plus Kim and Dirk."

"Derek," I corrected.

"Thank you, Craig," Mom replied. "It is a lovely invitation. However, tomorrow is my pinochle club. I couldn't possibly miss it. Amy is free though."

"Mom!"

"That's too bad, Barbara." Craig rose and refilled his glass from the open bottle on the kitchen counter.

I held up my glass for a refill, too, but either he didn't see the gesture or he chose to ignore it. I pushed my tongue to the bottom of my glass trying to reach the last remaining drops of golden nectar.

"Cindy got all excited. You don't want to disappoint her, do you?" Craig wasn't finished badgering me.

"It sounds to me like you're the one who's worried about disappointing the woman. Are you sure there isn't something you want to get off your chest?"

"Very funny. You get funnier with age, you know that?"

I bit my tongue.

Craig paced in front of me. "Come on, Amy," he wheedled. "Do this for me."

"Nope." I stood and stepped past him. I helped myself to the whiskey.

"Did I mention the duck?"

"I don't like duck." I had never developed a taste. Besides, ducks were so cute.

"You'd like this one," Craig said with a mysterious grin.

"I don't think so." I took a drink and then put a stopper in the bottle.

"I think it's sick or something."

I pulled my brows together. "You want to feed us a diseased duck?" First, he wanted me to come to dinner; then he planned to poison me? Was that what this whole dinner invitation was about?

"Of course not. What do you take me for?"

"I have so many answers to that question."

"Now, Amy," my mother said softly. "Craig is a guest."

"Not a welcome one," I said.

My insults seemed to bounce off of Craig—curse his thick skin.

"There are a few ducks at the tarn adjacent to the house. A couple of them look sick."

Craig gave me his puppy dog face. "I was hoping you might be able to take a look at the poor guys…or girls. I can barely tell a rooster from a hen. I don't know much about waterfowl, let alone enough to figure out what sex a duck is."

I found myself curious, which only made me mad at myself. "What kind of ducks?" I had a special fondness for waterfowl. Ruby Lake got its share. When the weather was nice, I often picnicked at the edge of the lake and watched them scooting along the surface and diving for food.

Craig shrugged his shoulder. "I dunno. There is more than one kind of duck, I think. But out of the sick ones, the one is sort of drab but the other is really colorful. But that's the duck that seems especially…I don't know, listless."

"It sounds like a pair, male and female. The male would be the more attractive of the two."

Craig snickered and I glared at him. He set down his glass. "There are a couple of guns up at the house, a rifle and a shotgun. If the birds are on their deathbeds and there's nothing you can do, I suppose I could put them out of their misery." He looked at me from under hooded eyes.

"You'll do no such thing." I slammed my glass on the counter. "You should call a vet. I know a good one right here in town. Buchman's Veterinary Medicine." The Buchmans, father and daughter, had helped me out a time or two in the past with injured animals.

"Can you come and take a look first? A veterinarian is going to charge a small fortune to make a house call."

"I sell bird-related merchandise. I'm no bird health expert, Craig."

"Just come take a look. Then, if you think I should call out the vet, I will." He raised his right hand. "I promise."

"Why not take a look, Amy?" Mom nudged. "I'm sure you have more expertise than you think. You know a lot about birds. And you'll get a nice dinner out of it."

"Right." Craig was beaming. "What harm could it do?"

"What you want, Craig, is free advice. You are too cheap to pay a vet, so you think you can bribe me to drive all the way out there and examine this supposedly ill waterfowl, just for the cost of a free meal."

"Is that a yes?" Craig asked.

I blew out a breath. “Fine.” Derek and Kim were going to kill me for getting them mixed up in a dinner with Craig and Cindy.

But what choice did I have? I couldn’t pass up a chance to help a sickly or injured duck. Assuming there were any waterfowl up at the Usher House. The whole story could have been a ruse to get me up there, but why, I had no idea.

“Great. See you at seven.” Craig handed me his empty tumbler. “Do you know how to find the place? It’s up Jefferson Mountain. If you take Dudley Road to—”

I held up my hand. “Never mind. I’m sure Kim can find it.” Not only had she grown up in Ruby Lake like I had, but she had sold real estate here for many years.

Princess followed Craig to the door. Craig reached for his scarf and gloves.

“By the way, how did you get in here?” I asked as he rewrapped his scarf around his neck and buttoned up his coat. “The house is locked up.”

Craig pulled a small ring of keys from his coat pocket and gave it a jingle. “These. Paul loaned me his keys.”

I grabbed for them, but Craig snatched his hand away.

“Uh-uh,” he said with a smile. “The keys to the biergarten are on this ring.” He stuffed them back inside the pocket and gave it a pat. “I need these.”

I closed the door on his smug face and slid the chain back in place.

“Why did you tell him I was free, Mom? I had this whole going-to-Charlotte-for-elective-surgery-and-spending-the-night-in-recovery story planned out in my head.”

Mom carried her empty teacup and saucer to the sink. I followed her with our glasses. “Because you need to let go of your animosity toward Craig, dear.” She patted me on the shoulder. “Trust me, you’ll sleep better. And besides, you won’t be alone. Kim and Derek will be there, too.”

I set the glasses at the bottom of the sink and squirted liquid soap into them. I grabbed the spigot and watched them fill and foam.

“For the record, I don’t have any animosity toward the jerk. I just prefer having nothing to do with him and keeping him out of my sight.” I dried my damp fingers on the towel.

Mom chuckled and said good night.

Leaving me to wrestle with my demons.

3

"This sucks big-time." Kim angrily flipped through the pages of a fashion magazine.

"I'm sorry." I apologized for the hundredth time. "Like I said, I thought we'd have dates. One of whom would be armed with a thirty-eight."

I had picked Kim up in my minivan and was behind the wheel. Kim played the role of the angry passenger.

"I told you, Dan is working nights this week." Kim recently had been dating Dan Sutton, an officer with the Ruby Lake Police Department. Dan had a license to carry a gun, always an asset when supping with an ex-boyfriend.

Both Dan and Derek had been unable to make it to dinner. Derek couldn't come with us because his daughter, Maeve, was spending a couple of nights with him while her mother was away. Derek's ex-wife was also an Amy.

To make matters worse, Amy the Ex lived in Ruby Lake and had opened up a high-end bridal boutique next door to Harlan & Harlan, the law offices of Derek and his father.

Sometimes I was convinced that life just liked to mess with you because it could.

"Besides," I said, leaving Kim's neighborhood and all thoughts of Amy the Ex behind as I headed toward the mountains, "it won't be so bad."

"In that creepy old house?" Kim gaped. "With that creep?"

I heard a tearing sound. A piece of a magazine page had come loose in Kim's fingers. "Sorry about that." She crumpled it up and tossed the wad behind her seat.

Not that I minded. The back of the minivan wasn't the cleanest place on earth.

"As for the 'creepy,' you'll get no argument from me when it comes to Craig. The guy is a bit creepy. Maybe even spooky, but the house is not haunted."

"You can't really be certain of that." Kim crossed her arms over her chest.

"No." I grinned. "I don't have to be certain." I tapped the tip of her nose. "I just have to get you to believe it."

Kim snorted. "It's not going to happen, so you can stop trying. In fact, you can stop this van and turn us around right now."

"I wish I could." My hands tightened on the wheel. I'd made the unfortunate choice of popping *Carrie the Musical* into the CD player. "A Night You'll Never Forget" was playing now like an ominous premonition.

"I sense a 'but.'"

"But I promised Mom I'd make an effort to be nice. She says I need to let go of my animosity toward Craig."

"Maybe she's right."

I swiveled my head in her direction. "Whose side are you on?"

"Think about it." Kim rolled up the damaged magazine and pushed it under her seat. "Maybe you should be thanking Craig."

"Thanking him? For what?"

"If Craig had not treated you so poorly, you might not have realized what a special guy Derek is now."

"I suppose." There were a lot of things wrong with Kim's logic, but, putting Derek and Craig side by side, it was easy to see their differences.

I turned off the car stereo. "So, what's the story on the Usher House? I heard that some guy had his head chopped off there." Just saying it aloud made me shiver.

Kim snorted. "Sort of." She pulled off her heels and rubbed her feet. "The way I heard it, Stanley Usher built the place around the time of the Great Depression. Usher had been a livestock broker, and he managed to succeed while others were failing. His family was moving down from up north someplace. Chicago, I think.

"Stanley Usher came down first to direct the construction of the house to his exact specifications. It was wintertime when he arrived with his family for the first time. Apparently the car he was driving hit a patch of ice and skidded off the road right at the edge of the property. Stanley Usher went through the windshield. Cars didn't have safety glass like they do now. The sharp glass cut half of his skull off." Kim folded her hands in her lap and stared out at the leaden sky. "His wife was with him. Miraculously, she was unscathed."

I gasped. "There must have been blood everywhere."

"There was." Kim nodded. "Stanley died on the spot. Even if there had been a hospital close by, there was no way his wife, Shirley, could have gotten him there in time."

"Why not?"

"Shirley never learned to drive a car."

I let the awful scene painted by Kim's words sink in for a minute. "What happened after that?"

"The wife and children moved into the house. People say that she went mad and was institutionalized within a year. The children were sent to live with some relatives." Kim leaned forward in her seat and pointed. "That's Dudley Road. Turn left."

I slowed and watched for oncoming traffic. There was no one else on the road, coming or going. "Who owns the house now?" I steered up a twisting road, tight against the edge of a rocky ravine on my right and a wall of granite on my left. The minivan groaned as it ascended the steep slope.

"Some distant relative. They've never lived in the house, according to Mr. Belzer."

Belzer was Kim's former boss in the real estate business. He had his own problems now. "That is, they came down once with the intention of moving in, stayed a couple of days, and then left abruptly. That must have been fifty years ago. Since then, they've been renting the place out when they can."

"I'm surprised they don't sell."

"It was one of our permanent listings, at a rock-bottom price, too. Few buyers have even been willing to look at the house. Those who have made the trip lost interest quickly once they laid eyes on the place and its remote location."

"Craig mentioned that he'd found and arranged the rental online." I could imagine the look on his face when he saw that his bargain was no bargain at all, but rather, a weird house out in the middle of nowhere. "This isn't the country club setting Craig generally goes for."

"Plenty of country"—Kim grinned—"no club."

The Kia's interior had grown cold. I turned up its heater and held my fingers in front of the vent for warmth. Old houses needed lots of maintenance. I owned an old house. I knew. "And the Usher House sits empty otherwise?"

"There have been a number of caretakers over the years."

We rounded a corner, and the road came to an abrupt end at a long, hard-packed track with knee-high stone columns on either side. There was a deep ditch between us and what lay beyond. A simple wooden bridge provided access.

"End of the road." I brought the minivan to a stop and put the gearshift in park, giving the Kia time to breathe and me time to reconsider my folly. I gazed out the driver's side window. It was dark now and the road ahead was unlit. The anemic yellow light from the Kia's headlamps did nothing to improve the scene. A dark forest; a dark road.

Dinner with my ex-boyfriend and his barely legal girlfriend who had an advanced college degree.

"There's still time to turn around," Kim said, reading my thoughts.

"One dinner," I said. "How bad can it be?" I put the car back in drive. "Besides, if there are some sick ducks out here, I want to see if there is something I can do for them."

"You'll be lucky to see them in the dark."

"I brought a flashlight." I pointed my thumb toward the rear of the van. "Craig told me they hang out near the house."

I lifted my foot from the brake pedal, and we slowly moved up the poorly maintained track. The Kia shook and squeaked with each bump. "If you see anything important fall off, give me a shout."

Kim giggled.

A minute later, the trees parted and we came to a tall dark silhouette. Several tall turrets stood out like arrows aiming for the stars. The house was big and clumsy-looking, not elegant at all. Smoke wafted from a stone chimney.

I couldn't help smiling. "Craig must hate this place."

"It's even more hideous than I had remembered." Kim leaned forward in her seat, pressing her nose to the glass.

"Leave it to Craig to rent such an abomination," I quipped. "And don't get so close to the windshield!" Kim's story of Stanley Usher's grisly demise was still fresh in my mind.

I pulled up to the ominous house. The minivan's headlights barely made a dent in the heavy, gloomy atmosphere. A long driveway wrapped around the house. I rumbled to a stop behind a sleek red Porsche Cayman. "That must be Craig's car."

I wasn't surprised by his choice of vehicle. I was also not surprised that it was a hardtop. Craig didn't like convertibles, because driving with the top down messed up his hair.

The guy was part lizard.

I killed the engine and turned off the lights. Two small gas flames flickered behind glass on either side of the house's massive front door. I grabbed my flashlight and tightened the collar of my coat around my neck.

I glanced at the sky. "It looks like snow," I remarked, stepping down to the ground.

Kim moved awkwardly across the uneven driveway. "I think you're right. It feels like it, too."

Walking over to the door, I saw a faint gleam of light to my left, probably the tarn that Craig had told me about. So, at least that much was true.

"I wish we had come earlier." It was the ducks I cared about, not dinner with Craig and Cindy. I hefted the flashlight in my hand, tempted to use it against the door, but I couldn't take a chance of breaking the bulb.

I reached for the heavy iron knocker.

"Look at that thing," exclaimed Kim. "It's hideous."

The face on the doorknocker was bizarre, to say the least: something between a gargoyle's and that of a cherub. "I barely can stand the thought of touching it," she said.

I turned to Kim. "You do it."

"Not on your life." She took a step back. "I didn't want to come here in the first place."

I frowned and placed my thumb and index finger on either side of the *chergoyle*'s chubby cheeks and swung it in and out hard a couple of times against the door.

When it finally creaked open. Craig stood in the entrance, of a dimly lit hallway behind him. He was dressed in dark slacks with cuffs, a white shirt with a wool vest, and a red cravat.

"Who do you think you are, a young Vincent Price?"

Craig ignored my jibe. "Welcome, ladies. You're late."

"We got hung up." I sent Kim a reproving look. Her indecision over what to wear had put us more than an hour behind schedule. If we had arrived earlier, I wouldn't have had to go duck hunting in the dark.

Craig planted a kiss on Kim's cheek and tried to land one on mine, but I dodged out of harm's way. He stepped through the door and peered outside. "Where are your dates?"

"Mine's working," Kim replied.

"And mine is spending time with his daughter."

"Pity." Craig rubbed his hands together. "The other guests will be disappointed."

Kim looked at me, and I passed the look on to Craig along with the question. "What other guests?"

Closing the front door behind us, Craig said, "Let me take your coats."

I removed my black coat and handed it to him. Kim did the same.

He tossed them on a tall wingback chair beside a small table and mirror. "You look lovely, Kim. You too, Amy." He gave me a quick once-over before returning his attention to my best friend. "It's wonderful to see you again, Kim."

"Thanks." Ugly and faded burgundy and gold wallpaper clinging to the walls, which might have been pretty in the house's time, added years to the appearance of the space.

Kim had opted for a black three-quarter-sleeve A-line dress and heels. I had chosen a fitted, army-green long-sleeved hoodie dress and flats. Dinner was supposed to be a casual affair, and I wouldn't have gotten dressed up for Craig even if it was formal. I was there for the waterfowl. I wasn't going to go traipsing down to a lake in high heels.

"*What* other guests, Craig?" I repeated. "You didn't say there would be others joining us for dinner."

Craig extended his hand, and I passed him my flashlight. He set it on a table beside the door.

"Didn't I?" Craig gave me a look clearly meant to imply innocence, but I knew better.

"No, you didn't." I was beginning to seriously regret my decision to come, ducks or no ducks.

"A few friends of Cindy's and mine. They are our houseguests, actually."

"I see." Craig had either lied or failed to include that tidbit of information, but it didn't seem to matter much. Besides, Kim and I had already driven all the way out here. A few more guests at the table was no reason to turn down dinner.

And I was famished.

Kim and I studied our surroundings. A broad staircase led to the second floor. The dining room was to the right. The long table was set, but the seats were unoccupied.

I hefted the flashlight. "Where are these sick ducks?"

"Aren't you going to say hi to Cindy first? Meet the others? The ducks can wait. Come on. Follow me." Craig motioned for us to go with him.

The man could be maddening.

I put the flashlight down. As much as I wanted to check out the waterfowl right away, I couldn't be rude. Kim took my hand and pulled me along with her.

We walked past the stairs and turned right. A hallway filled with doors ran the length of the house. Craig stopped outside a set of varnished mahogany-wood doors. I could hear voices coming from within the room, along with the gentle sounds of music playing. He pulled the door open and waved for us to enter.

"Cindy," Craig said loudly, following me and Kim inside the study. "Look who's here!"

Several strangers were standing or seated in the cozy, wood-paneled parlor. A large stone fireplace with sash windows on either side occupied the far wall. Green dimity curtains hung from the rods. Falling snowflakes were visible through the windowpanes.

The antique furnishings, like everything else I had seen so far in the house, from the somber carpets to the heavy paintings on the wall, seemed comfortless and out of place.

Two hideous paintings hung over the fireplace, and a row of duck decoys stretched across the mantel. I recognized wood ducks, harlequins, mandarins and mallards. Two more stuffed ducks hung over the bar, wings extended, forever in flight. There had been numerous duck decoys and stuffed ducks in the entryway, too. The taxidermist had also posed them in flight and they had looked to me like they were trying to fly out of the house.

Not a bad idea at all.

A sullen-looking woman with pretty features sat slumped in a tall, brass tack–studded purple velvet chair in the corner. Her legs were crossed. The most alive things about her were her bright-green-and-gold-flecked eyes. The woman raised her cocktail glass and drank as we stopped inside the doorway.

A glass-doored gun case to the side of the chair contained a pair of shotguns and a couple of rifles. Its heavy clasp was held in place with a padlock.

A redheaded man with longish locks and a bony frame was lazily prodding the logs with an iron fireplace poker. He reminded me of a woodpecker poking a decaying log in search of termites.

Cindy stood on a thick hearthrug wearing a bloodred dress with a surprisingly modest neckline and red stiletto heels, her svelte figure illuminated by the flickering blue and yellow flames.

"Amy!" Cindy flounced over and gave me an unrequested hug and a kiss on each cheek, as if we were devoted sisters or long-lost friends. "You must be Kim, right?"

"Right." Kim raised her eyebrow for my benefit. "And you must be... Cindy. I've heard a lot about you."

I jabbed Kim in the ribs.

"Hey!" squawked Kim, rubbing her side.

"That's me, Cindy Pym."

Craig stepped in. "Let me introduce you to the others. Everybody, this is Amy Simms and Kimberly Christy. Ladies, that's Mike and Helen Holberg. Mike runs the Holberg Group."

He pointed to a perfect-looking sixtyish couple in color-coordinated evening wear seated on the sofa. They could have leapt from the pages of a glossy magazine catering to the well-heeled over-fifty crowd.

Mike Holberg had black hair and a swarthy complexion. His wife was nearly his height and of medium build. Helen Holberg wore a mid-length blue dress and low black heels. He stood and firmly shook my hand while Kim said hello from the sofa.

The next couple was Robert Flud and Rosalie Richmond. He wore dark brown corduroys and a blue-and-white cotton sweater with comfortable boots designed for hiking but showing no signs of ever having set foot in the dirt. Her corduroys were the color of sandstone, and she wore a long-sleeved turtleneck sweater the color of sage.

"And this is Jackson and Augusta Canning." Augusta was the blonde woman near the fire. Both wore jeans and flannel shirts. His shirt was gray and white, and he'd tucked it neatly under his brown leather belt. Hers was red and black and fell loosely around her.

Jackson hung the poker in the wrought-iron tool stand. He pushed a hand through his hair and waved. "Hello, ladies. If there is anything you need, you just let me know."

"Jackson and Augusta are the caretakers," explained Craig. "They do everything around here."

"I'll bet." I couldn't imagine Craig lifting a helping finger.

"Welcome." Augusta waved from her chair by the fire. Her fingernails were clipped short and her palms were calloused. "Jackson, would you get me another?" She held out her glass.

"Are you sure you haven't had enough?"

She waved her glass. Jackson forced a grin and took it. He crossed to the bar along the back wall of the room. It was all glossy wood and polished brass. He mixed a gin and tonic and added a bit of lime.

The logs in the fire shifted, and I jumped. Sparks flew like angry wasps around the flames before settling once again.

"Here you go, dear." Jackson handed Augusta the fresh drink. "Shouldn't we be seeing to dinner?"

"I'm famished," Mike said, clutching his own drink.

Augusta sighed and rose. "Dinner will be in twenty minutes, everyone."

Jackson came toward me. “Don’t mind Augusta. Her mother recently passed.”

“Nobody cares about our personal business, dear.” Augusta had heard him.

“Can we do anything to lend a hand?” Robert asked.

“Thank you,” Augusta replied. “We have everything under control.” She and Jackson disappeared down the hall.

“Let me fix you ladies a drink.” Craig moved behind the bar. “What’ll it be?”

Kim and I studied the line of bottles. “Merlot for me,” I said.

“Double that,” Kim added. “What do you think of the house, Cindy?”

“It’s adorable,” Cindy replied. “We are a bit isolated, but I find it charming.”

My brow went up. “Charming” was hardly the word I would have used to describe the house. I found being inside the Usher House unsettling. But maybe it was the dwellers who unsettled me.

Maybe it was only Craig.

That and an empty stomach.

“And there’s plenty of room,” put in Robert, who had joined Mike at the ivory chessboard on a low table across from the bar. Helen and Rosalie hovered over them.

“It’s a good thing, too.” Craig poured himself a Scotch and water. “Because with the caretaker’s cottage uninhabitable, Jackson and Augusta have had to move into one of the spare rooms here today. This place has oodles of them.”

“‘Oodles,’ Craig?” Nobody seemed to want ice. Maybe it was the cold outside or the chill within.

“What’s wrong with the cottage?” Kim asked.

“No power, and Jackson says he can’t figure out what’s wrong with it. He’s called an electrician to come out and have a look. In the meantime, it’s too cold to sleep there, so Cindy and I told him to move into the main house with us.”

“The electrician was supposed to come today, but he called and said his truck wouldn’t start,” Cindy added. “He said he was confident he’d have the truck fixed today and that power to the cottage will be up and running by tomorrow afternoon.” She moved closer to the fire.

“I’ll be back in a moment,” Helen announced to no one in particular. She set her glass on the fireplace mantel and moved quietly out of the room, leaving a trail of floral scent that lingered.

I set my glass on the bar. "I'm going to go check on those waterfowl. Are you coming, Kim?"

"What?" Kim had been chatting with Rosalie, about what I couldn't imagine. I sometimes envied Kim's ability to make small talk with anyone at any time or place. Me, I had less skill at speaking with strangers. "No, thanks. It's freezing out there."

"Then bring your drink. It will warm you up." Mike and Robert were each staring intently at the chess pieces on the board as if each move was a life-or-death matter.

"That's a myth, Amy, and you know it."

"Fine. I'll go myself."

"I'll go with you, Amy," Craig offered. He tipped back his drink.

"No thanks, Craig. You're the host. You belong in here." No way did I want him tagging along.

"Let him go with you, Amy," Cindy insisted. "It's dark outside, and it can be quite dangerous if you don't know where you're going." She gave Craig a gentle push. "Get your coat."

"Dangerous how?" I asked.

"Well"—she tapped a manicured pink nail against her cheek—"there's the lake, or a 'tarn,' as Jackson and Augusta like to call it. It's cold and deep. The ground around here is horribly uneven away from the house."

"I've lived in North Carolina my whole life," I said. "I can handle a little uneven terrain."

"Okay," Cindy said. "But watch out for the ravine."

My brow went up. "The ravine?"

"It runs along the edge of the property, back all the way behind the barn," Craig explained. "It's deep, but it's not dangerous."

"Right. Unless you fall in it." I frowned. "Fine, you can come along." I wanted to add "*but keep your hands off of me*," but I wasn't going to say that in front of Cindy.

4

Craig and I retrieved our coats at the door. His was ostentatious, a big, puffy black coat with a fake beaver fur collar. At least I hoped it was fake.

Like him.

Okay, so maybe Mom was right and I still harbored Craig issues.

"We can't go out like this." He looked down at our feet. I was in dress flats and he was in wingtips. "I'll be right back."

I took my flashlight and tested it while waiting for Craig.

He returned carrying two pairs of floppy, fleece-lined rubber boots and handed me the smaller of the two pairs. We put them on.

Craig opened the front door and a blast of arctic air swept in. "Wow. It's really starting to snow."

I stepped onto the stone porch. "You're right." I bundled my coat around me and raised the hood of my hoodie dress over my head. "How far is it to this tarn?"

"A couple hundred yards maybe." Craig headed along the drive toward a line of dark trees. "Come on. Let's make this quick. I'm freezing my butt off already. Plus, you heard Augusta. Dinner will be ready in a few minutes."

"Have you and Cindy set a date yet?" I panted as I trailed awkwardly over the uneven terrain behind Craig. The wind was stronger than it had been when we arrived. Snowflakes fell steadily now.

Craig looked back over his shoulder even as he kept moving. "A date for what?"

"I noticed the diamond on Cindy's ring finger. Aren't you two engaged?"

The tarn was clearly visible now, shining dully. I moved my flashlight from side to side. I had a feeling the last thing I'd be seeing would be waterfowl.

Unless they were carrying LED torches around their necks.

"Sort of."

"'Sort of'? What does 'sort of' mean?"

"It means we haven't picked a date yet. But it's serious. We even took out million-dollar life insurance policies on each other."

Leave it to Craig to value love with dollar signs. "Who are these houseguests of yours?"

"Business associates." Craig stepped to the left. "Careful here. The ground slopes down fast toward the lake."

I slid down and came to a halt against the weed-choked shore. I moved the flashlight along the edges. A short wooden dock jutted from the shoreline a hundred yards to our right.

The snow was beginning to settle like dust on the cold earth. The dark trees rustled in the wind blowing from out of the north. The only other sound was our shallow breathing.

"I can't see a thing." I pushed the light out over the surface of the tarn. Then I held the flashlight steady. Near the shore, almost hidden in a thick patch of bulrushes, a tall, narrow wooden box on a pole sat several feet above the water. "Look at that."

"Yeah, I don't know what that's for," Craig replied. "There are a couple of them that I've noticed out here."

"It's a duck box. Waterfowl use them for nesting." If there were any ducks, they were surely already nestled someplace warm for the night. Like I should have been.

"The pole that box is mounted to ought to have a baffle, though, to keep out predators." I thought of such things as raccoons and rat snakes and wished I hadn't. I pointed the flashlight toward my feet, then the slope. "Let's go, Craig. This is useless."

"I thought you wanted to find the ducks." Craig started moving away, thrashing through the bushes. "I think they are this way. I often see them coming from this direction when I want to feed them."

"Forget it," I said. I was cold and I was hungry. And spooked. The bare tree limbs at the edge of the water danced like skeleton bones.

Despite Craig's sudden enthusiasm, I had little hope that we'd find the waterfowl now. "I'll drive up tomorrow and have a look." Maybe I'd even ask the vet, Jane Buchman, to come with me.

We trudged back to the house. There was a good-sized barn behind it. One section was open to the elements; the rest was closed up.

"When you say you 'feed these ducks,'" I huffed as I moved, "what exactly are you feeding them?"

"The usual stuff, you know."

"No, I don't know. Enlighten me."

"Bread, table scraps, donuts, chips."

I squeezed my eyes shut. "You can't feed ducks that junk."

"Why not?"

"It's not good for them. From the sounds of it, I'd say that's what's wrong with them. They're filling up on garbage. They might even have food poisoning."

I shook my head at Craig as he pulled open the front door. "I sell food at Birds and Bees for waterfowl." I wished I had thought to bring some. "I'll bring a bag of pellets when I come back. If you're going to feed them, give them that."

I unbuttoned my coat and tossed it on the wingback chair that Craig was using as a coatrack. "And plenty of fresh water. My guess is that on a regimen of balanced food and plenty of water, they will be back to normal in a couple of days. I wish I could say the same for you."

"Very funny." Craig dumped his coat on top of mine. "Come on, I smell dinner."

We removed our boots at the door, too, then joined the others in the dining room. The heavy crocodile-green draperies had been pulled tightly shut, but I could hear the wind beating against the windows and rattling the glass. It was all a bit unnerving.

A massive oil painting of ducks having dinner, at a table much like the one we were seated around, hung on the wall opposite the windows. Again, I recognized wood ducks, blue-winged teals, hooded mergansers, ring-necked ducks, and muscovies.

"That Usher guy was a bit daffy for ducks," Craig said as I stood inspecting the strange scene on the wall. "If you know what I mean."

"I do."

"Did you get a look at those portraits of him and his wife in the study?"

"You mean those two grotesque paintings above the fireplace?"

"Yep."

"The ones that look like half-duck, half-people?"

Cindy giggled. "The Realtor we picked up the house key from warned us about them. She said Stanley Usher loved ducks. That's why he wanted a house here. He had all this macabre stuff shipped down before he died."

"I think what he really loved about ducks was hunting them," Robert put in from the table. "Judging from the specimens scattered around the house."

"You mean they aren't all decoys?"

"It's a mixed bag," Robert said. "Pardon my pun. Get it?" he asked Rosalie. "'Bag,' like he bagged a duck."

Rosalie groaned.

"By the looks of it, I'd say he bagged practically every duck in the Great Lakes," quipped Craig.

"Stanley Usher wasn't only a hunter," explained Rosalie. "He was an amateur carver and taxidermist."

Stanley Usher had died in a car crash and never got the chance to pursue his avocations here. I had no doubt that had saved many a duck's life.

"That still doesn't explain the weird portraits," I said, moving to an empty chair.

Cindy picked up the thread of the conversation. "He wanted to surprise his wife, so he commissioned an artist in Chicago to create portraits of them as duck-human hybrids."

I furrowed my brow. That explained the grotesque human faces with the beaklike noses and eyes pushed out to the sides of their bulbous heads.

"Are we sure he died in a car accident and that she didn't murder him when she saw those paintings?" Kim giggled.

Rosalie raised her wineglass to Kim. "That's what I'm thinking."

"Stanley Usher was one odd duck," quipped Craig, taking a seat and reaching for the wine bottle.

"A real quack!" Mike added as Augusta walked into the room carrying a covered platter with both hands. "Tell me we're having duck."

"Sorry, sir." She set the platter near him. "It's beef."

"No matter." Mike lifted the cover and nodded appreciatively. "We can't always get what we want, can we?"

"No, sir." Augusta took the heavy silver cover from Mike and set it on the sideboard.

Jackson and Augusta served the meal but refused to join us, saying that they would eat in the kitchen.

Rosalie Richmond told us how she and Robert had heard a ghost walking down the hall the night before. "It was quite vivid, really." Rosalie's fingers tapped the side of her wineglass. "Wasn't it, Robert?"

Robert nodded and squeezed her other hand where it rested on the gold and turquoise damask tablecloth.

"It was probably just the house settling," Cindy said from the head of the table, where she sat opposite Craig. I got the feeling she was trying to convince herself with her words.

"The day we arrived," Craig began, "the caretaker told me that the guy who built this place had his head chopped off. According to Jackson, this Usher guy's ghost has been known to roam the house." Craig paused to look at us one by one. "They say his ghost comes looking for his lost blood. Only when he finds it will he be able to rest in peace."

Jackson and Augusta came in just then, carrying dishes of vegetables and a plate piled high with potato rolls.

"Isn't that right, Jackson?" Craig asked.

"Houses are full of stories." Jackson set the rolls within Craig's reach. "Including that one."

"Have you ever seen or heard this ghost?" Kim reached for a roll.

"We've only been here about six months. We've never seen anything out of the ordinary. Renters do come and go quickly. Some say folks are uneasy staying here. But we wouldn't know about that, would we, Augusta?"

Augusta shrugged as she refilled our water glasses. "We've never actually spent a night in the house. Not before today."

Helen gasped as Augusta overfilled her glass. Water spilled across the table, soaking into the cloth. Augusta set the pitcher on the sideboard and dabbed at the table with the hem of her apron.

"Careful," Rosalie said with a laugh, "we wouldn't want Helen to melt."

Helen's face darkened as she glared across the table at Rosalie. But Rosalie chose to raise her glass to Helen and drank.

Kim leaned toward my ear. "Let's eat faster."

Despite Craig and the others' unnerving stories, and whatever else was going on between the guests, everything went well enough until Cindy and Craig inexplicably began sniping at one another from across the table.

After dinner, the Cannings cleared the dishes from the table, then brought out dessert plates and a delicious warm peach shortcake with vanilla ice cream.

"This is excellent, Augusta, better than the one they serve at that diner in town." Mike shoveled a large forkful of shortcake into his mouth. He smiled as he worked his jaw muscles. "Thanks."

Augusta blushed. "I had to use canned peaches."

"Well, it's delicious anyway, Augusta." I was stuffed. And I was tired. "It's getting late." I shoved my plate away, dessert only half-eaten. Kim was seated to my left. I gave her a nudge. "We should be going." I wasn't looking forward to the drive back down the mountain, but I was looking forward to my bed.

I caught a look that passed between Craig and Cindy. Cindy seemed to be warning Craig of something with her eyes.

"One more drink for the road." Craig stood and pushed back his chair.

"Sorry. It's been wonderful, but all good things must come to an end." I wiped my lips one last time and stood. Kim drained the remainder of her Chablis and joined me.

"I insist," Craig said loudly. He'd been drinking heavily ever since we had arrived. In fact, it seemed like everybody had. "Come on, everyone. Drinks in the study."

Kim looked at me and shrugged. "What can it hurt?"

It was going to hurt in the morning when I had to get up early and open the store, but with everyone filing out of the dining room and moving toward the study, I had no choice but to follow.

Craig pulled a bottle of brandy from behind the bar and peeled off the foil seal. He set a row of brandy snifters atop the bar and poured a generous portion for each of us—except for Jackson and Augusta, whom I could hear washing dishes in the kitchen.

Craig handed a glass to Cindy. "Can I talk to you a minute alone, babe?"

Cindy pouted but nodded and left carrying her drink.

"We'll be right back," Craig promised. "Enjoy your drinks!"

Craig hurried from the study. I heard the sound of his steps fade in the distance. Kim and I huddled near the dying fire. "Drink fast," I said. "I've had enough."

"Me, too." Kim gulped her brandy. "You have to hand it to Craig, though." She licked her lips. "He buys the good stuff."

We heard the sound of shouting, both a male and a female voice. All of us turned to face the open doorway.

"That sounds like Craig and Cindy," Kim said, setting her snifter on the narrow mantel between a mallard and a harlequin duck.

"I wonder what those two are arguing about?" Helen Holberg asked, sounding amused rather than concerned.

I set my glass next to Kim's. "I think we should leave. Let's get our coats."

"I'm right behind—"

The sharp *crack* of a gunshot stopped all further speech. We all looked at one another in curiosity and fear.

"What the heck was that?" Robert awkwardly set his glass on the bar. His girlfriend, Rosalie, clung to his arm.

"I don't hear Craig and—"

Then we heard the scream.

We ran from the room en masse.

The sound of our pounding steps echoed through the house. We found Jackson and Augusta Canning standing at the entrance to a small library at the front of the house, to the left of the front door.

Augusta and Jackson clung to one another. Craig lay on the floor at the foot of a massive desk. A Tiffany lamp on the desk provided the room's only light. A single file of duck decoys edged the back of the desk.

Cindy stood, her arm dangling with a revolver in her hand. Her eyes were on Craig's motionless body.

Robert was the first to arrive, and we all pushed in around him.

I glanced from Cindy to Craig. A lovers' quarrel gone terribly wrong? "Somebody get the gun."

Mike Holberg bent in front of Craig, who was lying on his back.

"Is he dead?" Kim whispered.

"Nobody touch anything," I said. The tang of gunpowder hung in the air. "I'll call Jerry." Jerry Kennedy was Ruby Lake's chief of police. My purse was in the foyer. I asked Kim to go get it.

"Wait." Cindy set the gun on the edge of the bookcase. She looked contrite.

Mike grunted and stood. "You can forget the police." He shook his head and gave Craig a kick in the leg.

"Hey!" I protested.

"Nice try, Craig. Get up, you faker." Mike was grinning.

Kim tugged at my sleeve. "What the heck is going on?"

Suddenly, Craig moved and pulled himself up using the desk. He dusted himself off.

"Craig!" I glared at him. He was grinning stupidly. Everyone was talking at once.

"Got you good, eh, Amy?"

I locked my arms across my chest. "What do you mean 'got me good'?" I was furious.

Craig crossed to the bookcase and picked up the gun.

I flinched.

He opened the chamber. "Blanks, see?" he said cheerfully. He palmed the cartridges and showed them around the room. "I found a load of them in that bureau drawer." He pointed to a low chest of drawers near the desk.

"You moron." I was seething.

"Yeah," agreed Kim. "What a dumb thing to do."

"Sorry," Cindy said. "I warned Craig that it was a poor joke."

"Poor? It was a hoot!" Mike slapped Craig across the back.

Helen rolled her eyes. The corner of Rosalie's mouth quirked up in distaste.

Robert grabbed Mike by the collar and pulled him toward the alcove under the stairwell. The two started bickering, but I couldn't make out their words. The malice between them, however, was clear.

Cindy leaned close and whispered in my ear, "Why Craig invited those two I will never know. They are constantly at each other's throats."

Jackson and Augusta left. I heard them climbing the stairs to their room.

I fumed.

Craig dropped the blanks on the edge of the bookshelf. "Nice job, Cindy." He squeezed her slender waist.

"Why would you pull such a dumb stunt?" Kim's mouth hung open.

"I heard how Amy maybe helped solve a couple of murders and thought we'd have a little fun. End the party on a bang, as it were. Like one of those murder mystery parties."

I marched out of the room before there was an actual murder. Kim hurried after me.

"I am not staying here another minute!" I shoved my arms into my coat, not bothering to take the time to button up.

"Wait for me!" Kim struggled with her own jacket.

I threw open the heavy door and stormed out.

Into a literal storm.

Icy snow swirled through the air, stinging my face as if each flake had sharp, biting fangs. My first step was into a half foot of snow.

My second step sent me slip-sliding to the ground.

I felt a pair of strong hands reach under my armpits and pull me up.

"Thanks," I muttered, turning. Then I frowned. It was Craig. Cindy stood behind him. Kim lingered on the porch below the light, which was barely visible as it was shrouded by the heavy snow that was falling.

"It looks like you're stuck with us." Craig smiled smugly.

I shook myself free of him. "I may be stuck here, but at least I'm not stuck with *you*."

We retreated indoors and Cindy slammed the door shut.

"Now what?" Kim stood next to the wingback chair in the entry, half-in and half-out of her coat.

"I'd say the two of you will be spending the night in the Usher House," Mike quipped.

Helen rolled her eyes. "Join the party."

Rosalie had Robert cornered in the dining room and was stroking his chest.

"We do have plenty of room," Cindy said solicitously. "We would love to have you."

"I don't know…" My mind searched for an alternative to spending the night in this house with Craig and company. But I was having trouble coming up with anything that even made remote sense and didn't involve us freezing to death or running off the edge of the road in the dark.

I couldn't see the ducks, and I doubted whether I would be able to see the road.

"Please, Amy. I am sorry about Craig's little joke. I warned him it might be in bad taste." Cindy helped me out of my coat, and I didn't put up a fight. "He can be hard to say no to."

The poor girl had it bad. I found saying no to Craig easier and easier all the time.

"I'm not sure we have any choice, Amy," Kim added. "Mother Nature seems to mean for us to stay."

"Then it's settled." Craig clapped his hands. "You'll sleep in the room next to mine and Cindy's. It's the only room that's suitably furnished."

"I'll have to call my mom and tell her I won't be home." I didn't want her to wake in the morning and worry.

"There is no landline in the house." Craig pulled his cravat tight around his neck. "It was disconnected years ago. And there is lousy cell service out here."

Both Kim and I looked at our phones. Craig was right. Not even a smidgen of a bar.

"Reception comes and goes." Cindy didn't sound overly concerned. "The best spot we've found is out near the dock, or on it. You must be careful, though. The dock has a lot of loose or missing planks."

Craig nodded. "I wouldn't recommend walking out there this time of night, especially in this snowstorm."

Kim patted my arm. "You can text your mom in the morning, Amy."

"I suppose…"

"I'll show you the way to your room." Cindy started up the steps, one hand on the balustrade.

"Great," I muttered under my breath as we followed her wriggling butt up the stairs.

5

"This sucks," Kim said for the second time that day as she lay staring up at the ceiling.

And this time it really did.

Our room had twin beds and had clearly been decorated to accommodate a couple of young girls. A wooden rocking horse with a scrolled leather saddle sat in the corner. The two beds shared a long night table with a single lamp, its base also carved into the shape of a prancing horse.

The pink and blue wallpaper was yellowed and coming loose in the upper corners of the walls where it edged up to the crown molding. There was a long, jagged crack in the wall on my side. I reached out and traced it with my finger.

The bedding smelled stale but appeared clean. The room was cold but not unbearable beneath the covers.

"First thing tomorrow, we're driving out of here," I vowed.

"You'll get no argument from me." Kim yawned. "Good night, Amy."

"Good night." I turned off the lamp and began to nod off, listening to the wind howl against the house as if demanding to be let in.

"Oh no," Kim groaned.

"What is it?" I whispered, tucking the sheets tighter under my chin.

"I can hear them."

"Hear who?"

"Them," Kim replied. "Craig and Cindy. Their bed must share a wall with mine." She giggled. "It sounds like the two of them are—"

"No," I interrupted her. "Don't say another word." I pulled the covers over my head and prayed for sleep.

Not surprisingly, I slept uneasily. I was in a strange bed, in a strange house with strange people.

The sound of banging woke me. I raised up on my elbows and peered into the blackness. In the next bed, Kim's breathing came low and steady. The wind had not let up.

I fumbled quietly for my phone. I had set it near at hand on the table. I slid it out and checked the time. It was just past two in the morning.

I put the phone away and put my head back down on the feather-filled pillow. The banging continued irregularly, preventing my going back to sleep.

With a sigh, I sat up and rubbed my eyes. Whatever it was, it needed to stop. I fumbled around the floor with my feet until they landed in my shoes. I pushed my feet inside them and stood. I grabbed my phone again and went to the door.

I turned the brass knob slowly, not wanting to wake Kim. It was bad enough that one of us was awake. Once in the hall, I shut the bedroom door behind me. The hall and the house itself was in darkness. The house was colder than it should have been and I felt a draft. I turned on the flashlight app on my phone and peered over the rail. A soft glow seemed to come from the study. Probably the remnants of the fire.

Then I heard the bang once more, the one that had awakened me. It was the front door, swinging open and shut. "What the—" I tiptoed quickly downstairs as the door shot open again.

I reached for the handle and pulled it back, but it wouldn't latch. I tried again and again. Nothing. Then I noticed the scarf lying twisted against the floor sill and the side jamb. One end of it was caught outside in the twigs of a small brown bush rooted in a clay pot beside the door.

I pulled it loose. Before securing the door, I looked quickly across the drive. My minivan was half-buried but at least the snow had stopped falling. I prayed for sun tomorrow, the earlier the better. I couldn't stand the thought of another day stuck in the Usher House with Craig and the others.

I closed the front door and was relieved that it now held. Chilled to the bone, I decided to warm myself in whatever heat still remained of the fire before returning to bed.

I wasn't alone.

A couple of logs burned low in the fireplace. Two wineglasses rested on the coffee table in front of the velvet love seat.

"Good grief." I planted my hands on my hips. "Nice try, Mike. You about scared me to death." The shirt buttons at his neck were undone. The haft of a knife protruded from the middle of his still chest. There was a dark red blotch surrounding it.

I rolled my eyes. “You and Craig ought to be ashamed of yourselves—a couple of grown men acting like thirteen-year-olds. Where is Craig, anyway?”

I swiveled my head and moved the beam of the phone’s flashlight app around the study. “Hiding somewhere with a camera, getting ready to take a picture of poor, frightened Amy?”

I arched my brow and took a step closer, prepared to brace myself if he decided to leap up and attack me like some stupid zombie out of the movies. “Mike?”

I shook my head in disgust. At least I was no longer bothered by the cold.

I left in search of Craig. There was no sign of him in the hall. “Craig?” I whispered. I didn’t want to wake the entire house for another of his puerile jokes. I turned on the overhead kitchen chandelier. The room was dark and empty. Nothing but the lingering smells of roast beef and peaches.

A white glare off the snowy blanket outside was visible through the kitchen window. I turned off the phone’s light to conserve my battery and searched the remainder of the downstairs. Craig was nowhere to be found, not even in the library, the scene of his previous prank.

I peeked into the study once again, expecting Mike to have given up and gone back to bed. He remained on the love seat. I wasn’t certain, but I felt that he had shifted a little. “Good night, Mike,” I said from the door.

There was no reply.

“Fine. Be that way. I’m not talking to you, either.” I left him there and started up the stairs. “I can’t wait to get out of this house,” I grumbled.

I banged lightly on Craig and Cindy’s door. Craig answered, pulling his dark blue robe around him. “Amy?” He rubbed his eyes. “What’s up? It’s the middle of the night.”

I pulled my phone from the pocket of my hoodie dress and trained the flashlight app on him. Kim and I were still in our evening wear; neither of us had been willing to borrow a negligee from Cindy or one of the others.

Craig complained and covered his eyes.

“Tell your buddy Mike that he didn’t scare me in the least.” I jabbed Craig in the chest. “And you can both stop your juvenile jokes. They aren’t funny.”

I turned on my heel. Craig pulled his door shut and jumped in front of me. “Are you still mad about that? Come on, Amy. That was hours ago. It’s the middle of the night. You woke me up to give me a hard time now?”

He spoke in low, urgent tones, glancing constantly over his shoulder for fear of waking Cindy.

"I'm talking about now. You pretending to stab Mike."

Craig pushed his brows together. "Stab Mike? Why would I stab Mike? What are you talking about?"

"I'm talking about—" I pointed downstairs, but Craig cut me off with a lopsided grin.

"I know what this is. You were dreaming. That's it. You had a bad dream. What's the matter? Did all the ghost stories get to you?" He grabbed my shoulders. "Go back to bed, Amy. Get some sleep. You'll feel better in the morning."

"Get your hands off me, Craig," I whispered angrily. "I was not dreaming, and I know what I saw."

"And what exactly is it that you *think* you saw?"

I glared at him. "I *know* I saw Mike Holberg sitting on the love seat in the study pretending to be stabbed to death."

"Are you crazy?" Craig took a step back and dug his hands into the pockets of his robe.

"I was crazy to have let you talk me into coming all the way out here, just so you could play dumb gags on me. And close your robe. You're disgusting."

Craig sighed heavily and took my elbow. "Come on."

I pulled away. "Where?"

"Downstairs. You say Mike's there. Let's go talk to him. I want to get to the bottom of this." He frowned at me. "Maybe then you'll let me get back to sleep."

The bedroom door opened and Kim stuck her head out. "What the devil is going on out here? Amy? Craig? What are you up to?"

"Sorry," I said. "I didn't mean to wake you with another of Craig's lame gags."

"Huh?"

"Amy thinks Mike and I are playing some elaborate prank on her."

Kim wrinkled her forehead. "In the middle of the night?"

"That's what I said," Craig replied harshly.

The three of us heard a muted cough come from Rosalie and Robert's room.

"Let's go downstairs." Craig knotted the belt of his robe. "You're disturbing my guests."

Craig padded down the hall in his bare feet, grumbling all the way, and we followed.

Mike Holberg was precisely where I had left him. The flame in the hearth burned low.

Craig hit the light switch and snorted. "Very funny, Mike. I get it. Payback for my little joke."

"Uh, Craig." Seeing Mike in this light, and noticing how he hadn't moved at all at the sound of our entrance or at the light blinking on, made me look at him more closely.

The handle of the knife looked familiar. It matched the carving knife that had been used with the roast beef. I recalled it lying on the silver platter on the table. This was the very same knife, or one from a matching set.

I was beginning to think this was not a fake rubber knife handle that Mike Holberg had glued to his chest.

"What is it, Amy?" Kim pressed up against my back.

Mike's shirt was loosened, and he was in stocking feet. His shoes were upside down at the edge of the love seat.

Craig stepped over to the love seat. I intercepted him. "Mike?" I placed my hand on the side of his neck. "His skin feels cool."

Craig shoved me aside. "He's not sick, is he?"

"I wish he was." I felt the other side of Mike's neck and glanced nervously at his chest. "He's dead, Craig."

Kim screamed.

"That's impossible!" Craig grabbed his friend's limp arm and shook it. "Hey, Mike! Wake up!"

I ran to Kim to quiet her.

"You mean, he's really been stabbed with—with that?" Kim pointed nervously at the hilt of the knife in Mike's chest.

I held her hand. "It's real."

"We have to call the police," Kim said with a shiver. "We have to call Dan."

I looked at my phone. It showed no signal, but I tried anyway. Nothing. "I can't get through."

Craig paced up and down the study. "Tell me this isn't happening. Tell me this is a nightmare and that the two of you are hallucinations and that I am going to wake up tomorrow morning and laugh about this."

"I don't think so, Craig." I blocked his path. His pacing was driving me mad. "Calm down. What about your phone? Do you have reception?"

He pulled a face. "I don't know. I doubt it. My phone is up in my room. I'll go check."

"Okay. Kim and I will stay here with the body."

"We will?" Kim was shaking her head back and forth. "No, we won't." She backed out the door.

As Craig brushed past me, I put my hand on his shoulder. "And be quiet. There's no point in waking the whole house."

Craig nodded briefly and bounded up the stairs.

I cursed. "So much for quiet." I started snapping pictures with my cell phone.

"What are you doing, Amy?" Kim asked from outside the door.

"What does it look like?" I took a couple of closeups of the wound, then moved to get a wide shot of the study. "Taking pictures."

"That's morbid."

"It's evidence. I'll give them to Jerry when he gets here, which could be hours."

I joined Kim in the hallway. Mike Holberg wasn't going anywhere.

Kim was barefoot and her arms were wrapped tightly around herself for warmth. "What time is it? And what were you doing down here in the middle of the night?"

"Something woke me. A banging noise. I came to take a look."

The corners of Kim's mouth turned down. "Personally, I'd have hidden under the covers. Which is exactly what the two of us should be doing right now."

It was a little late for that.

"The front door was open when I came down. That's what woke me."

We both turned our eyes to the heavy door.

The sound of opening doors was followed by confused and agitated voices coming from upstairs. Soon, footsteps followed. Rosalie and Robert were at the top of the steps looking down. Jackson Canning appeared next in Scotch plaid pajamas and bare feet.

"Sorry, everyone," came the sound of Craig's voice, quickly followed by the man himself with Cindy gripping his hand. Even roused from a deep sleep, Cindy's blond hair managed to look perfect, and the short, thin black robe she was wearing left nothing to the imagination but the imagination. Black slippers with rose crystals covered her feet.

"Does anyone have a working cell phone?" I called out. There were confused murmurs. "Please, check your phones to see if you can get a signal, would you?"

Everyone disappeared except Craig and Cindy. They hurried downstairs still holding hands.

Under normal circumstances, I would have found it stomach-turning.

"I don't have a signal at all." Craig turned on the entry light and I blinked.

"Me, either," Cindy said, sounding frightened. "Are you sure this isn't another one of your jokes, Craig?" Craig must have told her about Mike.

"Trust me," I answered for him. "It isn't."

Kim fell onto one of the wingback chairs beside the front door.

The others came back within minutes, dressed in robes and long pajamas. No one claimed to have any phone reception.

Robert pushed up to Craig. "Do you want to explain what's going on? It's nearly three in the morning. What's happened? Why do you need a phone so desperately?"

I glanced at our small group. Helen Holberg was missing. So was Augusta Canning. Jackson Canning leaned against the wall beside Kim. "Mike is dead."

Rosalie gasped and hurried to Robert's side. She clutched his arm. "It can't be!"

"I'm afraid so," Craig said. "He's in the study."

Robert marched to the study. Rosalie hesitated a moment, then followed slowly behind. Kim and Jackson remained where they were.

I stepped ahead of Craig and Cindy as they entered the room. Robert was leaning over Mike. "I wouldn't touch anything," I advised.

Robert shot his eyes my way. "Dead, eh? I always figured it would be a heart attack or somebody he did business with." He stuffed his right hand into the pocket of his brown plaid robe. "I never figured he'd be murdered by a ghost."

"Robert," hissed Rosalie. "You shouldn't—"

He merely shrugged.

"Mike was not stabbed to death by a ghost, Robert," I replied. "Ghosts don't use knives."

"No," Rosalie said with a quiver in her voice. "They simply scare you to death." A sob escaped her lips. "I'm getting out of here." She released her grip on Robert's arm and fled.

"Where's Helen?" Robert asked, his eyes hovering over the two wineglasses.

"I haven't seen her," I said.

"Me, either," Craig said. "What about you, Cindy?"

Cindy shook her head once, her gaze fixed on the floor. Tears welled in the corners of her eyes.

"I'd better go check on Helen." Craig turned to go.

"I'll do it," I said.

"They're my guests. I—"

"Helen might not react well to you waking her in the middle of the night, Craig."

Craig acquiesced.

I told him to make sure nobody touched anything and left the study. Robert, Rosalie, and Cindy left, too.

"I'll make some coffee," offered Cindy. "I wonder where Augusta is."

"I'll help," Rosalie said, breaking away from Robert and following.

Kim was still seated in the corner near the door. She had wrapped her coat around herself. Jackson hadn't moved from his spot against the wall. "Have you seen your wife, Jackson?"

Jackson barely moved. Was he in shock?

I patted his arm. "Be right back." I moved upstairs and stopped first at Jackson and Augusta's room. The door was ajar, so I stepped inside. The bed had been slept in. There was no sign of Augusta.

There was a shared bathroom on the second floor. That door was open, too, and the room equally empty.

The Holbergs' room was directly across the hall from Jackson and Augusta's room. I knocked tentatively and received no answer. "Mrs. Holberg? Helen?"

I pressed my ear to the door and felt a chill pass over my legs, like a coldblooded serpent was coiling 'round them, then moving on.

I clenched my jaw and knocked again, a bit harder. "Helen? It's me, Amy Simms."

I felt an icy hand on my shoulder and whirled around. "Craig! What are you doing here?"

"You were gone a long time. I wanted to see what was happening."

"What's happening is that you're scaring me to death. I thought you were going to watch the body?"

"Bodies don't move much, Amy."

I couldn't argue with that. "Augusta isn't in her room. Helen isn't answering her door. I'm beginning to worry."

"Do you think something might have happened to Helen and Augusta, too?"

"I don't know." The possibility had crossed my mind. Could someone have wanted to murder the Holbergs and Augusta?

Craig gave me a nudge. "Open it."

I slowly moved my hand to the brass knob and turned it. The door opened quietly. No sound came from within.

As my eyes adjusted to the dark, I found my bearings. The king-sized canopied bed was to my left with a heavy dresser and mirror on the opposite wall. I made out the silhouettes of yet more duck decoys atop the dresser.

There were two windows in the back with the curtains pulled tightly shut.

I moved slowly around the bed. A figure lay under the covers. As I got closer, I recognized the face as Helen Holberg. I heard soft breathing and sighed with relief.

"She's sleeping," I whispered to Craig. I gave Helen a gentle shake. "Helen? Mrs. Holberg? It's me, Amy Simms."

"Wh-what?" Helen Holberg tossed her head across the pillow back and forth.

"Mrs. Holberg?"

"What is it?" she asked drowsily, cracking open her eyes.

"It's Amy Simms."

"What are you doing here?" Her hand reached out to her side. She turned, rustling the covers. "Where's Mike?"

"Is it okay if I turn a light on?" I asked softly.

"I suppose," she answered. I fumbled for the light switch of the bedside lamp. Harsh white light filled the space around the bed and created a halo on the wallpaper behind.

"There's been…" I couldn't say *accident*, could I? Mike Holberg hadn't tripped and accidentally fallen on a knife or something.

"I'm afraid Mike has been hurt," I finally said. I reached for her hand.

"Hurt?"

"I'm afraid he's dead."

Helen's hand went limp as she fainted.

6

"Is there anything I can do?" Craig called, full of apprehension, his hands gripping the door frame.

"Bring me a cold, wet towel," I ordered.

Craig ran down the hall and returned a minute later with a damp washcloth from the bathroom.

"Thanks." I took it and dabbed Helen's cheeks and forehead. She stirred. "I think you should leave us, Craig."

"Sure." Craig retreated to the door.

"Wait!"

"Yeah?"

"Have you seen Augusta yet?"

"No. I wonder what happened to her."

As Craig departed, I wondered, too.

When Helen came around, I offered her some water from a half-filled glass next to a bottle of pills on her bedside table.

Helen sat up and I propped two pillows beneath her back. "Thank you." She looked at me with trepidation. "What's happened to Mike?"

I sat on the edge of the bed. She handed me the glass and I set it back down. "There's no easy way to say this, Helen. Mike was stabbed to death."

"Oh!" Her hand flew to her mouth.

"I'm sorry."

Helen sobbed.

I excused myself and ran to the bathroom. I returned with a box of scented tissues. I handed the box to her. She pulled out two and wiped her eyes and nose.

"I know how hard this is for you right now, but I have to ask. Is there anyone staying here at the house who might have wanted to hurt Mike?"

Helen opened her mouth, then closed it again. She shook her head. "He thought Robert was nasty. I'm sure Robert felt the same about him. I can't imagine either one disliking the other enough to-to kill." She fell apart once more, her chin against her chest, in tears.

"Did Mike go to bed at the same time as you?"

"Yes. We always did."

"What time did Mike leave?"

"I don't know."

"Maybe he said he wanted to get a drink or a snack from the kitchen?"

Helen shook her head. "I-I didn't hear Mike get up or leave our room. I didn't hear anything." She brought her hands to her face and sobbed yet again. "I took a sleeping pill. I was out like a light. I fell asleep with Mike beside me and don't remember anything until you woke me." She pulled the covers up to her shoulders. "I'd like to be alone now."

"Are you sure? I don't mind staying the night." What was left of it.

She set her jaw. Her eyes were red and swollen. "I'm sure."

"Okay, then." I paused at the door. "Can I bring you anything?"

Her hand reached for the pill bottle on the table. "No."

* * * *

Craig was pacing in the kitchen when I returned downstairs.

Cindy, Kim, and Rosalie were seated at the porcelain-topped kitchen table drinking coffee with whiskey.

"Worst two hundred bucks a week I've ever spent," groused Craig.

I ignored him and felt no pity on his account. What did he think he was renting for two hundred dollars a week? The Biltmore estate?

"Are Jackson and Robert keeping an eye on Mike?" I inquired.

"Robert and Jackson moved Mike to the shed," Kim explained.

"You moved the body?" I gawked at Craig.

"It was Jackson's idea and we all agreed," Craig whined, always happy to put the blame on somebody else. "What were we supposed to do? Leave him here in the house?"

"It won't be before daylight that the police and an ambulance can get here." Rosalie leaned back in her chair, cup in hand. "The men discussed covering him up in the snow, but there could be coyotes or wolves or something else out there."

"Where is this shed?" I asked.

Craig answered. "Right outside the kitchen. Between the caretaker's cabin and the barn. It's freezing out there, Amy. It's the perfect place for him."

I was glad I had taken several photographs of the crime scene before they had moved the body. "I'm not sure Chief Kennedy is going to agree with you. But that's your problem, not mine." Thankfully.

Craig waved off my concern. "They wrapped Mike in a shower curtain before they carried him out. The police can't expect us to keep a dead body in the house with us overnight. Not even the Ruby Lake police can call me that dumb."

Craig grabbed a green apple from the basket on the table and tossed it in the air. "Besides, we all agreed to stay out of the study from now on until the police get here."

Heads nodded affirmatively.

That was good news. "I hope they didn't touch the knife," I warned.

"My friends aren't idiots, Amy."

My eyes fell on the knife block. "One of the carving knives is missing."

"We noticed that, too," Rosalie said. "It's a good thing I stopped Cindy from using one."

"What do you mean?" I asked.

"It's nothing," Cindy said, sounding tired rather than her usual chipper self. "I was going to make us some cold cut sandwiches. Rosalie warned me that I shouldn't touch the knives."

"We think the killer's fingerprints might be on one of the knives, as well," Kim added.

I nodded and helped myself to coffee. It wasn't a bad theory. "So, it's agreed. None of us touch the knives until the police get here." I joined Kim and the other ladies at the table.

Craig topped my coffee off with unrequested whiskey. I didn't protest.

"Where are Jackson and Robert now?"

No one knew.

"They did come back from the shed, didn't they?" I asked with concern.

"Sure." Craig squeezed himself onto Cindy's chair. "Maybe they went up to bed."

"I believe Robert said something about taking a look around." Rosalie yawned. "But bed does sound like a good idea."

"I don't think I'll be able to sleep a wink," replied Cindy with a well-timed shiver.

"They ought to be looking for Augusta." I drank. The whiskey was strong, and the coffee was weak.

"She isn't upstairs?" Kim turned to me.

"Not that I've seen or heard."

"That's weird." Kim pulled her brows together.

"Could she be at the cottage?" Cindy asked.

"Why would she go there? You told me the power was out." Nonetheless, I rose, walked to the sink, and stared out the kitchen window toward the caretaker's small cabin, now nestled in a bed of snow.

"Maybe she wanted to get something," Craig suggested.

Rosalie began to smile. "Maybe she wanted to hide."

"Hide?" Kim said.

"She kills Mike, then hides in her cabin. It makes more sense than staying under this roof, right?"

Rosalie seemed to delight in being controversial. Nevertheless, I had been thinking the same thing. "I don't see any footprints in the snow leading that way."

I returned to my seat at the white table. "When I came downstairs, the front door was wide open. Its banging was what awakened me."

"That's what Kim told us," Cindy said.

"You're thinking that maybe our little murderess ran out the front door after planting a carving knife in dear Mike's chest?"

I found Rosalie's grin disconcerting but her reasoning sound. "It could be. Or it could be that she was running from her killer."

Craig tilted his head. "You mean, some stranger could have broken into the house while we were sleeping?"

I shrugged.

"Mike might have surprised the burglar," Cindy suggested much to my surprise. "The burglar grabs a knife and attacks him. Augusta stumbles upon the body or maybe the two men fighting. Then the killer notices Augusta and chases her to keep her from talking."

That was a lot of conjecture.

"Do you mean that poor Augusta could be out there in the snow, trapped or hurt?" Kim gasped. "We have to go look for her!"

Kim pushed to her feet. I held up a hand to stop here. "Hold on, Kim. I'm not sure that all adds up, Cindy."

Cindy looked hurt. "I think it happened exactly that way, Amy." She rose abruptly, bumping Craig from the chair. A moment later, I heard her footsteps on the stairs going up.

"That wasn't very nice, Amy." Craig's lips tightened.

"Why is Cindy so sensitive? I wasn't trying to be rude."

"Whatever. Good night, ladies." Craig ran a hand over his head and went running after Cindy like a lovesick puppy dog.

Rosalie laughed and helped herself to the whiskey sans coffee. "Careful, Amy," she said. "You don't seem to be gaining any friends here yourself."

Was that a not-so-veiled threat? Was Rosalie hinting that I might become a victim myself?

I worried my hands. "As I said, I wasn't trying to upset Cindy. But there are certain things that don't add up in her theory."

"Like what?" Kim encouraged. "Tell us."

"Okay," I said. "Mike was seated on the love seat. If he had surprised the burglar or if the burglar had surprised him, why was he sitting rather than standing?"

"That makes sense," Kim said, stifling a yawn. She was still wearing her coat but had unfastened it.

"And he was sitting in the study, not here in the kitchen. That means the killer was carrying around the knife." That was Rosalie's contribution.

"Exactly," I said. "And then there's the big question…" I looked at them both.

"What's that?" Kim asked.

"If, as Cindy says, Mike stumbled on a burglar and Augusta then stumbled on them both…"

Kim leaned over the table. "Yes?"

"What was Mike doing downstairs in the middle of the night in the first place?" I asked.

Rosalie arched her brow and said slyly, "Yes, and what was Jackson's wife doing down in the study with him?"

"Well, I'll be," whispered Kim.

I drained my cup and carried it to the sink. "How well do you know Augusta, Rosalie?" I rinsed my cup and left it to dry on the drain mat hanging over the lip of the porcelain sink.

"Not well at all. You might have noticed, she doesn't speak much. She seems a bit aloof, frankly. Until she and Jackson moved into the house today, we only saw them when they were preparing meals or cleaning up around the house.

"Her husband seems like a decent guy." Rosalie rose and stretched her long arms over her neck, bending from side to side with catlike grace in her gray silk pajamas. "She likes to drink, I'll say that much. Why do you ask?"

"Just curious." I looked once more out the kitchen window. Mike Holberg was out there now, cold and dead.

Where was Augusta Canning?

Her disappearance had to be related somehow. It was too much of a coincidence to be anything else.

I wrapped my fingers around the cell phone in my pocket. "I'm going outside to have a look around."

"Now?" Kim said with surprise. "In the middle of the night? In a snowstorm?"

"The snow has stopped," I said.

"Can't it wait till morning? When the sun is out?"

"I'm with Amy." Rosalie put down her glass and pushed back her chair. "We should at least try. The sooner the police get here and we get off this mountain, the better."

I agreed 100 percent.

We went as a group to the front door. Rosalie and I bundled up.

Kim looked at her high heels. "I can't go out like this."

"I have a pair of hiking boots and a pair of duck boots in the back of the van. I'll get them."

I always kept extra shoes and some other hiking and bird-watching gear on hand. It paid to be prepared when you wanted to do a little bird-watching. In addition to the boots, I kept a small daypack, a few snack bars, a water bottle or two, a pair of binoculars, and a spotting scope with a tripod.

I hurried out to the minivan and returned with our shoes. I handed Kim the duck boots. "There should be a pair of thick socks rolled up in the bottom." Kim's feet were a little smaller than mine. The thick wool socks would help.

"Thanks." Kim sat on the bottom step of the stairs and changed her shoes.

I laced up my hiking boots. Rosalie had gone to the mudroom and returned with a pair of black fur-lined leather boots for herself.

I picked up my flashlight and flicked it on and off to make sure it was still working. "Perfect. Let's go."

"Go where?" came a man's voice.

We turned. Jackson and Robert were coming down the stairs.

"Where have you two been?" Rosalie directed her question to Robert.

Robert had swapped out his pajamas for a pair of jeans, a flannel shirt, and cowboy boots. Jackson had done the same with a black shirt beneath his open flannel one.

"We checked out the rest of the house."

"Any sign of Augusta?" I asked.

Jackson shook his head. "I'm worried."

"Did you find anything else?" I asked. "Like any signs of a break-in?"

"Nothing," answered Robert. "We poked our noses everywhere." He looked at our bundled-up selves. "What are you girls up to?"

"We wanted to walk down toward the dock and see if we could get any cell phone reception."

"That could be dangerous," Robert said.

Jackson said nothing. I thought he looked to be in shock.

"It's worth a try, don't you think, Robert?" Rosalie asked.

"Okay." He grabbed his coat from the pile near the door. "Let's go."

I pulled open the door. "Are you coming, Jackson?"

"No, I'll wait here."

"Okay. Who knows? Maybe your wife will show up in the meantime."

"Maybe." Jackson trained his eyes on the stairway for a moment, as if he expected Augusta to come traipsing down at any moment. She didn't. "Be careful," he cautioned, closing the front door behind us.

"Look." I aimed the beam of my flashlight at the snow-covered ground. "I hadn't noticed before. Those are footprints."

"Coming or going?" Kim said with a shiver.

"I'm not sure." The prints had been partially obliterated by the wind and snow.

"They are either coming or going from that direction." Robert pointed toward the lake.

We followed along on either side of the tracks as the Usher House grew smaller behind us.

"That's the lake there." I paused to get my bearings and pulled out my phone. Still no reception. The others did the same, and their results were no better. I didn't want to walk out to the pier for fear of falling into the near-freezing water. That could be fatal.

We moved on. The snow had gotten much deeper, and walking was difficult. Kim was huffing and puffing. I locked my arm with hers. "You want to go back?"

"Do you?" Kim asked.

I could hear the hope in her voice, but I wasn't ready to give up. "Not yet. I want to see where these footprints lead." By now, the only thing that was clear was that the footprints led away from the Usher House, not toward it.

"I am getting numb," Rosalie complained.

"Let's give it a couple more minutes," Robert suggested. "If we don't come to the end of the footprints or find anything interesting by then, we turn around. Agreed?"

We were all too cold to say no.

The footprints in the snow took a circuitous path, moving well past the lake and toward the rear of the property. The ground sloped gently downward.

I banged on the metal grip of the flashlight. "My batteries are getting low."

Suddenly a hand shot out and grabbed me. "Careful!"

I felt my right foot give way. Where I had expected solid ground, there was only air. "Thanks, Robert."

"No problem." He shouted to make himself heard against the mounting wind. "The ground looks treacherous here. We could use more light. There was a lantern in the barn. I wished I had thought to bring it."

"Be careful, everybody." I aimed the beam outward and down, but there was nothing to see. I turned to the right and left. The footprints had come to an end.

"It's like whoever made these steps vanished right into thin air," Kim remarked.

7

I woke up the next morning cold, cranky, headachy, and hungry.

Across the room, Kim lay sleeping, curled up in a ball facing me. I pulled away the bedcovers and stepped lightly over to the window, then peeked outside. The snow must have been a foot or two deep, with drifts much higher. The sky was leaden, and the sun was nothing but a blur.

I wondered how the devil we were going to get home. Ruby Lake had one official snowplow. To make up for the deficit, several farmers had snow-plowing attachments for their tractors. Would anyone of them make it up Dudley Road to the Usher House?

I tiptoed from the bedroom to the bathroom and found the door locked.

"I'll be out in a minute!" a woman's voice called.

I sighed and leaned against the wall to wait my turn. Portraits of two young girls hung in matching frames on the wall opposite, probably Stanley and Shirley Usher's children. A moment later, Rosalie threw open the door. Her hair was wet, and there was a damp bath towel in her hand.

"Good morning."

"Hello, Amy." Rosalie patted her dripping hair with the towel. "The bathroom is all yours. I wouldn't wait too long. There's only the one bath for everyone."

"Thanks. Have you been up long? Has there been any news?"

"I haven't heard a thing. No one has seen Augusta yet, if that's what you're wondering."

"It was."

Rosalie tossed her free hand into the air. "See you downstairs."

I washed up and rejoined Kim.

"Did I mention this sucks?" Kim stood at the window as I reentered the bedroom. She had opened the drapes.

"I believe you may have noted that once or twice." I leaned down and picked up my shoes.

Kim turned away from the window. "I hope the police get here soon."

"I do, too." There was no point in bursting her bubble, but I had a hunch it would be hours yet. "Let's go join the others for breakfast."

"I'm starved." Kim plucked at her dress. "If I had known we were going to be castaways out here, I would have packed an overnight bag."

"Not me."

"No?"

"Nope. I'd have stayed home."

Kim laughed as we followed the smell of food and coffee to the kitchen.

Rosalie and Robert sat side by side at the kitchen table. Jackson was preparing flapjacks at the gas stove. He wore the same clothes I had seen him in during the night, with the side addition of leather moccasins on his feet. Dark purple bags circled beneath his eyes.

Craig pulled a bag of ground coffee from one of the cabinets. "Good morning, ladies. Did you manage to get some sleep?"

"Barely," Kim said. She went over to the coffeepot, an old-fashioned stovetop percolator, and she poured us each a full cup.

As I carried my cup to the table, I noticed Cindy outside in the vicinity of the toolshed. "What's she doing out there?" She was bundled up in a puffy pink parka, leather gloves, and boots.

"She went to look for a snow shovel," Craig answered. He emptied out the used coffee grounds and refilled the aluminum filter basket.

"In the toolshed?" Kim made a face. "Where Mike—"

I matched her look.

"You wouldn't catch me out there," Rosalie quipped.

"I told her she wouldn't find one," Jackson answered without turning around. He flipped over a pair of pancakes, then moved them over to a plate beside him. "Who's ready?"

"I'll take those." Kim reached across him and grabbed the plate. "Unless somebody else was waiting?" She looked around to the others at the table.

"You go ahead," Robert answered. "We've had our share."

"And then some," Rosalie added.

"Amy?"

"I can wait."

I watched as Cindy returned from the toolshed empty-handed. She pulled open the kitchen door, letting in a wall of ice-cold air.

"Whew." She stamped her feet in the small mudroom and pushed back her hood. She unzipped her coat, pulled it off, and draped it over a brass hook on the wall.

"No luck, huh?" Craig handed Cindy a hot cup of coffee.

"Nope. You were right, Jackson."

Jackson nodded without turning around.

"Too bad." I carried my coffee to the table so I could sit. "If there was a shovel, we'd be getting out of here if I had to shovel snow and ice from here to Lake Shore Drive."

"Like I said, there's no snow shovel." Jackson placed another two buckwheat pancakes onto a plate and carried them to me.

I thanked him and picked up a fork from a pile near the center of the table.

"There is a big shovel in the barn. I believe they once used it for scooping horse manure," Jackson added.

I raised my brow in hope. "There are horses?" I had never ridden a horse before, but that wasn't going to stop me. "Maybe we can ride out of here."

"Sorry." Jackson curled his lip. "No. No horses." He returned to the stove and lifted his spatula.

"Rats." I grabbed the bottle of maple-flavored syrup and squeezed it over my breakfast. "I've seen Craig's car." It would be practically useless in the snow, as would my minivan. "Does anyone here have a four-by-four?"

"We flew into Charlotte and a service drove us up and dropped us off," Robert replied. "The Holbergs did the same."

Kim added a healthy helping of sugar from a small ceramic bowl and a dose of milk from the carton beside it to her coffee.

"I've got an old Jeep with four bald tires. I barely trust it to get me into town. I wouldn't trust it in this weather." Jackson held up the platter of pancakes. "Anybody want more?"

Everyone declined.

"Has anyone talked to Helen this morning?" I asked. "I wonder how she is doing."

Rosalie nodded and dabbed at her lips with a napkin. "Yes, the poor woman must be a wreck." There was ice in her voice, not compassion.

"I haven't seen her since I came down," Jackson answered. "And I got downstairs around seven."

"I guess she's still sleeping," Craig said. Cindy and Craig had joined us at the table. Craig had his hand in a bag of mini–powdered donuts from the market in town.

"I suppose I should check on her." Cindy turned her gaze toward the ceiling.

"I think we should let her sleep," I suggested.

Kim grabbed the bag of donuts from Craig and dropped several on her plate. She bit one in half and chewed, washing it down with coffee. "I agree with Amy." She looked down at her dress front. "Oh, great." She began wiping furiously at the powdered sugar she'd spilled on her chest.

"I have some things you can borrow, if you'd like a change of clothes," Rosalie offered. "You, too, Amy."

"No thanks," replied Kim. "I can last one more day."

Our clothing was looking wrinkled and loose, but I figured one more day wouldn't matter to me, either. "Same here."

"Let me know if you change your mind." Rosalie rose and carried her dishes to the sink. "What do you say, Jackson? I'll wash, and you dry?"

Jackson set down his spatula and turned off the burner. "You let me do that. You all are my guests."

"Are you sure?"

"I insist."

Rosalie shrugged and headed for the door. "Coming, Robert?"

Robert rose and followed.

"How are you holding up, Jackson?" I asked from the table. Only Kim, Craig, and Cindy remained, besides myself.

"I'm okay."

"I don't suppose…"

"No, Augusta hasn't reappeared." Jackson left the kitchen quickly.

"You know, if you and Kim would like to borrow an outfit from me"—Cindy batted her perfect lashes at me—"you only have to ask. Makeup, too."

"Thank you," I replied. "Like we told Rosalie, Kim and I appreciate the offer, but I'm sure that won't be necessary. In fact, I'm hoping we won't be here much longer." I looked at my ex-boyfriend. "Craig, is there a satellite dish in this place?"

Surely no cable company would run a line out this far. This was nowhere, and the Usher House was in the middle of it.

"Sorry. There is a portable DVD player and a collection of movies in the library, if you're interested." Craig grabbed the donuts back from Kim and popped another into his mouth.

I declined. What I wanted was some communication with the outside world.

I excused myself from the table. "I'm going out to call Mom. Coming, Kim?"

Kim's answer was to shove her two remaining donuts over her pinkie and follow.

We grabbed our coats and boots. “Let’s go out through the mudroom.” I led the way. Craig and Cindy had disappeared.

The thermometer mounted to the outside wall beside the kitchen door read 30 degrees Fahrenheit. That was both good news and bad news. The good news: The corpse would be well-preserved. The bad news: We were going to freeze our butts off.

“What for?” Kim hurried out the door behind me.

“The first thing I want to do is check on Mike’s body.”

“I say again, what for?”

I trudged toward the toolshed. “Don’t you think it’s odd that Cindy went out there earlier?”

“She said she was looking for a snow shovel. What’s so odd about that?”

“Number one,” I huffed, “there is a man wrapped in a shower curtain with a knife in his chest out in that toolshed. Number two”—I paused and turned to face Kim to better make my point—“can you picture Cindy shoveling snow?”

“I see your point.”

The first things I really wanted to do were to check on the ducks and then call my mother. They were alive, Mike Holberg was not.

But Cindy’s actions had me curious.

The ground all around the front of the gable-roofed shed was trampled, and the snow had been pushed away from the entrance. I pulled back the door and stepped inside. The shed was about ten by ten feet square. A bare light bulb hung from a low rafter in the center. There were no windows.

It was as cold inside the shed as it was outside of it.

Kim took one look at the interior, gagged, and ran back out-of-doors.

I didn’t blame her. Among the assorted tools and other items, such as metal buckets and chains, Mike Holberg stood out, wrapped in plastic on the cold, hard ground. His face was barely visible. The handle of the knife tented the shower curtain over him.

I took a step closer. The plastic didn’t seem to have been disturbed.

Looking at the body lying there stiff on the ground, I realized how little I had known of Mike Holberg, a rather ordinary, middle-aged man, married, an associate of Craig’s. Did he have children?

Could his wife, Helen, have stabbed him?

The spouse was usually the most likely suspect. They could have fought. Couples sometimes did.

Perhaps I’d ask Craig about that. He might have some knowledge of what shape the Holbergs’ marriage was in.

A lovers' quarrel could have turned violent. Augusta might just have had the misfortune to have been in the wrong place at the wrong time.

I remembered the two wineglasses on the coffee table in front of the love seat. They could be important and would need to be preserved for the police—eventually checked for fingerprints, and even lip prints.

8

Having seen enough and then some, I hurried from the shed and pulled the door tight behind me. Kim leaned against the side of the building, shivering.

"Now what?" she asked.

"I want to go check on the ducks." That was what had brought us to the Usher House in the first place—Craig's insistence that there were sick waterfowl on the property. "And call Mom." Hopefully, the stars would align and there would be cell phone service.

"Good idea. Maybe she can tell us when help will arrive."

"Besides, she's probably worried sick waking up this morning and discovering I didn't come home."

We walked toward the front of the house, where we picked up our trail from the night before. Seeing our tracks leading toward the back of the property, and with Augusta Canning still missing, my curiosity got the better of me.

I veered off from the tarn.

"Where are you going?" Kim demanded, taking awkward, lumbering steps behind me. Like she had the night before, Kim was wearing my duck boots.

I looked up. The sky was overcast. "I have a feeling it might snow again. I want to see if we can learn where those footprints lead before they get buried under another foot of flakes."

Our breath came out like clouds escaping our lungs for the sky.

Kim cursed but hung to my side.

We reached the point where we had stopped during the night due to the difficulty of the terrain and the lack of visibility.

Now I knew why.

The ground dipped, then rose again. After that, we reached a rocky precipice.

"Careful," Kim warned as I inched closer.

"This has to be the ravine Craig and Cindy were talking about." It was approximately thirty or forty feet deep and no more than fifty yards across. The ground sloped severely upward on the opposite side of the ravine and was tree-covered. A single set of footsteps led right to the edge.

Several icy brown rocks stood out above the snow. I planted my hand on a rock to steady myself, then I looked down and gasped.

"What is it?" Kim asking, standing well back from the edge.

"It's Augusta." My voice was deadened by the snow.

"You see her?" Kim approached slowly and stopped behind the rock. She followed my pointing finger.

"There."

Kim grabbed my arm. "I see her."

"Careful," I said, stumbling back to keep from going over the edge.

The body of Augusta Canning was partially visible at the bottom of the ravine, twisted against the rocks, half-hidden in the snow. Pieces of clothing remained visible. I could discern a bit of her red flannel shirt and blue denim pants—the clothes she'd had on last evening when I'd first laid eyes on her. Her head was buried in a drift of snow.

Augusta hadn't even been wearing a coat. She might have frozen to death. Not that it would have made any difference. Her plummet to the bottom of the ravine would have ended all hope of escape.

"She's dead, isn't she?" Kim said. "She's got to be dead, right?" Her voice was tight.

I nodded. "No one could survive a fall like that." And a night of exposure in subzero-degree cold.

"You would think she would have known better than to run out like that in the middle of a snowstorm."

I took a photograph of the body with my phone. "Augusta must have been confused, disoriented. I can only begin to imagine how upset she must have been after stabbing Mike Holberg in the chest."

"Is that what happened, then?" Kim asked me.

"It has to be. What else would have driven her to run out in the middle of the storm?"

"Maybe it's like Cindy said. She was running from the killer."

The cold reached to my core now.

"No. There was only one set of footprints in the snow. Nobody was with her or chasing her."

"True. Unless it was the ghost of Stanley Usher. Ghosts don't leave footprints."

I blew into my hands for warmth. "Can we not bring ghosts into the equation? There's enough to figure out without adding spirits to the mix."

Kim wrapped her arms around herself. "Could Augusta have committed suicide?"

"It's not impossible. But there are simpler, faster, and more certain ways of ending your life than throwing yourself into a ravine in the middle of the night."

Kim pulled a tissue from the pocket of her coat and dabbed at her red, dripping nose. "I guess you are right. Augusta must not have been thinking straight."

"Come on." I pulled Kim away from the precipice. In the distance, I saw a bundled-up figure standing at the edge of the dock and we moved toward it.

It was Craig. "What are you two doing out here?"

"Same as you," I said, gesturing to the cell phone in his palm.

"Then I hope you have better luck than I did. I couldn't get a signal. I wanted to check on the biergarten, make sure things are running smoothly."

I rolled my eyes. "Leave it to you to worry about business when there are two dead bodies lying practically at your feet."

"Money matters, Amy." His voice came out in puffy white clouds. "Everybody needs it—even you."

I refused to respond. We'd had this argument before.

"Craig," Kim said angrily, "what Amy is trying to say—"

Craig held up his hand to stop her. "Wait. What do you mean *two* dead bodies?"

"That's what we are trying to tell you." Kim turned to me. "You put up with this guy for six years?"

"And three months." I thrust my hands in my pockets for warmth.

Craig squawked. "If anyone put up with anybody—"

"We found Augusta," Kim announced.

Craig's his hands fell. "You did? Where?"

"Back there." I pointed. "At the bottom of the ravine."

Craig stomped off in the direction from which we had come.

"She's dead, Craig!" I hollered. He blew my words off with a wave of the hand.

Kim and I shared a look and trudged after him.

"You see?" I said, coming up carefully alongside Craig.

"Yeah, I see." He turned toward Kim and me. "What the heck happened?"

"My guess is that she stabbed your pal, Mike Holberg, then ran out of the house."

"Into a blizzard?" Craig's voice rose in disbelief.

"Maybe she thought she could run away. Maybe she got lost. I don't know. All we know for certain is that she ended up down there." I pointed. "End of story." The end of Augusta Canning's story, anyway.

Craig was pacing back and forth, and it was driving me crazy. "And for heaven's sake," I snapped, "get away from the edge before you end up like Augusta."

"Huh?" Craig looked at his feet, suddenly realizing that he was only inches from going over the precipice. And I was pretty sure he couldn't fly, despite his tendency to strut like a peacock. He jumped away from the ravine. "Why would Augusta stab Mike?"

"You tell us."

A lone hawk circled lazily overhead, seemingly undisturbed by the cold.

"How would I know?"

"Rosalie suggested that Augusta and Mike might have been having a late-night assignation," Kim said.

Craig frowned. "You think?"

"I'm just saying…" Kim spread her hands.

"Man." Craig chuckled. "Mike moves fast."

"Moved," I corrected.

"Right." Craig looked contrite and, dare I say it, a bit saddened.

Whether it was because he had lost a friend, he'd lost a business partner, or simply not have been the one to have had an affair with Augusta Canning, I couldn't be sure.

I looked at my phone. I had a smidgen of a signal. "Let's call the police, then get back to the house."

"Fine by me," Craig said. He whipped out his own phone. "I'm freezing my butt off out here."

As I brought my phone up to my ear, it beeped at me. I pulled it back and looked at the screen. I had two voice mails. I hit play. The first was from my mother, left about two hours before. As I expected, she'd discovered I hadn't slept in my bed last night and was worried.

The second call was from Derek, asking how I was doing and whether my power was out, too. I pursed my lips.

"What is it?" Kim asked.

"I had a message from Derek asking if my power was out. It sounds like the whole town has been hit pretty hard by the storm."

"Tell me about it," groused Craig, stuffing his phone back in his parka. "I just talked to my assistant manager at Brewer's. The power is out and most of the roads are blocked."

"How did he get to Brewer's?" Kim asked.

"The guy lives in a condo near the lake. He walked over. I told him to make sure everything was secure and go back home. We won't be selling any beer or food today."

I took a step away from Kim and Craig for privacy and dialed my mom. "Hi, Mom."

"Amy, dear. Are you all right? Where are you?" The cell reception was weak, and my mother's voice rose and fell sporadically.

"Kim and I are at the Usher House. We had to spend the night."

"I told Dan that was probably what happened. He sounded worried. Worried and tired. I think he was up all night."

"Dan Sutton?"

"Yes, he was looking for Kim. Apparently, she wasn't answering her phone."

"Phone reception has been tricky." I explained briefly about the storm.

"We are not much better off here," Mom explained. "Birds and Bees is snowed in. I'm afraid we won't be able to open today."

"Just stay safe and warm. It won't hurt to be closed for a day or two."

"Oh, Derek also called this morning asking about you and—"

"What? Hello, Mom?"

"I said Derek called this morning. I told him you weren't home and had probably had to spend the night at the Usher House." Meaning, to Derek, that I had just spent the night with Craig.

I winced. I hoped he didn't take the situation the wrong way. I didn't know how I might have reacted if the tables had been turned. "That's the least of my problems, Mom."

"Oh?"

I explained about the murder, and how I'd found one of Craig's houseguests stabbed to death in the study.

"Are you sure you're okay?" Mom sounded distraught. "Is Kim okay?"

"We are both right here, Mom. We're fine."

"Speak for yourself," Kim yelled at the phone. "I'm freezing, Mrs. S.!"

My phone beeped a warning and I looked at the screen. The battery was weak. "Mom," I said quickly. "I have to go. My phone is dying." Okay, that was a poor choice of words. "Do me a favor and call Jerry, would you?"

"Of course, Amy. I'll call right away. I'm sure the police are busy—but a murder! I'm sure that will be a priority."

"Thanks, Mom."

"I checked the weather report on my phone earlier. According to the news, there's another storm expected. Power is out all over town. Emergency crews are busy. It might be a while. Are you sure you aren't in any danger?"

I heard the fear in her voice.

"It's okay, Mom. Really. We're safe. We are not in any danger. We found the body of the woman who stabbed Mike Holberg. She is at the bottom of a nearby ravine."

"*Two* bodies!" Mom squealed.

I held the phone away from my ear a moment. "Yes. So you see, we are completely safe." My phone gave me another annoying beep. "Gotta go, Mom. If I don't answer, it's only because reception is spotty or my battery is dead. So, don't worry, okay?"

Mom promised she wouldn't, but I knew that she would.

We said our good-byes. Kim and Craig were watching me. "The town got hit pretty badly by the storm. Mom said power is out there, too. She's calling the police now."

"How long before they arrive?" Kim slapped her arms against herself for warmth.

"We'll see," I replied. "As soon as they can safely get here."

"Great," Craig snapped angrily. "Paul is in Eleuthra working on his tan and I'm stuck here on this freaking mountain with two dead bodies."

Kim walked slowly to the brink of the ravine. "Speaking of which, how are we going to get her up here?"

"Get her up here? Impossible!"

"Impossible?" I asked.

"There is a trail leading down." He waved. "Back that way. But it's narrow and steep, treacherous at the best of times. I tried it myself when we first arrived. You want to risk your necks climbing down in this snow and ice? I don't." He made a beeline for the house. "Let the police deal with the problem. That's what they get paid for. At least we don't have to worry about being murdered in our sleep anymore."

Kim looked at me for guidance.

After a moment's hesitation, in which I weighed our options for retrieving Augusta Canning's body—without injuring or killing ourselves—I started after Craig.

9

We shrugged off our overcoats and boots at the kitchen door. A glance at the thermometer told me that the outdoor temperature had risen to a balmy 32 degrees.

Cindy sat at the table touching up her fingernails with a slender nail brush and a bottle of coral-colored nail polish.

“Any luck?” she asked.

“Do you mean good or bad?” asked Kim.

Craig bussed Cindy’s cheek.

She pushed him away. “Your nose is cold, honey bear.”

“Sorry. Is there any hot coffee?” He looked at the unlit stove.

“I’m afraid not.” Cindy focused on her nails. “Shall I ask Jackson to make some?” Apparently making coffee was beyond her abilities, or her job description.

“No!” the three of us answered at once.

“I’ll make it,” I offered. Hopefully, the smell of brewing coffee would sweep away the pungent chemical stench of acetone that her polish was emitting.

Kim pushed me aside. “No, no. Let me do it.” She wasn’t a fan of my coffee. I left her to it. I wasn’t a fan of my coffee, either.

“Where is Jackson?” I asked. I closed my eyes for a moment, letting the warmth of the house sink down to my bones. I should have opened a store for bird lovers in the Bahamas. Preferably beachside: Birds & Bees & Beach Bums. I could practically see my open-weave hammock strung between two swaying palm trees right now, while colorful hummingbirds and parrots flitted overhead in the bright, clear blue sky.

"I haven't see him." Cindy screwed the cap onto her nail polish bottle. She caught the look that passed like a hot potato between me, Kim, and Craig. "Is something wrong?"

"Augusta's body is lying in a heap at the bottom of the ravine," Craig said. He stuffed his left hand in his jeans. "Looks like she took a nosedive." He mimed a dive with his right hand.

"Oh!" Cindy's hand flew to her mouth. I noticed she was careful not to mess up her fresh coat of nail polish. "She's dead?"

"Dead as a duck. Dead and frozen." Craig was as callous as a barefoot marathon runner's feet. He pulled open cabinet doors and rummaged around. "Is there anything to snack on around here?"

Cindy pulled at the collar of her turtleneck sweater. Her lower half was covered in a pair of sexy, skintight leggings. They were black, so maybe she was in mourning for Mike Holberg. "Was she stabbed, too?"

"We can't tell." I found myself placing a hand on Cindy's shoulder. There were tears welling up in the corners of her eyes. "She's at the bottom of the ravine. Half-buried in snow."

Kim spoke up from the stove where she was fiddling with the percolator. "We think she was running away, got disoriented, and fell to her death."

"That's awful," whispered Cindy.

Craig found a package of wheat crackers and ripped into it. "What's awful?" We were exposed to a mouthful of wet crackers as he talked. "Augusta stabbed my business partner and then paid the ultimate price. Saves the taxpayers money, and we don't have to worry that she might go after one of us next."

"Coffee's ready." Kim carried the percolator to the kitchen table.

"Did you move her body to the toolshed?" Cindy asked.

"Are you kidding, babe? She's a hundred feet down in a ravine!" A slight exaggeration.

"You just left her there?" Cindy looked stricken.

"We had no choice," I said, not that I wanted to defend Craig, but it was the truth. "The police will deal with the body when they arrive."

"Personally, that's not soon enough to suit me." Kim fell into a chair at the table and filled an empty coffee mug.

"Especially if the charge is led by a certain police officer?" I asked with a grin. On the walk back to the Usher House, I had told her how Dan had called my mom looking for her. She had looked pleased.

"It couldn't hurt." Kim's eyes twinkled.

"Somebody has to tell Jackson." Why was Cindy looking at me while she said that?

“Fine. Better me than Mister Sensitivity over here.” I left to take a look for Jackson. I checked the library, study, and dining room. I couldn’t find him in any of those rooms.

I climbed the stairs to Jackson and Augusta’s room, trepidation weighing down my heart. The door to his room stood open. “Jackson?”

I crossed the threshold. The room was empty. A large desk was situated under the front window. The bed was unmade. Men’s and women’s clothing lay on the floor and on the two chairs in opposite corners separated by the window that overlooked the front of the house, more stuffed ducks and duck decoys were on display. You couldn’t go anywhere in the house without practically tripping over a duck.

There was a narrow curtain hanging on the wall facing me. If it was like the bedroom I was staying in, it hid a small closet. I heard the sound of voices as I turned to leave, feeling like I was invading Jackson Canning’s privacy.

I stood outside his door. The voices were coming from across the hall, from behind the Holbergs’ closed bedroom door. Jackson Canning and Helen Holberg were talking loudly. Not shouting, but it wasn’t exactly a polite conversation.

It definitely didn’t sound like Jackson was paying his condolences to Mrs. Holberg on the death of her husband.

The old floorboards creaked as I inched closer. I pressed my ear to the door carefully and shut my eyes to concentrate. It was no use. Their words were muffled noises, nothing more.

“Amy?”

I jumped and backed away. Kim stood at the top of the stairs giving me a quizzical look. “Kim. Shh.” I held my finger to my lips. But it was too late.

Helen’s door shot open.

Jackson’s eyes were dark, and his cheeks and forehead were mottled red. His white fingers tightly gripped the edge of the door. “What are you doing here? Trying to listen in on our private conversation?” He glanced across the hall. “Were you in my room?”

“No, of course not. I-I came looking for you.”

“Well, you found me.” He crossed the narrow hall in two long steps, then he entered his room, slamming the door behind him.

Helen Holberg stood in the center of her bedroom watching me through bloodshot eyes.

“Hi, Helen.” She was wearing a long white housecoat. The bottoms of green pajamas protruded from the hemline and cuffs. Her face was swollen, but her hair was neatly combed. “How are you today?”

Kim came up beside me. "Hello, Helen."

Helen took a single step toward us. "Mike is dead, isn't he?"

I frowned. Was Helen confused? Disoriented?

"Yes." I nodded. "Last night. Remember?"

"Mike took such good care of himself, too. Always exercising. He was a fanatic, wouldn't miss a day at the gym."

Kim and I shared a troubled look.

Helen twisted her wedding band. "I remember you coming into our bedroom. Mike wasn't here."

"That's right."

"If it's any consolation," Kim said gently, "Augusta Canning is dead, too."

Helen Holberg's green eyes flickered briefly. "He killed her, you know."

"Excuse me?" Kim's voice rose.

"*Who* killed her, Helen?" I felt a frisson of fear work its way under my skin. "Who killed Augusta?"

"She killed him and he killed her," Helen said emphatically.

"Helen, that doesn't make any sense. Who—"

"They know." Helen pointed. "You can't hide from them."

Kim whispered to me, "Is she pointing at the ducks?"

Sure enough, Helen's finger pointed at the row of ducks atop her dresser.

"We should never have come." Her hand played with a loose thread on the lapel of her robe. "I told Mike we should never have come, but he insisted."

"Helen—"

"I'd like to be alone now." Helen cut me off. She walked over to the door and closed it quietly in our faces.

I waved Kim back away from the door. "That was weird," I whispered.

"No kidding." Kim shook her head. "What's wrong with Helen?"

"She just lost her husband, unexpectedly and savagely at that. She must be in shock. She's going to need some time to process her grief."

"I suppose," agreed Kim. "And it can't help being cooped up here with her husband's dead body."

"Hopefully, she can get some grief counseling when she gets back to Raleigh."

"Speaking of grief, did you break the news to Jackson about his wife?"

"Not yet." I pointed to Helen's room. "He was in there."

"What were you doing with your ear to the door?"

"Trying to hear what Helen and Jackson were arguing about."

"They were arguing?"

"By the sounds of it. They sure weren't talking about the weather."

I motioned for Kim to follow me back to our bedroom. Helen and/or Jackson might be standing on the other side of their doors listening to our conversation right now.

We stepped inside, and I closed the door behind us for privacy. "Let's sit."

We sat on our respective twin beds and faced one another.

"Something odd is going on around here," I began. The bedroom window curtains were open now, letting some welcome light into the claustrophobic space.

"Gee, you think? I'll make a pact with you." Kim swung her legs over the edge of the bed. "The next time one of us gets the bright idea to go to dinner with one of our ex-boyfriends, the other one gives them a dope slap."

I leaned back on my elbows and laughed. "Deal."

"So now we wait, huh?"

"Now we wait." Sooner or later the police would arrive. I leaned back and stared at the ceiling. "This being cooped up inside is making me crazy. What do you say we go look for the waterfowl? That's what got me up here in the first place." I rolled over to face Kim. "Every time I start out to find them, something pops up."

"Something like a dead body," Kim quipped.

"That's not even remotely funny," I replied. "True, yes. Funny, no." I grunted and came to my feet. "Are you in?"

Kim shook her head. "I'm out. Like a light, that is. I'm going to lie down and see if I can nap a bit." She fell back on her pillow. "A girl cannot survive on three hours' sleep."

"Okay. I'll be back in an hour."

"Wait!" Kim lifted her head from the pillow. "When are you going to tell Jackson about Augusta?"

"When I came upstairs, he was already in Helen's room, and when he came out he looked so angry that I was afraid to tell him anything, let alone that Augusta was dead. I thought I'd let him cool down first."

Kim rolled onto her side and propped up herself up with her elbow. "He looked like he wanted to hit somebody."

"Exactly. Maybe I should send Craig upstairs to break the news to him. What's the worst that could happen?"

"Jackson lashes out and punches Craig in the nose?"

"I said, what is the worst, not the best." I smiled, and Kim laughed.

I was only half-joking.

I started down the stairs and stopped halfway, my hand on the rail. My conscience got the better of me. I sighed and turned around.

Jackson Canning needed to know what had happened to Augusta. And like it or not, I was the best person for the task. Besides, to be fair, his flash of anger could have been sparked by his agonizing over his wife's disappearance.

I would have been angry and frightened, too, if Derek had suddenly gone missing. I tapped my knuckle on Jackson's door. "Jackson? It's me, Amy."

There was a moment of silence, then he said, "Come on in."

I pushed open the door. Jackson was leaning over picking up a pair of trousers from the rug. He tossed them on the bed. "Sorry about before. I didn't mean to—"

I put up my hands to stop him. "That's okay. You don't have to apologize."

Jackson sighed and pulled his hands roughly down the sides of his face. "How can I help you?"

"Actually, there's something I need to tell you."

He shrugged. "Spit it out. You don't have to beat around the bush with me." He scooped up a couple of balled-up socks near the dresser and put them in a drawer.

"Maybe we should sit down," I suggested.

"Okay." Jackson picked up another pile of clothing from the seat of the chair in the corner. "Here you go."

He moved to the other chair. There was a beautifully carved cinnamon-teal duck sitting atop a poorly folded wool blanket, as if it were nesting.

Jackson picked up the decoy and moved it to the dresser next to the others. "You'd think these ducks were alive." He returned to the chair and sat down atop the blanket.

I folded my hands in my lap. "Jackson, it's about Augusta."

Jackson pulled in a sharp breath. "Yes?"

"There's no easy way to say this. I'm sorry, but she's dead."

Jackson's Adam's apple bobbed up and down. His fingertips bit into his knees. "Are-are you sure?"

I nodded. "I saw her body myself."

"You saw her?" He leapt to his feet. "Where is she?"

"She's at the bottom of the ravine, Jackson." I looked down at the floor, unable to face the grief on his face. "She must have fallen."

Jackson groaned. "And you're certain she's dead? She couldn't just be hurt? Because if she is—"

"No, Jackson. I'm sorry. I wish it wasn't so."

Jackson fell into his chair so hard that the back of it hit the wall with a bang. "I can't believe it." Tears ran down his cheeks. He pushed them aside with trembling hands.

"Jackson, if there is anything I can do..." I sat there helplessly, watching him shudder and cry.

"No." He sniffed. "Who would do such a thing?" he asked. "Who?"

I didn't know how to answer. As far as I was concerned, Augusta had stabbed Mike Holberg to death and then died herself. Whether she had been trying to flee or trying to kill herself afterward, I had no idea.

"I'll bet it was Helen Holberg." Jackson's voice was suddenly as cold and hard as ice.

"What?"

"I'll bet she did it." He stared venomously across the hall toward the Holbergs' room.

"Jackson, I don't believe—"

He chopped his hand in the air to cut me off. "She accused Augusta of sleeping with her husband."

I bit down on my lower lip. "Is that what the two of you were arguing about?"

Jackson hesitated only for a second. "Yeah. She said that Augusta went downstairs last night to meet up with her husband. She accused Augusta of leading him on, luring him in like she was some kind of succubus or something. Then she claimed Augusta went mad and stabbed him." Jackson shook his head. "The woman is crazy. I told her, Augusta was with me all night. I think Helen stabbed her husband. And now she's just trying to cover for it." Jackson was seething.

"I know this is a terrible thing to ask you, and please, don't take it wrong," I said, knowing full well that there was no chance of taking what I was about to say any other way. "Could Augusta have snuck out after you'd gone to sleep without you hearing her?"

Jackson glared at me fiercely, and then his anger subsided like a retreating ocean wave. "I'm a light sleeper. I'd have known if she left the room. And she didn't."

He rose and adjusted the spacing of the ducks on the dresser. "She wouldn't."

"Do you know anyone else here who would have wanted Mike Holberg dead?"

Jackson turned quickly, knocking a duck decoy to the floor. "Augusta and I hardly knew these people!" He clenched his hands. "But..."

"But what?"

"Augusta and I took this job about six months ago." Jackson picked up the fallen duck and set it with the others. "It was her idea, not mine. I'd been laid off from my job. This offer of working as caretakers came up, and she thought we should take it.

"Personally, I wanted to get out of North Carolina completely. Ruby Lake is hours from Pittsboro, but I wanted something even farther away. Like, Alaska. We could have started a new life there. Climbing, hiking, fishing. We could have had a farm of our own."

Jackson rested his elbow on the corner of the dresser. "Now she's dead because of our coming here. It's not perfect, but it's not so bad, either, when there's nobody around but us.

"But the people who rent this place? Some of them are nice enough. Some you barely see. Others, they barely see you. Do you know what I mean?" He arched his brow.

"I'm not sure that I do."

"I mean, they act like you hardly exist unless they want something from you: clean sheets, dinner, to fix a lousy clogged toilet." He kicked the nearest chair with his boot.

I held my breath.

"And sometimes, sometimes they talk."

"Talk?"

Jackson grinned enigmatically. "They talk, and they say things to each other and about each other like we are no more important than the furniture." He struck the back of the chair with his fist. "But there's a big difference." He tugged his right earlobe. "We have ears."

"And the people staying in the house now?"

"Oh, they say all kinds of things."

I tilted my head. "What kinds of things do they say?"

Jackson opened his mouth, then snapped it shut. "What's the difference? It doesn't matter now. Augusta is dead. Mike Holberg is dead."

I thought for a moment. "Jackson, please, if Augusta didn't kill Mike Holberg—and I don't know if I can believe that Helen did—"

Jackson threw back his head and snorted.

"Then who?"

It took a moment before he answered. "Robert Flud, maybe. He and Mike Holberg were always arguing. If not Helen or him, take your pick. All of these people hate one another. No offense, but your ex-boyfriend, too."

"None taken."

"The way they feel about one another, I don't know why they all came up here together in the first place." Jackson ran his hand along the wall. "Then again, maybe it's this house that makes them that way."

Jackson's words suddenly gave me goose bumps. Did he really think the house had some sort of supernatural influence over its occupants?

"What exactly were Mike and Robert arguing over?"

"Money, from what I could gather."

"Money?" Not women?

"I got the feeling that Robert owed Mike a bundle and that Mike was tired of waiting for payback." Jackson sneered. "Maybe payback is exactly what he got."

That made a certain amount of sense, but Robert was here and it was Augusta who was dead.

"You don't believe that Augusta would ever…hurt herself?"

Jackson snorted. "Augusta? Not in a million years. Now, if you don't mind, I'd like you to show me exactly where you saw her."

"She's very far down, Jackson. I don't think there is anything we can do until the police and fire rescue teams arrive."

Jackson stared at me grimly. "I have to try."

I stood. "I understand. I'll take you."

"Thanks." Jackson started for the bedroom door and I followed. "Augusta and I should never have come here." He glanced at me over his shoulder. "And neither should you."

I was about to tell Jackson just how much I agreed with him when the house shook.

I squeezed my brows together. "What's that noise?"

10

A loud, coughing metallic din came from the side of the house. The windows vibrated like angry glass bees.

Jackson ran to the bedroom window. He leaned over the desk and threw open the curtains. "That's Craig!"

We both stood transfixed as Craig came rumbling around the side of the house in a big, rusted-out red tractor spitting blue-black smoke.

"Is he crazy?" Jackson gasped.

"Is that a rhetorical question?" I asked.

The tractor slid sideways and bumped the corner of the house before straightening. That was going to cost Craig his security deposit.

While the tractor was having trouble negotiating the snow, Craig was managing to move forward a few feet at a time.

"What is he up to?" I flew down the stairs. I heard Jackson's pounding steps behind me. At least I hoped they were Jackson's. If it was the ghost of Stanley Usher trying to catch me, I planned to keep running until I hit the county line.

I had a remote, yet fervent hope that ghosts couldn't cross county lines.

I threw open the front door, unprepared for the cold and the racket that assailed me. I spotted Robert waving his arms and jumping up and down. I cupped my hands at my mouth and shouted, "What's Craig up to?"

"Hi!" Robert waved at us. "Isn't it great?" he shouted.

I waded through the snow to Robert's side. Craig chugged past and waved. There was a big, dumb grin on his face.

"Get off that thing before you kill yourself!" I jogged alongside the tractor. Smoke billowed from the engine.

Craig made a face at me. "Give me a break. I know what I'm doing, Amy!"

"How about telling me, then?" I huffed. Craig had sped up and I was forced to drop back.

Robert approached. "We found the tractor in the barn. Craig offered to go for help."

"He'll never make it."

"I don't know." Robert had his eyes on the slowly moving tractor. "He seems to be making out all right."

"I'm not sure that old tractor will make it down the mountain." Jackson had thrown on his jacket and joined us. Others were gathered at the front door.

"I'm not sure it will make it down the drive," I replied.

"You're being too pessimistic." Then, as if noticing Jackson for the first time, Robert laid a hand on Jackson's shoulder. "Hey, Jackson. Sorry about Augusta."

Jackson's mouth flattened. "I'll bet you are." He turned and stomped off.

The sound of splintering wood and a muffled *thud* caused Robert and me to look toward the edge of the property. The tractor lay on its right side.

There was no sign of Craig.

We both took off as fast as we could. Given the deep snow, I stuck to the tractor tracks as much as possible. My heart was beating fast as we approached the wreck.

"Where's Craig?" I shouted.

Snow hissed at us and turned to steam that melted into the air. The tractor's engine had died, although black smoke billowed from its side.

It was clear what had happened. The wooden bridge crossing the ditch had been unable to support the weight of the tractor.

Now we were really stuck.

If Craig wasn't dead, I was going to kill him.

"There he is!" Robert pointed and leapt into the snow-filled ditch.

Craig lay sprawled out about six inches deep like an upside-down snow angel. Together, we flipped him over.

"Are you okay?" Robert asked.

I gave Craig a slap on the cheek. I didn't know if it would help bring him around or not, but it sure made me feel better.

I was about to hit him a second time when he raised his hand and stopped me.

"Okay, okay. Quit that, Amy!" He rubbed his cheek. "I'm okay. I'm okay."

I yanked my arm free. Robert and I helped Craig to his feet.

"Nice going, Craig," I said. "Not only are we trapped now, but you've succeeded in busting the bridge and blocking the drive. Nobody can get in or out."

Craig frowned at the tractor. "I warned Cindy this might happen."

"Come on," I said. I had run outside without a coat. Hoodie dresses were hardly snow-worthy. If I wasn't careful, I was going to end up with frostbite. It was time to borrow some proper clothing.

"Let's get you back to the house," I said. "Are you sure you can walk?"

"Yeah."

Cindy was waiting at the front door. "Are you okay, honey bear?"

"Good as new," Craig replied, stamping his feet and stepping inside.

"Yeah," Robert said, pulling off his coat, "but the bridge isn't."

I shivered and closed the door behind us. "Cindy, have you got some warm, dry clothes I could borrow?"

Cindy beamed. "Of course. Come on. Let's go upstairs and shop!"

Five big black, designer-labeled suitcases were open on the floor of Cindy and Craig's room. Two were filled with Craig's clothing; the other three overflowed with Cindy's belongings.

"Wouldn't it be simpler to keep your things in the bureau?" I stood in awe at the amount of clothing they'd brought. There was also an open jewelry box on the bureau—next to an assortment of stuffed and carved ducks, of course. After all, why should this room be any different from the others?

The small bedroom I was occupying with Kim had its share of waterfowl, including an eerily lifelike pair of diminutive stuffed buffleheads on wooden mounts attached to the wall.

Cindy's jewelry box contained all manner of baubles. Expensive baubles at that.

"I suppose." Cindy was kneeling in front of the suitcases. "I never got around to it." She turned and appraised me. "These might do. The jeans are practically new and stretchy. They would look good with this turtleneck."

She held up the suggested outfit for my consideration. There wasn't a chance of me fitting into a pair of Cindy's tight denim pants no matter how much she claimed they stretched.

"Let's keep looking." I squinted as she rifled through stacks of slacks. "How about a nice pair of sweatpants? And maybe a second pair for Kim, if you're sure you don't mind."

"I don't mind at all." Cindy scooted over on her knees to the suitcase at the end of the row. After a careful search, she pulled out one purple outfit and a pink one. The purple outfit consisted of a sequined, cashmere, zippered hoodie and drawstring track pants. I'd keep that one for me.

"Thanks." I took the clothes in my arms. "These will be perfect."

The pink velour track suit I would give to Kim. One of us was going to have to walk around with a "Juicy" butt—better her than me. She also handed over underwear and socks.

It seemed the humiliation would never stop. Now I was being forced to borrow clean underwear from my ex-boyfriend's new girlfriend.

Cindy put the remaining clothes in her suitcases back in order. "Did you tell Jackson about finding Augusta?" she asked without turning around.

"Yes. He seemed pretty shaken, but I'm sure the news wasn't unexpected at this point."

"I suppose." Cindy sat cross-legged on the floor facing me. "It must be hard when you learn someone you loved is a murderer."

"Jackson doesn't think she is."

"Oh?"

I shook my head. "He thinks Mike's wife might have stabbed him." I watched carefully for Cindy's reaction.

"Helen?" Cindy leaned back, using her arms for support. "She doesn't seem the type, if you ask me."

"Is that your professional opinion?" I had practically forgotten that Cindy was a psychologist. I had let my feelings for Craig color my opinion of her. As a psychologist, she might have some insight into these people I was trapped with, including their motivations and desires and maybe even their potential to commit a murder.

"I guess it is."

"What was your opinion of Augusta Canning? Professionally, I mean."

Cindy leaned farther back and blew out a breath. "Well, we didn't see much of her. She was officious, good at her job. She seemed to want to do well."

"In other words, she seemed completely ordinary. Not unstable in any way?"

"She did seem a bit put out when our guests arrived."

"Speaking of your guests, Mike Holberg didn't say or do anything to Augusta that would have made her mad enough to kill him?" Could he have insulted her badly enough or even physically attacked her, thus provoking her to retaliate?

"Not that I ever saw." The beginnings of a smile formed on her face. "Robert, on the other hand…"

"You alluded to something going on between Robert and Mike before. What is it?"

Cindy leapt lightly to her feet and sat on the edge of the bed. She patted the mattress for me to join her.

I laid my borrowed clothes on a chair by the door and did so. "I'm listening."

"Craig is trying to get a big Chatham County land deal together between his investment group and Mike's."

"I heard that. Helen said Mike had already turned him down. And Jackson told me that he overheard Mike and Robert arguing. He got the impression that Robert owed Mike a lot of money."

"I know all about Mike turning Craig down. Craig told me. I've heard nothing about Robert owing Mike money. Craig put a lot of money down on a big development deal and then Mike backed out of promised funding. Honey bear's got less than sixty days to make his next payment on the property or he loses everything—the down payment and the property."

"What does Robert have to do with any of this?" I asked. Cindy was talking in circles. Circles leading nowhere.

"Robert is Mike's VP. He's very much in favor of the deal."

"I wonder why Mike Holberg and Helen came on this trip if he already told Craig no."

"Craig says he was hoping to get him to change his mind," Cindy was quick to explain. Then she narrowed her eyes at me. "You're not suggesting that Craig had anything to do with Mike's murder, are you, Amy?"

"Of course not." I felt myself blushing.

Cindy stood and planted her fists on her hips. "Oh, Amy." She shook her head in disappointment. "I was hoping we could be friends." She took my hands in hers. "And we still can. But you really need to get over this jealousy of yours."

"Jealousy?" I tried to get my hands free, but Cindy wasn't letting go.

"Craig and I are in love. You need to move on. Trust me, as your friend, when I say you'll find somebody." She pushed her brows together, but only momentarily for fear of permanent wrinkling. "What about this Dirk fellow?"

"That's Derek." I yanked and succeeded in breaking free.

"Yes. I'm sure if you give him a chance—"

I scrambled to my feet. "Thanks, Cindy. I'll keep that in mind." I ran to the door before we bonded even further.

"Wait!" Cindy came running after me. "You forgot these!"

She thrust the clothes into my arms and left.

In the hallway, I ran into Helen coming out of the bathroom. “Do you know when we will be able to leave?” She played with her wedding band. “I need to make arrangements.”

I smelled alcohol on her breath. Her eyes were streaked with red.

I explained about the weather, the power outages, and the rough condition of the roads. “I’m sure it won’t be much longer.”

“I hope so.” Helen started for her room and I followed along.

“It must be a blessing to have friends like Robert and Rosalie here to support you in this awful time.”

Helen swung around, her eyes slits. “The only thing those two care about is themselves. They certainly don’t care about me.”

I couldn’t pass up an opening like the one Helen had just given me. “Is it true that Robert owed your husband a lot of money?”

A small smile showed on her face for the first time since the news of her husband’s death. “I’d call a half million dollars *a lot*, wouldn’t you?”

“Yes, I would.”

“It’s a pity Mike didn’t have time to do what he intended. That would have served them right.”

“Them who? You mean Robert and Rosalie?”

“That’s right. Mike was going to dissolve the company, leaving Robert and his floozy high and dry.”

Helen pushed open her bedroom door and retreated once more into her private world.

11

I went to the bedroom Kim and I shared. Kim was still snoring, so I left the pink Juicy track suit and some clean socks and underwear at the edge of her bed and quietly tiptoed out.

I knew she would thank me for it later. Not.

I changed quietly in the bathroom. Catching an unfortunate glimpse of myself in the bathroom mirror over the sink, I was horrified to see a human-sized eggplant with appendages looking back at me. "Thank you, Cindy," I muttered, then turned quickly away.

I headed back downstairs and went straight to the study. With everything going on, I had forgotten about the wineglasses that had caught my eye the night before. I could be proven wrong, but they might provide some clues as to what had gone on the night Mike was stabbed.

I was going to set them aside for the police to examine.

But when I got to the study, the coffee table was empty. Hearing voices in the kitchen, I headed that way. Cindy, Jackson, Craig, Robert, and Rosalie were all present. The two couples were playing a card game at the kitchen table. Jackson was chopping carrots on a cutting board beside a pile of damp romaine leaves.

"Has anybody seen the glasses that were in the study?" I asked, popping my head around the corner.

"What glasses?" Craig asked.

"The two wineglasses that were on the table when I found Mike."

"The ones on the coffee table?" Cindy asked.

"Yes."

"I carried them to the kitchen," she answered brightly.

"And I washed them and put them away behind the bar," Jackson added.

"Why do you care, Amy?" Craig asked. "We've got plenty of glasses. If you want a wineglass, just grab one from behind the bar."

"Because those glasses could have been evidence."

"How do you mean?" Cindy tilted her head.

"I mean they could have had fingerprints on them or maybe the state crime lab could have found some DNA in the wine." I had no idea if that was even remotely possible. I was trying to impress on them all just how crucial it was to maintain the crime scene for the Ruby Lake Police when they arrived.

"Gee, that's too bad." Craig returned to his hand and took a card from the deck. "Gin."

I fumed. "I thought we'd all agreed to stay out of the study." I pointed. "It's a crime scene."

"I only wanted to clean up a little." Cindy pouted.

"Yeah, lighten up, Amy." Craig tugged on Cindy's chin and she smiled at him.

Since when did Cindy stoop to housecleaning?

"I'm going out to the tarn," I said, grabbing my coat and duck boots. I needed some fresh air and a change of scenery. Craig and his cronies were getting under my skin big-time.

"Whatever for?" Rosalie looked amused.

"Bird watching. I want to observe those wood ducks some more." I glared at Craig. "You haven't been feeding them any more table scraps, have you?"

"Of course not. You think I'd go hiking out there in this weather?"

"Silly me. Driving tractors into ditches is more your speed," I said with a smile.

"It wasn't my fault the tractor slipped off the bridge," Craig huffed.

"I don't suppose there's any way of getting the tractor out of the ditch and safely out onto the road?" Hopes of driving the ancient tractor down the mountain simmered in the back of my brain.

"Nope." That answer came from Jackson. "I took a walk out and looked at it. She's too heavy for us to lift. It's going to take a tow truck or another tractor to free her."

Jackson dumped the chopped carrots and lettuce in a bowl and covered it with plastic wrap. He set the bowl in the refrigerator. "By the way, Craig, I took a look at the side of the house where you clipped it with the tractor."

I snorted, and Craig looked affronted.

"It's going to need a couple of replacement boards, but you didn't break through. It's all superficial damage. Still, I'll have to let the owners know.

But, in my opinion, it should be as good as new with a little work and minimal expense."

"That's a relief," Craig sighed.

"Don't forget the little matter of the broken bridge and the beached tractor," I added.

"Yeah, the bridge…" Jackson appeared troubled. He had probably been hoping that we would all drive quickly away at the first sign of a thaw.

"And so we remain castaways." Rosalie thumbed her playing cards.

"Well, this castaway is going bird-watching." It was a lot better than being cooped up with this sour bunch of grapes.

Robert pushed back his chair. "Hold on, Amy. I'll go with you."

"Are you sure?"

"Yeah." He looked at Rosalie. "I could use some fresh air."

"Take him, Amy." Rosalie studied the playing cards in her hand and rearranged two of them. "He could use the exercise."

"What about our fourth?" Craig complained.

Rosalie smiled at Jackson. "Come join the party, Jackson. You can play with me."

"How's Helen holding up?" Robert asked as we neared the tarn. The sky was dark gray, and a few fat flakes fell silently around us.

"To tell you the truth, I'm worried about her."

"Oh?" Robert shifted the collapsible tripod from one shoulder to the other. We had stopped at the minivan first for my binoculars and spotting scope. The scope was mounted to a collapsible tripod. Robert had offered to carry it for me.

"She seems to be very fragile right now."

We came to a stop near the edge of the tarn, at least as close as I planned to get. Snow and ice extended over the water, making the boundary between tarn and land difficult to distinguish.

One wrong step could prove disastrous.

"Have you and Rosalie tried talking to her? The four of you must have been close." Since Robert had brought up the subject of Helen and Helen had said some interesting things about him, I thought it would be good to hear his side of the story.

"Yeah." Robert set up the tripod and swiveled the spotting scope in the general direction of the ducks. "We tried. She refused to talk." The tripod wobbled and he jammed the legs deeper into the snow. "The woman can be difficult."

I could see duck and other bird tracks in the snow along the edge of the water. Then I spotted a pair of beautiful wood ducks moving out toward the center of the tarn. More followed.

I pulled the lens covers from my binoculars and zoomed in on the wood ducks. I counted eight of them now, moving lazily offshore. There were also two pairs of mallards near the opposite shore.

"Everything looks fuzzy." Robert held one eye closed and was squinting through the viewfinder of the scope.

"Let me adjust the focus for you." Robert stepped aside and I trained the scope on the tightest grouping of wood ducks. I turned the focusing ring until the water fowl came in sharp and clear. "Take a look now."

"Thanks."

Robert stuck his eye over the eyepiece once again. "Hey, what are those?" He pointed. "Beautiful, aren't they?"

"Those are the wood ducks."

"I saw some fake ones in the house, but until you see them for real, well, it's hard to believe that they really existed out here in nature."

I chuckled. The wood duck was one of my favorite birds. They, meaning the male of the species—yes, Mother Nature had a sick sense of humor—were stunningly beautiful with their distinctive metallic purple and green head, white stripes and ruddy brown chest and buff sides. This was particularly true during mating season, a time when males of most all bird species were at their brightest. The male wood duck was also notable for its bold red irises.

I had seen Kim's irises look like that a time or two, but those times had involved tequila and not necessarily mating.

Female wood ducks, on the other hand, were nothing to write home about, although if I knew Mother Nature's address, I had a few choice words to send her concerning the relatively drab appearance of the female wood duck, with their grayish-brown heads and white speckled bodies.

The only thing, besides the essentials, of course, that the female shared with the male wood duck were the boxy heads, broad tails, and stout bodies. The females also had a white ring around the eye, although this turned yellow during mating season. Mating season was yet months away, so these females had the white rings.

"Wood ducks are year-round residents in the Carolinas. However, I rarely see them." I planned to make the most of my visit. I was determined to get something good out of this unplanned overnighter.

"Are they legal to hunt?"

I bristled as I brought the binoculars back to my eyes. “I spoke with Helen myself a little.” I wanted to keep the subject of our conversation on the Holbergs, not hunting.

I also knew I had to proceed carefully in my questioning of Robert. If I said the wrong thing, made him suspicious or angry, he’d shut me out. “She seemed confused. I’m not sure what to make of half the things she said.”

“What sort of things did she say?”

“First she accused Augusta of stabbing Mike.”

“Wow! Really?” Robert pulled his eyes from the scope and looked directly at me.

“She also said her husband was a fitness freak.”

“True. He exercised every day.”

“Yet there was no sign that he even tried to fight off his attacker.”

“Maybe he didn’t see the attack coming.”

“He was struck in the chest.”

“Then I guess it happened quickly.”

Robert had an answer for everything. “Then she said something about how maybe you and Rosalie were involved.”

Robert frowned. “Me and Rosalie? That’s nuts.”

“She also said that her husband was going to dissolve the company and…how did she put it? I remember now. Leave you ‘high and dry’.”

“That’s crazy, too.” Robert squinted through the eyepiece once more. “Mike and I had our differences, but it was all small potatoes. In fact, Mike was planning to retire.”

“He was?”

“Yep.” He maintained his gaze on the wood ducks. I did the same. “In fact, he agreed to let me buy him out.”

“You mean he was selling you his business?”

“That’s right. Lock, stock, and barrel, as they say.”

“That’s funny. Helen didn’t mention anything like that to me.”

“Maybe he hadn’t told her yet.”

“I don’t think so. In fact, Helen told me you owed her husband a half million dollars. If that’s true, how could you afford to buy him out?”

Robert seethed. “That’s a lie. Sure, I borrowed some money from the company but I paid it back.” He stuffed his hands in his coat pockets. “In full.”

“I’m impressed. A half million dollars is a lot of money to come up with.”

“It just so happens I made a killing in a private deal of my own,” Robert gloated. “Mike Holberg wasn’t the only guy who knew how to make money.

Despite his thinking so." Robert's cheeks were deep red, and I didn't think it was merely from the cold.

"Not to speak ill of the dead"—Robert sneered—"but his company is going to be better off without him. So is Helen." He snorted.

"How do you figure?"

"Two million dollars buys a lot of solace."

"Two million dollars?" That would buy a lot of tissues for the grieving widow.

"Yeah, and that's just the life insurance. She's also got the business assets, the house, and everything else in his personal bank accounts."

"Two million dollars is a lot for a life insurance policy."

Robert shrugged me off. "Not really. I had a company-paid policy, too, only for a million, though. That was Mike's way of telling me I was only worth half as much as him, I guess."

It sounded like Robert fostered a lot of resentment for the dead man.

Craig and Cindy had million-dollar policies, too. What was that all about?

I had zip for life insurance. Maybe it was about time I had some, for my mom's sake. If anything happened to me, she could be stuck with my mortgage and having to run Birds & Bees herself. At her age and with her illness, even with the assistance of Kim and Esther, that would be challenging.

"Cindy told me that Mike had backed out of a deal with Craig on some property in Chatham?" I said.

"Yeah. Craig was furious, but I told him not to sweat it. I told him everything would work out." A smile broke across his face. "I guess I was right."

"Why did Mike come on this trip?"

"You want my opinion?" I nodded and he gave it. "Because he liked to watch people squirm. He enjoyed people fawning all over him and making them jump through hoops for him."

Was that what Mike Holberg had done to Robert Flud?

I was about to ask the question when a sudden gust of wind sent me sideways. I dropped the binoculars, letting them dangle around my neck by their nylon strap. The snowfall was getting denser.

"Maybe we should head back." Robert was looking at the quickly moving gray clouds overhead. It seemed much darker now than it had been five minutes earlier.

"In a minute. I want to get a couple of photographs first for the wall."

"Wall?"

I explained about the bulletin board in Birds & Bees. “My customers will love to see these wood ducks.”

I pulled out my cell phone.

“A bit far away for a good photo, don’t you think?” Robert looked doubtfully at my phone. “Especially in this light.”

“Sometimes you have to work with what you’ve got.” I fished in my coat pocket for the item I had also fetched from the minivan. “I can’t do anything about the light, but I can get closer.”

I had a small, clever attachment that hooked my cell phone to my spotting scope. This allowed me to zoom in close on my target and use my cell phone’s camera to take photographs. “I use this.”

“What is that?”

“Watch.” I placed the phone mount on the scope’s eyepiece. I pressed the button on the side of my phone to bring it to life. I had shut the phone down earlier to conserve my battery. With no cell reception at the Usher House, there was no point in wasting what little battery life remained.

As the phone sprang to life, several text messages popped up. I scrolled through them. Several were from customers asking when we would be open, one from Chief Kennedy wanting to talk to me—about the murder, no doubt—and another from Derek telling me that he had talked to my mom and he hoped I was safe—he was such a sweetie.

Cousin Riley had texted to say that he was busy helping the town clear the streets, but he promised to come shovel out the Birds & Bees as soon as he could. My cousin owned a tractor and served as one of the town’s many volunteer snow-plow operators.

The last message was from my mom, checking in on me. “It’s my mother,” I told Robert, holding the phone up to my ear and listening to her message. “Hold on a second.” I stepped away and dialed her back.

My call went straight to voice mail. I left her a quick message assuring her that everyone was fine and that I was happy to hear that everybody in town was, too.

I hung up the phone.

“Everything okay?” Robert asked.

“Yes. The town is still mostly snowed under. On the plus side, Mom said that Jerry promised that help would be here tomorrow.”

“Who’s Jerry?”

“The chief of police.”

“I see.” Robert stabbed his toe in the snow.

I gazed up at the ever-darkening sky and the quick-moving clouds. “I think we are in for round two.”

"I believe you're right." He grabbed the tripod. "Let's go."

I stilled his arm. "Just a couple of quick shots." I raised my binoculars. The ducks were working their way toward the safety of the shoreline.

"Okay, but make it fast." Robert held the tripod steady while I hooked the phone onto the mount.

I focused in on the slow-moving group and managed to get what I hoped would be at least a few decent photos for our bulletin board.

As we hurried back to the safety of the Usher House, Robert resurrected the conversation on Helen Holberg. "You know, it really bugs me…"

"What's that?" I spoke loudly over the rising storm.

"All that talk of Helen's. I mean, I know she just lost her husband, but she still shouldn't go around slandering people."

"I'm sure she's just upset. You know she's going through a lot right now, Robert. And being confined here, in the very place where her husband was just killed, can't be helping. Once we get out of this house, we'll all be better off."

"Tell me about it." Robert trudged forward ahead of me.

12

Later that afternoon, with the snowstorm blowing outside, I cornered Craig in the library, where he sat watching a kung-fu movie.

He barely looked up at me from his slouched position on the small sofa near the TV. "What's up, Amy? How are your ducks?"

"Time for a heart-to-heart." I planted my hands on my knees. "Why am I here, Craig? Why are all these people here?"

Craig blinked. "Uh, the snowstorm?"

"That's not what I mean!" I moved to stand in front of the DVD player and watched his head dodge my body left and right in an effort to keep up with the action on the screen. I made it easier for him by pressing the power button on the DVD player, bringing his movie to a halt.

"Hey! What did you do that for?"

I crossed to the library door and closed it. "Why did you invite all these people out here? Cindy told me all about this fiasco of yours."

Craig appeared flummoxed. "What fiasco?"

"The big deal you were trying to put together between your company and Mike's." I tugged on his shirtfront. "You're about to lose your shirt, aren't you?"

Craig straightened. "Like I told Cindy, it's all under control, Amy."

"How do you figure? By stabbing the man who was impeding you?"

"Hey!" Craig spread his hands. "That really hurts. How could you think that about me?" He shook his head in disgust. "You know me, Amy. I wouldn't hurt a fly."

"Really?" I couldn't keep my voice from rising, despite my best efforts to keep this conversation between ourselves. "Well, you sure hurt *me*, Craig!"

I turned and stomped out of the library, having accomplished nothing more than venting my frustrations, and okay, I'll admit it, some ill will that I might have still been harboring toward my former boyfriend.

I bumped into Cindy on the way out.

"Everything okay in here?" she asked. "I could hear you from the kitchen."

I blushed.

"Amy!" Craig rushed out of the library, then stopped when he saw Cindy. "Uh, could you give us a minute here, babe?"

Cindy tilted her head. "Of course, honey bear," she said sweetly. Patting my arm, she added, "I know how hard it must be for you to see me and Craig together. But think of us *both* as your friends, Amy."

I raised my arm as if to strike her, but Craig had preempted my move and held my arm in place as Cindy smiled and sashayed off to wherever it is that blondes masquerading as redheads sashay off to. Okay, so maybe I was still harboring some lingering ill will toward Craig's girlfriend, too.

Then again, I *was* wearing the woman's underwear.

I glared at Craig's fingers wrapped tightly over my forearm. "Let go of me, Craig."

"Sure." He held up his hands in surrender.

"What do you want?" I wasn't in the mood for an apology. Besides, as much as I hated to admit it, I probably owed him one myself.

"There's one small problem." Craig shifted from side to side. I knew that move. He wanted something from me.

"Problem? What sort of problem?" Being trapped in a cursed house full of quacks and ducks, with a dead body lying in the toolshed, wasn't problems enough for him?

"People have to eat."

"Not exactly a newsflash, Craig." We hovered in the entryway, which had to be the coldest spot in the house at the moment.

"Augusta is dead, and Cindy can't cook."

So, that explained why I hadn't smelled any food. "Jackson made pancakes this morning. I'm sure he intends to make dinner for us, too."

"No, he says he's only in charge of the physical property. Augusta's job was to cook. And after his argument with Helen, he said he's not inclined to cook for her at this point. He's been locked in his room most of the afternoon."

"Well, I guess I can't blame him. What about your other houseguests? Can't they cook for themselves?"

"I can't ask them to cook. Like you just said, they are my guests."

"Kim and I are your guests, too." Albeit unwilling ones. Frankly, I was beginning to feel more like I was under house arrest.

"The Holbergs, Robert, and Rosalie are my biggest investors. I need you and Kim to handle dinner."

"Not a chance."

"Do this for me, Amy, please? I'll pay you both."

"You can't afford us!"

"One hundred dollars each."

I shook my head. "What's so important about this dinner that you're willing to pay *us* to cook for you?"

"There's a lot of money at stake here, Amy."

"You are still hoping to get Mike's company to invest in your deal? Don't you think that deal is as dead as Mike Holberg himself?"

"Two hundred dollars!" Craig pleaded.

Two hundred dollars was a lot of money for cooking a single meal. "Each?"

"Each." Craig whipped out his wallet and gave me a handful of cash. "That's all I've got on me, but I'll give you the rest when we get into town."

"Fine, but we're not washing the dirty dishes." I had to draw the line somewhere.

"No washing of the dishes." Craig held up his right hand. "I promise. I'll do them myself if I have to."

I stuck the bulk of the money in my pocket. "That I'd pay to see," I said, stuffing five dollars of his cash back into his shirt pocket with a flourish.

"Are we done here?"

Craig bit his lip. "There is one other thing."

"Spill it."

"We are getting low on supplies."

"By 'supplies,' I take it you mean food?"

"Yes. My suggestion would be to keep the portions on the smaller side."

I closed my eyes and counted to ten. When I opened my eyes, Craig was gone.

I went to give Kim the good news.

I found her staring at herself in the antique floor mirror that was standing in the corner of our bedroom. "Good news. I heard from Mom. Jerry promised we'd be rescued tomorrow."

"I look like a giant stick of bubblegum," was Kim's reply.

"I don't know…" I fought to control the smirk that was trying to take over my face. "I think you look adorable."

She twisted around and looked over her shoulder at her reflection. "I am not leaving this room with 'Juicy' written across my butt."

"You have to. We're in charge of dinner, and I believe the natives are hungry."

"Let them eat snow."

"Another day or two in this house, and that might just be what we are reduced to."

"Is it that bad?"

"Let's hope not. Craig mentioned we are getting low on supplies. I guess he and Cindy never thought to stock up."

I couldn't blame them for that, as much as I would have liked to. They couldn't really have foreseen being trapped on top of a mountain with a houseful of guests. No one had predicted the severity of this storm.

Kim tugged up her pants leg. "And brown wool does not go with pink velour." She pouted as she looked down at the thick socks on her feet.

"Would you rather have Popsicle toes?"

Kim let her pants leg fall back down. "What's this about us being 'in charge of' dinner? Isn't that Jackson and Augusta's job?" Her hand flew to her mouth. "Oops!"

"Jackson is refusing to make dinner."

"Why?" Kim pulled a hairbrush from her purse and stroked her tresses while watching herself in the mirror.

"I guess it's because he's upset about Augusta. Plus, he's mad at Helen and apparently refuses to cook for her."

"I can understand Jackson being upset about Augusta, but why is he mad at Helen? She lost someone, too." She returned the brush to her purse.

"Because Jackson said she accused Augusta of killing her husband."

Kim scrunched up her nose. "Isn't that what happened?"

I shrugged. "Maybe. Probably." I stepped in front of the mirror Kim had vacated and immediately wished I hadn't. Lack of sleep and strain showed in the dark circles under my eyes and in the lines on my face.

My hair looked like I had been out in a snowstorm.

Oh yeah. I had been out in a snowstorm. I pulled Kim's brush out of her purse and worked my hair back into some semblance of style.

"Look." I placed my hands onto Kim's shoulders. "You know how I feel about Craig, but let's do it just this once. All we have to do is get through this night. Tomorrow we'll go home and put all this behind us."

"I don't know…"

"Did I mention he was paying us?"

Kim pulled her brows together.

"Two hundred dollars."

"Each?"

"Each." I raised my eyebrows. "What do you say?"

Kim grabbed the hairbrush back out of my hand. "I don't do dishes."

"Don't worry. I've got that part covered."

"Whose underwear are these, anyway?" Kim fingered the elastic waistband of her track pants and pulled, revealing the top edge of a pair of leopard-print panties.

She let them go with an accompanying *snap*. "Wait, don't tell me. I *do not* want to know."

As we moved downstairs and neared the kitchen, we heard loud voices: first, a male's and then a responding female's.

"I don't care what Helen says, I—"

Kim and I looked at each other as we turned into the kitchen. Rosalie and Robert were huddled in the corner near the stove, red in the face and as rigid as stick people. Rosalie held a wineglass by its stem. Then she lifted her chin and took a defiant sip.

"Everything all right here?" I asked. Walking in on an arguing couple was never pleasant.

Robert forced a smile. "Of course." He rubbed his hands together. "Craig says that you ladies are in charge of dinner and so we're in for a treat tonight."

Kim tossed her hair and laughed. "You mean we're ordering in pizza?"

"I wish," Rosalie said. "That would mean the road was clear enough to get out of this dump."

"Did Robert tell you? I heard from my mother. She says that the police have promised to have us out by tomorrow." I pulled open the refrigerator to see what Kim and I had to work with.

"Isn't that great news, Rosalie?" Robert poured himself a glass of wine from the open bottle of pinot on the counter. He topped off the glass in Rosalie's extended hand. "Can we help with dinner?"

"That's not necessary," I replied. "You two go enjoy yourselves. We've got this."

Behind me, Kim was opening and closing cupboards in a search for ingredients. Or for cookies. Kim loves her cookies. She set a bag of rice and a box of spaghetti noodles out on the counter, then resumed her investigation.

"Shall we leave them to it, then?" Robert reached for Rosalie's arm, but she pulled back. Apparently, the two lovebirds were going to be on the outs a bit longer if Rosalie had anything to say about it.

She grabbed the wine bottle by the neck and left the kitchen.

"Don't mind Rosalie," Robert apologized, already halfway out the kitchen door. "She gets cranky sometimes, but she doesn't mean anything by it." His empty hand gripped the door frame. "I'm sure whatever you come up with will be very...*juicy*."

Robert winked at Kim and left.

Kim blushed and pressed her rear end back against the oven door.

I grabbed a skillet from the peg over the stove. "Sometimes I think we're the only two people in this house who actually like each other."

I set the cast-iron skillet on the front burner. From what I'd seen so far, it looked like dinner would consist of beef burgers, potatoes, and carrots, because I hadn't seen anything that paired well enough with the rice or pasta—at least not anything that I was up to preparing.

"Do you like me well enough to switch clothes with me?"

"Sorry," I teased. "Not quite." I grabbed a blue-and-white-checkered apron from a hook beside the refrigerator. "Put this on. It'll cover the 'juicy' parts."

"I swear..." Kim said as she fought to tie the apron behind her back, "I *will* get even with you, Amy!"

Sadly, I knew that she would. Like the time in high school when I convinced David Bremmer, a gangly boy who preferred the violin to football, that Kim was in love with him. David spent the next week serenading her outside her bedroom window with selections of Bach and Stravinsky.

Kim was livid. Her parents had thought it was a hoot.

After a week of Kim's sometimes pleading and sometimes screaming at David to take his violin elsewhere—like to the bottom of Ruby Lake—David finally took the hint and returned from whence he had come, band class. But not before complaining that a certain Amy Simms, *moi*, had confided in him that Kim was in love with him.

The saying goes, "Don't get mad, get even." Kim doesn't put much stock in sayings. Instead, she did both: She got mad *and* she got even. A month after the David incident, with me having already forgotten all about it, Kim switched out my body lotion with self-tanning lotion.

It wasn't that I looked hideous after innocently applying it all over my body. I mean, for a pumpkin, I looked pretty darn good. That had been the nickname bestowed on me by my classmates, too—Pumpkinhead Simms—

until the bright orange finally faded away, along with the nickname, although the sobriquet lingered far longer than my orange skin.

That's why there is no photograph of me in the eleventh-grade class yearbook.

Fortunately, this time, I considered that Kim's being forced to wear a pink velour outfit with the word *Juicy* on her butt would not rise to the level of me ending up with a face the color of a ripe mango.

Not that I was going to take any chances, though. I'd be checking my lotions and potions carefully before applying them for a long time to come.

"Even for what?" a voice asked.

Kim and I spun around.

"Hi, Jackson. I wasn't expecting you." I turned back quickly and stuck my tongue out at Kim. It was only fair—she'd just done the same thing to me.

Kim put on her solemn face. "I was very sorry to hear about Augusta."

"Thanks." Jackson slouched against the counter. I noticed the edges of his hair were damp. He ran the palm of his hand over the small square tiles that lined the countertop. His eyes were puffy, and he sounded tired.

"Can I get you something?" I laid a hand on his back. "Would you like a drink?"

"Or maybe a snack to last you until dinner?" Kim added.

"No, thanks. I came down to prepare supper." The harsh kitchen lighting made his complexion appear sallow.

"Oh, great!" Kim started untying her apron.

I shot Kim a quick look. "Actually, Kim and I were going to take care of the meal ourselves. We heard you wanted to rest."

Of course, what I'd really heard was that he was refusing to have anything to do with pretty much anyone, let alone preparing our dinner, but I could hardly say that to his face.

"Why not join the others in the dining room?" I suggested. "Let us serve you for a change."

Kim was too polite to complain.

"I think what I really need is to keep busy." He lingered, standing where he was.

I thought for a moment. "How about giving us a hand, then?"

"I can do that. How about if—"

The lights flickered and went out.

13

"Hey!" Kim dropped a dish on the floor and it shattered. "What's going on?"

The whole house had gone black.

Jackson cursed. "The generator must have gone out."

I navigated toward the blue flame of the stove with my arms extended. The sounds of commotion came from the direction of the dining room and upstairs as everybody stumbled about in the dark, wondering aloud what was going on.

"Ouch!" That was Jackson.

"Sorry, Jackson." I had poked him in the chest. I bumped against the counter and slid over to the window. It was pitch black both outside and in.

"No problem. There are some candles around here someplace."

I heard the sound of a drawer opening and the rattle of hands searching.

"Got one." Footsteps shuffled across the kitchen floor. Jackson lit the candle using the burner's flame. "That's better."

"I can barely see," complained Kim. "Have you got any more of those?"

"Let's take a look." Jackson carried the candle to the drawer and shuffled more utensils around. He came up with two additional long, tapered candles and a packet of twelve previously used, multicolored birthday cake candles.

"What's this about a generator, Jackson?" He handed me a candle, and I held the wick to the flame until it caught.

Craig bounded into the room carrying my flashlight. "What the heck is going on now?"

I set my candle inside a tall glass. "Jackson was just about to explain."

"Oh. Hi, Jackson." Craig aimed the beam of the light at Jackson's face. Jackson squinted and threw up his hands. "Good to see you."

"Give me that thing before you blind somebody." I took the flashlight from Craig and switched it off. It was mine, after all.

"Tell us about the generator," Kim urged.

"There's not much to tell. We aren't exactly hooked up to the power grid up here. The Usher House is too remote. There's a propane tank on the side of the house."

"I've seen it," I said. "There's a big silver tank on concrete blocks and a smaller one next to it."

"That's right. The big one supplies power to the generator that produces the electricity—"

"So, what happened?" interrupted Craig. "Something broke? Can you fix it?"

"You want Jackson to go out and work on the generator in this weather, Craig?" I said. "Jackson, you stay right where you are."

"Listen, Amy." Craig's voice rose. "I'm the one paying the bills here and—"

"It wouldn't matter if I did go out," Jackson interrupted in his turn. "I'm sure there's nothing wrong with the generator."

"There isn't?" Kim said.

"Nope. My guess is that the tank is empty."

Craig groaned. "Empty?"

"Then how come the stove is still working?" I pointed to the gentle flame coming from the burner.

"The secondary propane tank works the stove and the water heater." He made a clicking noise. "That's about it."

I was afraid to ask the next question, but it escaped my lips against my better judgment. "What about the heat for the house?"

"I'm afraid not."

Craig groaned, louder this time. "Are you telling me there's no heat? It's freezing outside."

Jackson held his hands open over the pot on the burner. "This house isn't too badly insulated. We ought to stay warm. Sort of."

"Don't worry, honey bear. We can snuggle."

I was surprised to see that Honey Bear's mate, Perky Cindy, had joined us. She locked lips with Honey Bear like they were a pair of hormone-driven teenagers. I thought I'd puke.

Once Cindy let go of Craig's face, he turned back to Jackson. "Can't you go take a look at the generator and this propane tank?" He was breathing heavily. Apparently, a little Cindy went a long way. "There must be some way you can get the smaller tank to operate the generator." Craig clapped Jackson on the back. "What do you say we give it the old college try?"

Jackson pulled his hands back from the stove. "Sorry, the equipment isn't set up that way. We'll be fine. We have a stove and hot water. There's dry firewood for the fireplace in the storage room."

Jackson held a flickering candle up in front of his face and looked at me. "Of course, that will mean using the study."

"Fine by me," I said, albeit reluctantly. "The crime scene has been compromised so much already, I suppose we might as well."

"It beats freezing," Kim said. "Not that I feel like spending any time in a room where a man has just been stabbed to death."

"I'll gather up some wood and set up a supply pile in the study." The door to the storeroom was accessible from the mudroom, and Jackson went that way.

Craig snatched the candle from my hand and headed for the hallway. "I hope dinner won't be long. I'm famished."

Our make-do supper was served by candlelight. The others had found four candles and holders in the sideboard and spaced them out across the table.

Kim and I brought the simple fare over to the table. Nobody complained, so it couldn't have been too bad. There was some peach shortcake left over, so I brought that out, too.

I didn't bother with the ice cream. I had made the executive decision that we had all had enough cold things in our lives for the time being.

Rosalie whispered in my ear as I served the potatoes, "Talk to you after dinner, Amy?"

"Sure," I muttered back. I had no idea what was on her mind, but she certainly seemed to be one to speak it out and I couldn't wait to hear what she had to say.

"Where's Helen?" With all the food on the table, I took my chair beside Kim and helped myself to the cabernet.

"I haven't seen her all afternoon," Craig said.

"Me, either," piped in Cindy.

Jackson sat woodenly near the end of the table. Cindy set some food on his plate, which was yet untouched.

"I went to her room," Robert said. "It must have been a couple of hours ago. She refused to talk to me or even open the door."

Rosalie coughed. "I'm sure she's fine. Trust me, when she gets hungry enough, she'll put in an appearance." She turned to her husband with a small smile. "And everybody gets hungry eventually."

"Everyone with a stomach…and a heart." Robert raised his glass and drank. Judging by the bottle beside him, it was whiskey.

Dinner was awkward and the conversation sparse. Two members of our party were dead. And one refused to join us. A snowstorm raged outside, and the Usher House was without electricity.

Under the glow of the weakening candlelight, everyone's faces appeared otherworldly, slightly menacing. Even when they were smiling, it seemed sardonic.

Or perhaps it was my imagination. Perhaps it was the house and the storm having an ill effect on my state of mind.

I helped myself to a piece of shortcake, hoping to improve my state of mind, then stood. I felt a little woozy. I blamed it on the lack of sleep. But I knew that part of the blame had to be laid on the fact that I had had too much to drink.

Judging by the empty wine bottles littering the dining table, we all had.

"Are you okay, Amy?" Kim asked.

I pressed my fingertips to the table to balance myself. "Yes. I'm fine." I picked up my plate and set my glass and silverware on top of it. "I'll help you clear the table later."

"Where are you going?"

"I want to check on Helen. I'm going to prepare her a plate and take it to her."

"Good idea," Craig called out. "Tell her to come down. We can all watch a movie together. Something fun."

"Yes," Cindy said. "Please tell her to join us. I told Craig to move the DVD player to the study, where we'll be more comfortable."

I arched my brow. "More comfortable, at the scene of a murder?"

"It's the only room in this drafty old house with a fireplace," Robert said.

"Yeah. If you'd stop talking about…what happened…all the time, Amy, maybe we could *all* forget it and try to make the best of things." Craig tilted his head in Jackson's direction.

"I agree, honey bear." Cindy planted a kiss on Craig's cheek.

Jackson pushed back his chair. "Not me. I'll be in my room."

"Jackson, wait!" said Rosalie.

He left without another word.

I saw his dark silhouette moving toward the staircase as I carried my plate to the kitchen in one hand and balanced a tapered candle in the other.

I took a clean plate from the upper cabinet next to the sink and loaded it with meat and vegetables, then filled a glass with water from the tap. I had noticed some black lacquer serving trays in one of the lower cabinets earlier. I placed everything on the tray.

My candle was fixed to a small blue and white ceramic holder. I set it on the tray, as well. I picked up the tray and walked slowly, for fear of the flame going out, pausing several times on the stairway as the candle fluttered and flared.

The hallway was dark and silent and not just a little spooky. I moved to the left. Jackson's door was closed. I assumed he was inside. Helen's door was also shut.

I set the tray on the floor and knocked. "Helen? It's me, Amy. I brought you some dinner." I tilted my head and listened. Nothing. I knocked again. "Helen? Are you awake?" Okay, that was a stupid question.

I tried the doorknob. It turned easily in my hand. The hinges creaked as I pushed the door open a crack. The room was shrouded in darkness. I stuck my head through the opening. "Helen?" I whispered.

There wasn't a sound. Not a rustle. Not a stirring. Not even a gentle breath.

I looked up and down the hall. It was too dark to see anything or anyone. But I thought I saw...something. I reminded myself that there were no such things as ghosts. "Helen?"

I received no answer.

The candle on the tray on the floor illuminated only my feet. I picked up the candleholder and pushed it through the door. "Helen?"

Nothing.

I pushed the door open far enough that I could step inside. The heavy drapes were shut. Not that having them open would have made any difference to my ability to see.

I moved cautiously over to the bed.

It was empty.

I stared, frowning, at the bed, the flame flickering in my hand.

Where was Helen?

14

There were no other doors in the room. No closet. No balcony. Not that anybody would have been foolish enough to go out on a balcony in this blizzard.

I doubted Helen was hiding from me under the bed, but I dropped to the floor and looked anyway.

No Helen.

If there were any dust bunnies, or dust rats, lurking under the sagging old bed, it was too dark to notice them.

Where had Helen gone?

I looked at the bed once again. The pillow held the impression of her head. The heavy comforter was pulled back. The sheets were tousled.

On the nightstand were the bottle of pills I had seen earlier, a glass containing a couple of ounces of water, and a pitcher.

The room was warmer than I would have expected it to be, and I wondered why. I moved slowly around the room. It wasn't a small space, but the heavy furniture made it seem so.

There were two hard-shell silver suitcases to the left of the six-drawer bureau. One bore the initials *HH*; the other, *MH.* Neither was open. Atop the bureau, the ducks looked at me through glassy, deadened eyes.

I had seen enough.

I left the bedroom, closing the door behind me, picked up my tray and returned to the kitchen.

By candlelight, Kim tossed a handful of utensils in the sink with an accompanying *crash*. "What's up?"

I set the tray on the counter. "I can't find Helen."

Kim ran the faucet over the items in the sink, then dried her hands on a dish towel. She had placed a lit candle on the window ledge above the sink. "She has to be here someplace."

"I know. The question is where."

Kim picked up a glass of wine and sipped. "I wouldn't worry about it. She's bound to turn up sooner or later."

I set the plate of food I had prepared into the cold oven. It wouldn't keep warm, but the oven would keep it safe until I found Helen. "I'm worried about her. I don't like the idea of her wandering around alone in her condition."

"What do you mean?" Kim leaned back, resting her elbows on the counter. I noticed she had removed the apron. I guess that with the lights out, she figured nobody would notice her *Juicy* butt.

"She's been really upset. What if she decided to do something stupid?"

Kim pulled her brows together. "Like what?"

"Like go for a walk?"

"Outside? In this weather?" Kim sounded incredulous. "That would be crazy!" She shook her head. "It would be suicide."

"Exactly."

Kim's hand flew to her mouth. "Oh. You don't really think she'd do anything like that, do you?"

I could only shrug and speculate. "She's just lost her husband, and brutally, don't forget. We're also cooped up here in this creepy old house."

"With a bunch of creeps," Kim couldn't resist adding again.

"There is a certain 'creep factor' present," I agreed. "Who is to say how either of us would be holding up or behaving if we had just lost our husbands here?"

Kim took another drink. "I'm beginning to wonder if we'll ever *have* husbands, let alone lose them."

"Give it time. I've seen you with Dan. I think there is the seed of a real relationship there."

"Maybe," Kim conceded. "What about you and Dirk?"

"Ha-ha. Very funny. *Derek* and I may have had a couple of bumps in the road—"

"Your fault completely," Kim couldn't help but interrupt.

I folded my arms over my chest. "Yes. Fine. My fault completely. But…"

"But what?"

"Never mind."

"What? Come on, Amy. What were you going to say?" She pulled on my sleeve.

"It's not important." Okay, so I was going to say, "*but I love him*." It was sort of important—okay, very important. I just hadn't even said it to him yet. I wasn't about to tell Kim first.

Not to mention, I'd be mortified if she spilled the beans to Derek. And after this whole *Juicy* butt incident, she just might be tempted to.

"What is important right now is that we find Helen."

"We?"

"You are coming with me, aren't you? Maybe you would rather hang out with the so-called *creeps*? They are probably in the study together right now—the room where Mike Holberg was just knifed in the chest—probably watching a cheesy kung-fu movie marathon.

"Or," I taunted, "maybe you would rather go back to our cold, lightless bedroom and wait for the headless ghost of Stanley Usher to show up looking for a blood transfusion. Remind me again, what blood type are you?"

Kim planted her hands on her hips. "Amy Simms, sometimes I think you are evil incarnate."

I grinned. "It's a gift."

"So, what are we going to do?"

"Like I said, we're going to go look for Helen." I picked up my flashlight from where I had placed it earlier beside the toaster. With its weak batteries and the power outage, I had been saving it for emergencies.

In my book, Helen's disappearance qualified as one.

I clicked it on and off. Nothing. I hit it with the palm of my hand, and the bulb flickered to life.

"Let's go." I waved the flashlight in front of me. "We are going to search this house from top to bottom."

"Maybe we should check to see that she didn't go outside first."

"Good idea. There are only two doors in and out of this house." Kim followed me to the mudroom off the kitchen. The door opened easily. Snow was piled deep all around. There was no sign of footprints, human or otherwise.

We moved to the storeroom. The room was filled with stacks of boxes, miscellaneous furniture, an old canister vacuum cleaner, and a cord of firewood.

There was no sign of Helen.

We went straight to the front door. I turned the knob. The door stuck.

"Hold this." I gave Kim my flashlight and banged my shoulder against the door. This time, the door opened. The snow had to be two feet deep in drifts up around the house. The surface of the snow was undisturbed.

Kim stuck her head outside. "She didn't leave this way."

"On we go," I said. I had an idea. "Let's check Helen's room again. Maybe she stepped out to use the bathroom or something and I just missed her." That was the best-case scenario.

We padded down the hall once again and stopped outside Helen's door. I knocked impatiently. There was no answer, so I wasted no time in entering. "Shine the light around."

Kim obliged. "Her bed has been slept in."

"It was like that before. Don't forget, she spent most of the day here."

"I've seen enough, or, in this case, nothing." I left the door hanging open as we left.

Kim clung to me like a shadow as we moved through the house. We went from room to room, calling Helen's name every few minutes as we did.

Helen never answered. All of the upstairs rooms were closed up except for the bathroom. Kim and I crept into that room together. The smell of minty toothpaste hung in the air.

Kim's cold, trembling hand clung to my shoulder. "What if she's waiting behind the shower curtain with a butcher knife?"

"Must you?" I hissed. "This place is creepy enough." I was not going to let Kim scare me. But just to be on the safe side, I gave the tub-shower combo a wide berth as we approached.

I held my breath and gingerly pulled back the curtain. The metal hooks rasped, making my skin crawl as I drew them across the metal rod.

Kim aimed the light inside the tub.

"Empty." I breathed a sigh of relief. "That just leaves the downstairs." And I didn't have much hope for finding her there. Unless there were rooms we hadn't discovered yet.

"Don't you think Helen would have heard us looking for her by now?" Kim asked as we proceeded down the staircase.

"Probably. Which could mean that she's avoiding us."

"Why would she do that?"

"Maybe she's hiding from all of us." We moved into the dining room and shined the light around. "Empty."

"She's not hiding under the table." Kim moved the beam back and forth across the floor.

The library was also quiet. We heard the sounds of a movie playing in the study, so I knew Helen wasn't there or somebody would have told us she'd been located.

We swept through the downstairs hall once more. The house was cooling down, and the downstairs was already several degrees colder than the upstairs.

There was a closed door near the corner. "What's in there?"

"Beats me." Kim shined the flashlight beam at it.

I turned the knob. "It's locked."

"Maybe it's a downstairs bathroom."

"I can't remember who told me, but there's only supposed to be one bathroom in the entire house."

"Maybe whoever told you that meant a *full* bathroom."

Kim made a good point. I knocked. "Hello?"

"I noticed some keys on a ring in a junk drawer in the kitchen."

"Show me."

We hurried back to the kitchen, and Kim rummaged around until she came up with a set of keys. We carried them back to the room at the end of the hall.

I picked what I thought was the most likely candidate and tried pushing it into the keyhole. Of course, it did not even remotely fit. "Too big." I grabbed another key and tried again. And another.

"Bingo." I finally turned the key in the lock and heard a *click*.

Kim shined the light past the door, running the beam up and down the long, narrow space.

"What is all of this?" The tight, little room was filled with floor-to-ceiling shelves holding everything from canned food, bed linens, bath towels, a toaster, flatware, and dishes. "Why would anybody lock up all this stuff?"

"Owner's closet," Kim answered.

"What?"

"Owners of rental properties often keep a locked room for their personal supplies on hand for when they use the property."

That made sense. "At least we know where we can find some extra food, if need be."

"There's enough canned ham and sausages here to live on for a month." Kim spotlighted row after row of canned meats.

"I see some candles here, and batteries." I checked out the batteries. They were the wrong size for my flashlight.

"I wonder what the others are up to." Kim yawned.

"Are we giving up the hunt for Helen?"

"Can you think of anyplace else to look?"

"No, but—"

A loud, bloodcurdling scream suddenly pierced the air, the kind of which horror film legends are made and horror film actresses meet their violent, bloody, and untimely deaths.

15

"What was that?" Kim dug her fingers into my arm.

"I have no idea." My heart pounded in my chest.

"It came from down there."

I nodded. "*Down there*" was the study.

Rubbing shoulders, we tiptoed toward the study.

Kim's breath tickled my ear as she said, "You don't suppose somebody else was just stabbed to death, do you, Amy? I mean…" She stopped dead in her tracks, forcing me to do the same.

"Of course not," I said bravely. "What are the odds?"

"I don't care about the odds. I care about saving my neck."

"Turn off the flashlight," I whispered.

Dim light skimmed the hallway floor, emanating from the study. I leaned against the wall and slowly poked my head around the corner, ready to pull back at a moment's notice should there be any sign of murderers, vampires, werewolves, ghosts, or even stray poodles.

Craig sat alone in a chair in the corner of the room near the fireplace. The flames danced briskly. His eyes drooped. His gaze was fixed on the DVD player atop the bar. The screen flickered, creating dancing images on the paneled wall.

"It's Craig." I let out my breath and stepped into the study.

Craig just about jumped out of his skin and his chair. "Amy, Kim. You scared me." He blinked rapidly.

"Where is everybody else?" I asked.

"They all went to their rooms. A bunch of party poopers."

Who but Craig Bigelow could ignore all the misfortune going on around him and talk about partying?

"Even Cindy?"

More screams came from the TV.

Craig loved horror movies almost as much as he loved Asian martial-arts movies.

"Even Cindy," Craig said with a yawn "She claimed she was tired and had a headache." He stood and stretched. "I might as well turn in, too."

"Hear that, Kim? Maybe you won't have to worry about hearing strange noises when you're trying to sleep tonight."

Kim chuckled.

"Very funny."

I turned my attention to the screen. It was an old black-and-white movie and I recognized it: *House on Haunted Hill*, starring Vincent Price.

As I remembered, it was the disturbing tale of a psycho millionaire who paid a group of supposed strangers, three men and two women, ten thousand dollars apiece on the condition that they spend the night locked up in some strange old house.

To make matters more interesting, he gave each guest a pistol for protection. If anyone died during the course of their overnight stay, the survivors would split the pot of money.

If memory served, the mad doctor's wife and her lover ended up in a vat of acid conveniently located in the creepy house's basement.

Craig smothered a yawn and turned off the DVD player with the remote. "I'm out of here. If you do hear any strange noises," he said, turning to Kim, "use your imagination."

Wait. "The basement."

Craig stopped in the hall.

"Is there a basement in this house, Craig?" I asked, excitement rising. "I mean, there must be a basement, right?" I looked from Craig to Kim.

"Don't look at me," Kim said. "I have no idea."

"Now that you mention it, there are some doors almost under the kitchen window." Craig tapped his chin. "I think Jackson said they go to a root cellar or something."

"Is there any way to get into it from *inside* the house?" I asked.

"Beats me." Craig threw up his hands and disappeared into the darkness.

I sat at the edge of the fireplace, feeling the warmth of the hearthstone work its way into my flesh. "Okay, let's think this through."

Kim helped herself to a handful of popcorn from the bowl on the edge of the bar, then spit it out. "Too much salt." She poured herself a drink to wash it down.

A creaking noise came from above us, and we both looked up.

"Please don't let that be Stanley and Shirley Usher," Kim grumbled, falling into the chair Craig had vacated and crossing her legs.

"I think it's just the house settling."

"It's had about a hundred years to settle."

"Yeah, but now it is adjusting from the weight of all that snow that must be up there."

Kim's eyes widened. "You don't think the roof is going to collapse on us, do you?"

"Like you said, the house has been here forever. It has stood just fine through countless storms."

Although, perhaps never one as severe as this. This one had all the makings of what the meteorologists labeled a *"hundred-year storm."* "It survived all of them. There's no reason it shouldn't survive this one now, too."

My eyes flicked up to the ceiling, and I waited anxiously to see if the house would contradict me.

Kim shook her legs nervously. "Did it? How do we know the roof hasn't crashed down a dozen times before and simply been repaired?"

The house shrieked again, as if Mother Nature were testing its limits.

Kim was right, but telling her so would only frighten her more. "Let's focus on finding a way into the basement."

"If there is one."

"You heard Craig. There is. If there is a root cellar, surely the original builder would have wanted to have access from inside the house. Especially in the winter."

I rose, reluctantly leaving the warmth of the fire, which had nicely toasted my back. "Follow me." I picked up the flashlight.

"The kitchen is over there," I said softly, thinking aloud. "The study. The owner's closet." I moved the light to my left.

"And that's the back of the stairs. This is hopeless, Amy. I say we go to bed and say our prayers that when we wake up in the morning, the storm is over, we haven't been buried under a mountain of snow and rafters, help is on its way, the sun is shining, the snow is melting, and Helen Holberg is bringing us hot breakfast in bed."

I chuckled. "Look at this." Like much of the rest of the house, the wall along the back of the stairs was paneled. But there was a tapestry hanging near the center with a narrow, hip-high table bifurcating it. The heavy wool tapestry hung from a thick iron rod, situated about six inches down from the ceiling. The busy tapestry scene featured fruit, flowers, and birds in shades of yellows and greens.

"Hideous," Kim remarked.

I pulled back the edge. "This is it."

"This is what?"

"A door. And if I'm right, it leads to the root cellar." It made sense, too. The entrance to the kitchen was only a couple of steps away. "Help me move this table."

"Okay," Kim agreed. "But the only thing we are likely to find down there are some rotten vegetables and fungus. And spiders. You know how I feel about spiders." She shuddered.

Kim and I didn't agree on everything. But we did agree on spiders.

"Okay, if we see any big spiders, any really, really big spiders…or any rats—"

"Rats?!"

"We turn around."

"Deal. But you go first."

"Why me?"

"This was your idea. Besides, you found the door. You deserve to go first," Kim said smugly.

I frowned and laid the flashlight down on the hallway runner. I grabbed one end of the table. It held several old travel books relating to Chicago, New York, and Boston, all placed on their sides and stacked one on top of the other. The table also held a miniature spinning wheel and a pewter-framed photograph of the house that must have been taken just after it was completed.

The house looked so clean and the grounds so well-kept. It was a very different scene from the Usher House of today. Even with caretakers, the house wasn't being maintained as it should have been. The owners had probably been unwilling to spend the money on upkeep. Unable to sell the property, they were then forced to rent to cheapskates like Craig.

We set the table to one side. I retrieved the flashlight with one hand and slid back the tapestry. It moved easily across the iron rod. A wooden door was visible now, flush with the wall. It had a black iron handle.

"It's locked. Where are those keys you got from the kitchen?"

"I think you left them in the closet door."

"Right." I hurried up the hall and pulled the key ring from the lock.

"Try the skeleton key," suggested Kim.

I grabbed the big, primitive iron key hanging on the ring. It slid smoothly into the keyhole.

The lock turned easily, and I tried the handle. The door came toward me. I slipped the keys in my pocket and then aimed the beam of the flashlight downward into the pit. It was like peering into the bowels of the earth.

"There's a wooden staircase," I said. "But it's steep and the treads are narrow. Be careful."

"Trust me."

I took a couple of steps and felt Kim's breath against my neck. "Any sign of spiders or bats?"

Bats! Goose bumps rolled over my flesh. I did not want to see bats. I mean, I knew they were harmless. "Even vampire bats are harmless," I said aloud, to assure Kim, but mostly to reassure myself.

"Are you sure?" Kim trembled. "They suck blood, Amy."

"Animal blood," I replied. "Not human blood."

"Humans *are* animals, Amy."

"It doesn't matter. Vampire bats live in Central and South America. Can we talk about something else please?"

"Okay. Let's talk about the house. Because I'm pretty sure I just heard a sound like one of the rafters or maybe even the ridgeboard splintering."

"Cut that out. You are going to scare us both to death." My feet touched solid ground. "We've hit bottom."

"Tell me about it," quipped Kim.

"No." Kim bumped into my backside. "We've struck ground." I aimed the beam down. "And I mean *ground*, literally." The floor was packed earth. The air was damp and musty.

I intended to keep one eye open for any bubbling pits of acid like the one lurking in the basement of the *House on Haunted Hill.* People went into that pit. Skeletons came out.

"It's freezing down here."

The flashlight fizzled, then went out.

"Oh great." I banged the handle with my free hand. "I think the batteries are kaput."

"You pick now to run out of batteries?" Kim complained.

"It's not exactly something I got to choose." I banged the shaft again, harder. The beam again sprang to life. Well, sort of. At least we could see our outstretched hands.

But not much farther.

"Can we get out of here now? This place is dark, it stinks like there's a nest of dead raccoons living here, and it is freaking cold."

"In a minute. We're here now. We might as well take a look around."

"Your flashlight is on its last leg."

"When it dies, we'll leave. Okay?"

"In the dark? How will we find our way out of here?" Kim moaned. "We could be trapped down here forever. My ghost will be forced to haunt this house."

"Then Stanley Usher will have some company. That ought to cheer him up." I edged away from the stairs. Kim's remark about the flashlight had sunk in. I did not want to be down here without a light.

There could be spiders. There could be rats. And there could be bats, vampire or otherwise.

Given a choice, I'd rather see them before they got to me.

Bang!

"What was that?" Kim whimpered.

I looked out into the darkness. "It was nothing. The basement door banged shut."

"By itself?" Kim let out a yelp that was deadened by the damp, packed-earth floor and walls.

"It was probably just the wind."

"What wind?"

"Then it was the air pressure." I pulled my arm free of Kim's viselike grip, pretty sure her fingernails were leaving tracks in my skin.

I moved through the small space carefully. The weak light didn't let me see far. There were moldy boxes, an old ice chest, and pieces of broken furniture. Heavy iron pipes hung from the low ceiling. I knew that because I'd just hit my forehead against one. "Watch your head," I cautioned after enduring my teeth-jarring second blow.

There were several rickety old shelving units under the stairs, holding a mishmash of stained and faded canisters, rusty tins, and cloudy glass jars.

I heard a squeak in the corner.

"Was that a mouse?" Kim stopped and sucked in her breath.

"No." It was probably a rat. Maybe even a blood-sucking, cheese-loving, bat-rat hybrid.

There were more rough-hewn wooden shelving units along the wall to the right side of the stairs. Mason jars filled the shelves. Whatever was in them was long expired. The contents were muddy and gelatinous-looking.

"Look." Kim kicked a wooden bin.

I aimed the light inside.

"Rotten vegetables. I told you, Amy."

I rubbed my nose with my free hand. "No wonder it reeks down here."

"Let's go."

"Fine." I lazily swung the light around to the next bin. I had seen, heard, and smelled enough. The light flickered and went out. I jiggled it furiously, and it responded with a dull glow.

I almost wished it hadn't.

I screamed.

This made Kim scream twice as loud.

I backed into her, and we fell to the ground together. I dropped the flashlight.

"What's wrong?" Kim cried.

I scrambled on hands and knees for the light, wrapping my fist around it. I pulled myself up using the side of the vegetable bin for support.

I slowly brought the light to bear on its contents.

My breath caught in my throat.

Helen Holberg lay inside the box, atop a pile of long-rotten vegetables. Her eyes were half-open. Her lips were parted. But I did not think she was breathing.

She was still in her green pajamas and her long white dressing gown. The gown's belt was loose and lay beside her hand, coiled like a snake about to strike.

Her hair was matted, and there were streaks of dirt or blood on her face. It was too dark to be sure which they were comprised of.

"Helen…" Kim whimpered. "What happened, Amy? Did she fall in there and hit her head?"

"I don't think so," I said with a tremble. I held the flashlight as close as I dared to Helen's neck. "See those marks? I think she was strangled."

"But why? Who?"

"I don't know." My head was spinning. I was sure that Augusta Canning had stabbed Mike Holberg to death. I didn't know exactly why, but she had to have committed the crime. It was the only answer that made any sense at all. "I don't know why, and I don't know who."

Kim retched. "Let's get out of here. I don't feel safe."

"I hate to say this, but I don't think any place in the Usher House is safe anymore."

"Don't say that. Don't even think it."

We shuffled toward the stairs in the near darkness. No longer were we cognizant of the claustrophobic space and the stench of rotten food, decay, and mold. We were only mindful of the dead body we had just discovered.

"Think about it. We searched the house from top to bottom, Kim." My foot found the bottom step, and I started upward. "Take my hand."

Kim locked her fingers with mine, and we climbed slowly, listening to the dull *clomp* of our feet moving up the rough, wooden steps.

"We're snowed in. There were no footprints outside the doors, either coming or going," I said.

Kim stopped, forcing me to do the same. I turned the dully glowing light on her.

"What does it mean?" Kim asked, fear etched on her face.

"It means"—I was sorry to reply, but there was no other answer to give—"that the killer is one of us."

16

Kim blew out a breath, then flew past me. "I've had enough. Let's get out of here!"

Kim hit the door and jiggled the handle. "It's locked!" she cried frantically.

"Let me try." Kim moved aside. I tried the handle. It turned freely. "It's fine." I gave the door a push. It resisted. "What the—"

I tried harder, this time hearing a scraping sound as the door resisted my efforts. The tapestry hit me in the face as I shoved, giving me a mouthful of old wool. I spat. "Somebody put the tapestry and table back in place, that's all."

"Who would do that?"

"Good question." And a scary one. Was somebody simply putting things in order, or had they intended to keep us in the root cellar?

Kim stumbled into the hallway, breathing heavily. "We need to wake everybody. Let them know what's happened."

"Wait." I held her back. "Let's check the windows and doors first. I want to be sure there's no way for anyone to have gotten in or out of this house."

"Now? In the middle of the night? With a killer on the loose?"

"That's just it. The killer might be long gone. We don't even know when Helen was strangled, let alone who is responsible. We don't want to create a panic."

"Why not?" Kim whispered harshly. "I'm panicked. Why shouldn't everybody else be?"

"Come on," I urged. "It won't take long. We'll split up. I'll take this side of the house and you—"

"Split up? That's crazy! You might as well invite an ax murderer to split our skulls in half, because that's practically what you are promoting."

Kim crossed her arms in defiance. "Splitting up," she continued firmly, "is for people with a death wish. And I, for one, Amy Simms, have only one wish at the moment. And that wish is to live!"

Kim could exaggerate like no one else. But I could see where she was coming from. I wasn't in the mood myself to be cleaved, stabbed, or strangled.

"Okay, we stick together."

"You bet your life, we do. Let's go get a fresh candle and a nice sharp knife, or that fireplace poker, to protect ourselves."

There was no chance that I was going to use a knife on anybody. I knew Kim would never be able to, either. The most we could do was keep a killer away by waving a knife in their face. "We'll get the poker in the study."

If there was a murderer on the loose in the house and we happened upon them, I could swing a poker.

We heard a heavy banging toward the front of the house. We ran to the front door. The noise was coming from outside.

"What the heck is that?" gasped Kim.

"I have no idea. A bear?"

"Why would a bear be pounding on the door?" Kim sounded derisive and terrified all at once.

"Looking for someplace warm and dry to spend the night?" My heart lurched as the doorknob shook.

"Or a meal!" Kim hissed. "Did you lock the door?"

"Of course, I—" I froze. I had forgotten to lock the front door the last time I opened it to check to see if Helen might have gone out. "No."

"No?" Kim grabbed the chair next to the door and held it in front of her, whether as a weapon or a shield, I wasn't sure.

What I was sure of was that it would be useless against a determined attacker, either man or beast.

"What would be the point?" I ran for the door. "We're in the middle of nowhere."

"The point would be to keep ghouls and bears out!"

We heard yelling. At least it didn't sound like fierce growling. I reached for the door handle just as it shot open. A dark, heavyset figure in a black mask and black gloves hurled itself inside.

I wasn't sure whether I was happy or not that it wasn't a big black bear.

Kim pushed the chair at whom or whatever it was.

"*Oof!*" The figure stumbled. He reached out and grabbed Kim. "What are you—"

Kim punched wildly at his bulky chest and arms.

"Stop it! Ouch! Hey!"

"Get away from her!" I hit him in the shoulder with the flashlight, then kicked him where the sun doesn't shine. Unfortunately, it was merely a glancing blow.

Nonetheless, our attacker grunted in pain and surprise and released his or her or its grip on Kim. Kim fell back, crashing into my arms.

Our attacker dropped to his knees and held up his hands. "What's wrong with you two?"

"Dan?" Kim was breathing heavily. So was I.

"Yeah. Have you two gone crazy? Can I get up now?"

"Oh, Dan!" Kim threw herself into his arms. They tumbled to the rug together.

"Dan? Is that really you?" I aimed my flashlight on him, forgetting that it was near death and useless. I ran to the dining room, grabbed a candle, and lit it. The candle sputtered wildly in the wind and threatened to extinguish.

I hurriedly shut the front door.

Dan pulled himself to his feet unsteadily. Big, clumsy snowshoes were fixed to his boots. He pulled off his ski mask. "Is this how you welcome guests up here? Because if it is, remind me to stay home next time."

Kim was in tears. Tears of joy. "Oh, Dan. I am so glad to see you." Her arms held tightly around his neck.

"Yeah. I can tell." Dan kissed the top of her head. "I say again: What the devil is wrong with you two?" He looked at a sobbing Kim, then at me for an answer.

"Th-there's a dead body in the cellar." Kim sniffled.

"Yeah, I know. Chief Kennedy told me what happened. A Mike Holberg, right?" He held Kim steady in his arms.

Kim shook her head violently from side to side.

"The body in the cellar belongs, or should I say belonged, to Helen Holberg."

Dan looked nonplussed. "*Helen* Holberg?"

"Mike Holberg's wife," Kim said, landing on her feet as Dan set her down.

"So, it was Helen Holberg who was stabbed, not Mike Holberg?" Dan's brow was deeply creased.

"No," I answered. "Mike was stabbed. I think Helen was strangled."

The corners of Dan's mouth turned down. "I don't understand. How hard did you two hit me?" He smacked his open palm against the side of his head.

Kim grabbed Dan's hands. "There's a killer in this house, Dan." Her face was pale and ghostly in the candlelight, and while she was obviously relieved to see Dan, I feared Kim was on the verge of a nervous breakdown. "Somewhere…" Her eyes darted about.

"Relax." Dan squeezed her hands. "Let me get out of these things." He raised his left foot, clamped tightly to a snowshoe. "Then we can sit down and talk about this."

I was beginning to get the feeling that Dan thought we had gone off the deep end—a couple of hysterical women whose imaginations had run horribly wild.

Kim snuffled. "Okay." She retrieved the ski mask that Dan had dropped and stuffed it in her coat pocket.

Sitting in the chair by the door, Dan unsnapped the bindings of his blue and black snowshoes. Sturdy steel teeth protruded from the bottoms.

He pulled off his thick black gloves, then unzipped his black parka. Next, he wormed himself out of a pair of elastic-banded black snow pants. Kim took the parka and pants and shook the melting snow off of the items before draping them over the banister.

Dan is about our age. He is stocky, but fit, with large brown eyes and short dark hair—the chief of police wouldn't tolerate anything else. His father was Hawaiian, but his mother was a pure Carolinian.

Under his snow pants, Dan was wearing heavy denim jeans. Green flannel lining protruded from the cuffs. His shirt was gray flannel. A waffled, long-sleeved black T-shirt showed through. "It's cold in here," he remarked. "I was hoping it would be warmer."

"We've lost power," Kim explained. "Amy does have a flashlight."

"It's not much use. It's on life support," I added. Not to mention, I might have broken the light bulb by slamming it into Dan's shoulder. "We do have gas for the stove and wood for the fireplace, though."

"Hey." Kim pulled Dan up from the chair. "You must be freezing. Why don't I make us some tea?"

"Good idea,' I said. Helen wasn't going anywhere, and there was a lot to talk about. The first matter of business might be to get Dan to realize we were sane.

Dan agreed.

Holding the candle close to my chest, I led us to the kitchen. Kim held his hand all the way.

I lit a few more tall candles and spread them throughout the kitchen to chase the spooks away. One near the stove, another on the other end of the counter, and the third at the kitchen table.

Kim ordered Dan to sit while she filled the white enamel teakettle from the tap. She lit the stove and set the kettle on the burner to boil.

I grabbed a box of assorted teabags and a package of sugar cookies from our dwindling stores and put them within Dan's reach at the table.

Kim brought cups and a plastic jar of honey to the table, then sat beside her boyfriend.

"Thanks." Dan wrapped his fingers around the cup, absorbing the heat while Kim squirted a generous dollop of honey into his tea and stirred.

"Can I fix you something hot to eat?" Kim asked solicitously.

"No, thanks."

"Are you sure? There's a plate all prepared." Kim started to rise. "All I have to do is warm it up."

Dan laid one hand on Kim's arm to hold her down and set his other hand on the cookies. "These will do."

"How did you get here?" I asked, helping myself to a cookie and dunking it into my hot tea before popping it in my mouth.

"I drove as far as I could. Dudley Drive is still snowed in pretty good. When my truck refused to go another foot, I switched to the snowmobile."

"You drove a snowmobile up this mountain in the dark?" Kim laid her hand atop his. "In this weather? You could have been killed!"

Dan tried to laugh off her concern. "It wasn't so bad. At least, not until the snowmobile ran out of fuel."

We both gasped.

"It was a good thing I'd thought to bring the snowshoes."

Dan lifted his cup to his lips at the same time Kim threw her arms around him. Warm tea spilled from the cup, spreading across the table. I ran to get a towel.

"You are the sweetest, bravest man in the world!" Kim kissed him repeatedly while he blushed. "Isn't he, Amy?"

"That he is." I soaked up the tea and poured him a fresh cup. "Please tell me that the cavalry is right behind you."

Dan popped a couple of cookies into his mouth and chewed before answering. "I'm afraid not, Amy." Dan added honey to his cup and stirred. "I'm sure the chief will get here in the morning. I just couldn't wait any longer, especially after he told me about the murder.

"I knew the killer was dead—at least that's what your mom told the chief—but I still didn't like the thought of you being stranded out here."

By "*you*," I was sure Dan meant Kim more than me, but that was to be expected.

"Thanks for coming," I said. "I don't know whether I could have made it. Climbing up a snow-covered mountain in the dark—that really is above and beyond the call of duty."

"Yes, Dan." Kim rubbed her hand up and down his arm. "We're glad you are here."

It might have been the boyfriend rather than the cop inside Dan that had spurred him to action. Either way, we were grateful beyond words.

"Derek begged me to let him come, too, Amy. I convinced him to let me handle it myself. He's been worried sick about you."

I felt tears welling in the corner of my eyes and rubbed them away with my knuckles.

"Right." Dan laid his palms flat on the table. "Now, tell me what's going on."

Kim looked at me. "You tell it, Amy. I'll boil a second kettle." She pushed back her chair and refilled the teakettle, setting it once more on the front burner.

"Mike Holberg was stabbed to death in the study last evening. The storm came, and we were trapped. The men moved his body out to the toolshed, where it would be safe and stable. It's like a refrigerator out there."

"More like a freezer," Kim corrected me.

Dan reached for the cookies. "And you say there's another dead Holberg?"

"Helen Holberg, Mike's wife. Kim and I had just discovered her body in the root cellar when you showed up."

"That's why we were so freaked out when you rattled the door," Kim added from the stove.

Dan blew out a breath. "I thought the killer was dead?"

"So did we," Kim said rather unhappily. She returned with the kettle and refilled all three cups.

"Do either of you have any idea who might be responsible for these murders, then? And what about this person whom your mother told the chief was dead?"

"Augusta Canning," I said. "She's lying at the bottom of a ravine at the edge of the property."

"Who was she? And what does she have to do with this?"

"She was the wife of the caretaker." Kim said.

"And somebody pushed her?"

"Actually, we thought she might have fallen to her death by accident." I explained how I had theorized that Augusta had stabbed Mike Holberg to death, then run out in the middle of the night and fallen to her death.

"A single set of footprints led from the front door to the ravine," I continued. "We found her the next day when the weather cleared and the sun came up."

"Her body is still down there." Kim visibly shivered at the thought.

"According to Craig, there is a path leading down to the bottom, but it is treacherous at the best of times."

"I see." Dan nodded. "I'll take a look at that in the morning. Maybe I can reach her."

"After what you went through to reach us up here, that wouldn't surprise me one bit." I punched Dan lightly on the shoulder.

"Ouch!" Dan rubbed his shoulder. "I guess I'm sore from the beating you two ladies gave me."

"Sorry." I found myself blushing.

"Forget it. I'm only teasing." Dan traced the edge of his cup with his finger. "Why would this Augusta Canning make for the ravine?"

"We think she was trying to escape," Kim added.

"Or she decided to end her life after realizing what she had done."

"Overcome by remorse, you mean?" Dan said.

"Yes. Maybe." I sighed in frustration. "I don't know."

"Those are reasonable assumptions, Amy." Dan snapped a cookie in two with his front teeth. "Except…" Dan's fingers drummed the table. "Now you are telling me there has been another death. Are you sure it was a murder?"

"Helen is lying in a vegetable bin in the root cellar. The door to the cellar was closed. I suppose she might have gone down on her own to explore or something."

"And had something like a heart attack or a stroke," suggested Kim.

I squirted a generous blob of honey into my tea. "Someone, not knowing she was down there, could have shut the door."

I pictured Helen Holberg lying in the bin. "But I don't think she would have fallen in like that. Plus, I think she was strangled. It was dark. My light was weak. But I saw what I think are marks around her neck."

"Okay." Dan nodded thoughtfully. "Do either of you have any idea when she was killed?"

"We don't know," I answered. "Not yesterday. I saw her today. So, she was alive at least until this afternoon."

"I only saw her briefly today," Kim told him. "She locked herself in her room after her husband's death."

"Do you think she was afraid she might be next?" Dan asked.

"I hadn't thought of that," I answered. "I assumed she was shaken up by her husband's death and just couldn't face being around the rest of us."

Dan's comment raised the question now: Was Helen afraid more than sad? If so, who or what was she frightened of?

Dan brushed cookie crumbs from his lip. "So, we have a dead man and a dead woman, man and wife, killed within a day of each other in the same house."

"Yes."

"And you say this Helen Holberg's body is still in the cellar? Nobody moved her?"

"No. We just found her, like I said. We haven't told anyone else yet. Nobody knows about it but us."

"And the killer." Dan's tone was grim.

"Yes."

"Amy thinks the killer is in the house with us."

"It snowed again today, and there were no footprints at the front or back doors." I explained my thinking. "The snow was completely undisturbed—until you showed up."

"You didn't see anyone or notice anything as you approached, did you, Dan?" Kim wondered.

"No. Nothing out of the ordinary." He chuckled. "Except for a tractor lying on its side in the ditch at the end of the driveway. Then again, I wasn't looking for anything in particular, except for this house."

"The tractor in the ditch was my ex-boyfriend Craig's doing."

"What was he doing?"

"I think he thought he was going to ride into town on that tractor like some cowboy in a white hat on a stallion and bring back help."

"Are you sure he wasn't trying to escape?"

"Because he's a murderer?" I tilted my head and thought about it. "Craig is a lot of things, but I don't think he's a killer. And I don't think he would have left Cindy behind."

Although I still wasn't sure whether Craig was better off now that Mike was dead or when he had been alive. There were too many unanswered questions about the business dealings between Mike, Craig, and Robert.

"Cindy?" Dan asked.

"Cindy Pym. She's his sexy new girlfriend." Kim supplied the answer.

"She's not *that* sexy." I supplied the catty commentary.

"Who else is here?"

"There's Robert Flud and Rosalie Richmond," I answered. "They are a couple. They share a room, but I do not believe they are married."

"Plus Craig and Cindy. Then there's Jackson Canning, Augusta's husband." I shrugged. "Everybody else is dead."

"Hey!" Kim said. "That means that one of *them* is the murderer!"

"And a stranger couldn't have gotten in and out some other way? You didn't see any other tracks leading to or from the house?" Dan quizzed us.

We shook our heads in the negative.

"What about an unlocked window?"

"It's possible," I admitted. "I'll go check."

"No," Dan said. "I'll check later. That's my job. I want you two to stay out of this."

"Understood," I said.

"Good. First, I want to see Helen Holberg." Dan pushed back his chair. "How do I get to this root cellar?"

Kim and I bristled, both of us picturing Helen's limp form lying alone in the dark cellar. It hadn't been a pleasant death.

"It's just down the hall," I said. "We'll show you."

Dan and I stood and moved to the kitchen entrance. Kim followed.

"Here." Kim handed him the candle that she had been using beside the stove.

"Thanks, but you'd better keep this." He handed it gingerly back to Kim. "I can use my flashlight app."

We moved as a group down the dark hall and approached the door to the basement. The cellar door had swung shut, but the table still sat askew in the middle of the hall. The tapestry that hid the door was still pushed back along its iron rod.

"This is it?"

I nodded. "When Kim and I came up after discovering the body, the door was shut, and someone had placed the table and tapestry back in place."

"I don't like the sound of that. Did you ask any of the other guests about it?"

"We haven't seen any other guests," I answered.

Kim cupped her hand around the flickering candle. "Not since Craig left the study."

"Alone?" Dan seemed suspicious of Craig. "What was he doing there?"

"Watching a movie. Then he went to bed," I replied.

"And that had to be an hour ago or more," Kim filled in.

"And the others are all in bed?"

"I guess so."

"Okay." Dan plucked his cell phone from his shirt pocket and turned on the beam. "I left my snowshoe poles and flashlight outside the front door.

I want you two to go get them. Leave the poles at the door, but bring the flashlight. We might need it."

We agreed.

"After that, I want the you to go to your rooms—"

"We're sharing a room," Kim whispered.

"Better yet." Dan shot the beam of light across the steps leading down into the damp black cellar. "Lock yourselves in, and wait for me to come get you. Do not open the door to anybody, you hear me?"

"We hear you." And everything he was saying was making us nervous.

"Good." With a brief, reassuring smile for Kim, Dan turned and started down the steep, narrow steps.

"The body is a few steps to the left in the bin near the wall." My voice was deadened by the packed-earth floor and walls.

"Right. Stick together," Dan ordered as he disappeared. "Do not go anywhere in this house alone."

17

"Come on."

Kim's feet were glued to the runner. "Are you sure he's going to be okay down there?" Kim's voice quavered.

"Of course he is going to be okay. He's a trained, experienced police officer. He goes into dangerous situations all the time."

Kim's fingers dug into my forearm. "'Dangerous'?"

I winced. "Did I say dangerous? I meant dark. I'm sure he goes into plenty of dark spaces all the time. It's probably part of his cadet training. He's going to be perfectly fine."

"If you say so," she said uneasily.

I hooked Kim's free arm with mine and pushed her along the hall to the entryway. "There's nothing down in that root cellar but rotten vegetables and a dead woman."

"I guess you are right."

"I know I am." I grabbed the knob to the front door. "Maybe Dan will be able tell us more about how Helen died when he gets back."

I opened the door and spotted the snowshoe poles leaning against the wall, their sharp ends thrust a foot deep into the snow. I yanked them free and laid them on the floor. In a pinch, they could be used as weapons.

"Hold the candle closer to the ground, Kim."

Kim complied. "What are you looking for?"

"The flashlight. I'm not seeing it."

Kim bent her knees and held a hand in front of the candle. A gust of wind snuffed the flame. "Rats. I'll be right back."

I closed the door to keep out the elements and heard the sound of footsteps as Kim shuffled to the kitchen, returning with a lit candle. "I brought a box of matches in case it goes out again."

I opened the door and searched once more. I thrust my hands into the icy cold snow. "Nothing." I stood and dusted myself off. "I don't get it."

"It's got to be there someplace." Kim peered over my shoulder.

"Well, it's late and my fingers are about to fall off." And I was scared witless that while we were staring out the door, a killer might come up from behind and slay us.

Not that I was going to mention that fear to Kim.

"Let's forget it. Dan can look for it when he gets back. I think we should go to our room and lock ourselves in, like Dan suggested."

"Okay." Kim sounded unsure. She turned her head in the general direction of the root cellar. "Don't you think Dan should have been back up here by now?"

"He's probably searching for clues."

"Maybe we should go help him," Kim suggested.

"We've already botched up one crime scene. I don't think the police would appreciate us tainting another. No, the best thing we can do is to wait for him in our room." Best and safest.

I made sure to lock the front door—wondering, as I did, whether I was locking a murderer in or out.

We did the same thing upstairs. We locked ourselves in and threw ourselves down on our narrow beds.

"I am exhausted," I said, staring at the ceiling as shadows danced in the candlelight.

"Me, too." Kim let out an audible sigh. "When we get home, I am going to sleep for twenty hours straight."

"Me, too." I wiggled my toes. "And when I wake up, I'm going to take a nap."

Kim tittered. Fear and fatigue were taking a toll on both of us. Mental and physical.

She was silent after that, and I dozed off to the sound of the wind whistling outdoors and the occasional creaking of the old house.

"Amy? Hey, Amy?"

I pushed my eyes open. The candle atop the dresser was visibly shorter than it had been the last time I had seen it. "Yeah?" I yawned. "What is it?"

"What time is it?" Kim whispered, turning toward me.

"I don't know." I struggled to my feet and moved closer to the candle. My watch did not have an illuminated dial. I turned the crystal toward the light. "After two."

That meant an hour or so had gone by since we had last seen Dan.

It also meant we were entering the second day in a row without enough sleep.

Kim sat up quickly. "Amy?"

"Yes?" I ran my hands over my face and sat up on the edge of the bed.

"Aren't you worried?"

"About what?"

"About Dan. Don't you think he should have been up here by now?"

"I'm sure he wanted to take his time in the root cellar. And secure the crime scene for when Jerry and the others arrive. And, remember? Dan said he was going to check all of the windows."

"Then why hasn't he checked ours?"

"He probably meant the downstairs windows. There's no way somebody could get up or down from the second-floor windows."

"Unless that somebody had a ladder."

"Point taken, but it isn't likely, especially in the snow." I laid my hand back on my pillow. "Dan told us to wait for him here with the door locked. You don't want to go wandering around this big house in the middle of the night with a killer on the loose, do you?"

After a moment, Kim answered me softly, "No."

"Right." I pounded my feather pillow. "Let's get some rest. If Dan does not come in the next half hour or so, we'll go looking for him. In the meantime, let's get a little rest, okay?"

"Okay." Kim turned over on her side.

A half minute later, the bedclothes rustled as she turned back toward me. I braced myself.

"Amy?"

"Yes?" I was tired and tense and losing patience quickly, best friend or not. A little sleep would have done us both a world of good.

"Dan forgot to ask where our bedroom was, and we forgot to tell him."

I groaned. "Bird poop."

I threw myself out of bed and scrounged around on the floor for my shoes. "What are you waiting for?" I said. "Let's go."

Kim practically shrieked for joy as she leapt from the bed, still fully clothed and shod. She grabbed the candle.

I unlocked the bedroom door. Together, we crept out into the hallway. All was quiet and calm.

But was there trouble lurking?

Who knew? Not me.

I paused outside our door and listened hard. “I can’t hear a thing.”

“Me, either,” Kim whispered in my ear.

Craig and Cindy’s door was firmly shut. As we worked our way up the hall to the stairs, I noted that only the bathroom door stood open.

At the top of the stairs, we stood shoulder to shoulder.

“Do you hear anything?” I asked.

“No.” Kim peered over the railing. “Dan?” she whispered. “Dan, can you hear me?”

“We’d better check the cellar first.”

“Okay.” The candle went out. Kim cursed, grabbed the matches from her coat, and relit the wick.

At the bottom of the stairs, we turned past the empty dining room, and began to move down the connecting hall leading to the long hall running parallel to the length of the house.

With a shaky arm, Kim held the candle extended in front of us. The table and tapestry were just as we had left them—the table partially blocking the hallway, the tapestry pulled back to reveal the door.

The door to the root cellar was closed. Either somebody had closed it once again, or it had swung shut on its own.

Maybe Stanley Usher’s ghost was trying to tell us to keep out of his cellar.

I pulled the door open toward me. “Dan? Are you down there?”

Kim’s free hand was on my shoulder. “He isn’t answering.”

“Shine the light in here.”

Kim pushed the candle past me, illuminating the steep, narrow staircase. “Dan?” She turned toward me with worry written across her face. “Where could he be?”

“I don’t know.” I turned her around. “Let’s check the rest of the downstairs rooms.” I pulled the cellar door closed, and we continued to the kitchen.

It was dark and quiet.

“There’s nobody here,” I whispered.

“I wouldn’t say that.”

Kim and I shrieked.

Kim whirled around, and the candle went out again. We heard laughter coming from our left, echoing eerily off the tiles.

There was the sound of a flick. Rosalie Richmond’s grinning face was lit up like a ghostly apparition.

“Relax,” said Rosalie, quietly. A small flame swayed in front of her narrow nose. “It’s only me.”

Kim shakily lit a match and relit her candle. She set it down on the edge of the counter.

"What are you doing here?" Kim gasped.

"In the dark," I added.

Rosalie flipped her lighter shut and rested it on the table among the remains of our tea and cookies. "I woke up hungry. I thought I'd have a little late-night snack." She waved her hand at the bag of cookies. "I see I wasn't the first person to have that impulse."

No, but she had gone another route. In front of Rosalie sat an open can of bite-sized sausages. Apparently, she had found the owner's closet, too. Her snack also appeared to include brandy. A bottle of the spirits and a half-filled glass were within easy reach.

I picked up our candle and walked over to Rosalie. She was wearing a pink and gray, Fair Isle print pair of flannel pajamas, over which she had donned a beige down vest. A small knit cap was on her head. There were soft-soled slippers on her feet.

No doubt she could move around the house quietly in those slippers.

"Have you seen Dan?" Kim asked, hopefully.

"Who?" Rosalie's hand languidly fell around her glass, and she picked it up and drank.

"Dan Sutton. He's my boyfriend."

"He's with the Ruby Lake Police Department." A fact I wanted her and everybody else in this screwy house to know ASAP.

"He's here?" Rosalie sounded surprised. She grabbed a sausage in her fingers and popped it into her mouth.

"He got here a little while ago," Kim said. "We're looking for him."

"You mean, we can finally get out of this house?"

"No," I replied. "Dan came up by himself to make sure we were all okay."

"How on earth did he get here?"

"It wasn't easy," I said.

"I'll bet." Rosalie lazily licked her fingers.

"The police will rescue us in the morning." Kim picked up the bottle of brandy and poured some into the teacup she had left behind earlier on the table. She sipped. "So, you haven't seen him?"

"Kim, I haven't seen any new man around here. Believe me," she said with a grin, "I'd remember it if I had." She pushed off from the table. "I'm off to dreamland." She picked up her glass and headed for the door.

"Don't you want a candle?" I said.

"I've got this." She flicked the lighter in our faces.

"What do you make of her?" I asked after Rosalie's retreat.

"I think she's weird."

"I think she's keeping secrets," I said. "And lots of them."

"Like what?"

"I have no idea," I was forced to admit. "When I was serving dinner, she whispered in my ear that she wanted to talk later."

The frown line, which Kim claimed she didn't have between her eyebrows, deepened. "What did she want to talk about?"

"I don't know," I said with a shrug. "We never got the chance to talk."

"Too bad."

"Yeah, I was going to track her down the first chance I got."

"Do you believe her when she says she hasn't seen Dan?" Kim asked.

"I am not taking anything Rosalie Richmond says at face value—or what anybody else says, for that matter."

"Why do you say that?"

"Because people are dropping like flies around here."

Kim sucked in a breath.

"And killers have a tendency to lie."

Kim finished her drink and set her cup on the counter near the sink. "Amy, I'm getting a funny feeling about this. Where is Dan? He couldn't have simply disappeared. He wouldn't leave us after coming all this way."

"No. He wouldn't." I thought a moment. "Do you think he might have gone outside to take a look around?"

"His outer coat and pants are still on the newel post where I put them."

"Are you sure?"

"Yep. I saw them when we passed by."

I picked up the candle. "Okay. Let's start with the last place we saw him."

"You mean—"

"Going down into the root cellar."

"First, let me put Helen's meal in the fridge before it spoils." I moved to the oven and opened it. "It's gone." I pulled open the refrigerator and shined the candle inside. I saw no sign of my plate of food.

Kim looked over my shoulder. "I guess Rosalie or somebody else got hungry, too."

I shut the refrigerator. "That's for the best. If the power doesn't come back on soon, everything in it will spoil anyway."

"We can always store food in the snow."

"Good idea, Kim, provided no curious, hungry critters dig it up. Hopefully," I said on my way out of the kitchen, "we'll be out of here in the morning and it won't even matter."

"Hallelujah." Kim grabbed a second candle and followed me.

18

My blood went cold.

The reflected light had come from Dan's silver belt buckle. I lurched and bent down to him. His face was pallid and his lips unmoving. "Dan?"

I reached out a hand. A draft from the cellar doors extinguished the flame, and I tripped against the side of the wooden bin, dropping the candlestick.

"Kim! Are you there?" I scrambled on hands and knees for the candle among the rotten veggies. The pile was slimy, smelly, and disgusting in uncountable ways.

Light feet raced up my back, and something ran into my hair. I screamed and flailed at it with my hands. "Get off me! Get off me!"

Kim's steps pounded down the stairs. "Amy! Amy?"

"Over here." My butt was on the cold, hard earth. My back rested against the bin. My eyes fixed on the smudgy dark blur that was Kim as she approached. There was gunk all over my hands.

"What's happened? What happened to you?"

I steeled my chin and looked up at her. "I found Dan."

"You found Dan?" Kim looked quickly side to side. "Where is he? Dan?"

"He's here by me. Bring the light."

"I don't understand. Dan, are you okay?" Kim scooted closer.

"He's unconscious."

"He's not dead, is he, Amy? Please, oh please, tell me he isn't dead."

"No, I don't think so." I found my candle on the ground. I wiped the dirt from it and relit it from the flame of Kim's candle.

Kim had spotted Dan and was leaning over him. "He's hurt. There's blood on his head."

I stood over Kim and Dan. Kim's hand held fresh blood. "You're right. We've got to get him out of here."

"Yes," Kim agreed quickly. "Let's carry him."

I gripped Kim's shoulder. "We'll never be able to move him ourselves, let alone get him up the steps."

"But we have to."

"Kim, I need you to go wake up Craig. It will take the three of us together to move him."

Kim fought back a flood of tears and brushed her hand across her face. "No. I'm staying here with Dan." She twined her fingers with his and held on.

Kim sniffled. Her face was a blanket of tears. "You go, Amy. Please?"

I nodded once.

Kim laid her hand on my arm. "You should get Robert, too."

"No. Just Craig."

"But—"

"I think we can trust Craig. I'm not certain we can trust anyone else."

"Hurry back." Kim turned her attention to her boyfriend.

I smiled grimly. "I will."

Heart racing, I climbed the cellar stairs. I started down the hall, then stopped and turned around. I wedged the table between the door and the frame.

I went to the front of the house and climbed the main stairway. The long hallway was as silent as a tomb. I could not even hear the sounds of sleeping penetrating from the thick walls or doors.

I stopped outside of Craig and Cindy's room and knocked lightly. The door remained closed. I rapped a little harder and pressed my ear to the door.

The door popped open, and Cindy appeared, clutching a bathrobe to her chest.

She didn't look happy to see me.

"Amy, it's the middle of the night. What are you doing here?" She took a sudden step back. "Eww, what's all over your hands? You smell funny."

Even at this ungodly hour, Cindy's hair and face looked all too pretty. Whatever deal she might have made with the devil might be worth considering for myself.

Then again, if that deal meant having to sleep with Craig, I wanted no part of it.

"Never mind that." I wiped my hands on my pants. Well, they were Cindy's pants, actually. Better hers than mine. "I need to speak to Craig."

"Now?" Cindy frowned. The robe slipped from her fingers, and I saw more of Cindy than I ever wanted to.

I averted my eyes. "Yes, please. It's important." How could she sleep like that? Maybe she had a six-inch-thick down-filled quilt comforter.

With a high-pitched sigh, Cindy pulled her robe closer and turned around—showing yet another side of Cindy. "Honey Bear is asleep. He's not going to like this."

"I know. But I really need to see him. Now."

"Give me a minute." She pushed the door shut, leaving me alone in the hall.

True to her word, Craig appeared, thankfully wearing a robe and pajamas. "What the heck, Amy?" he whispered harshly. "Are you nuts?"

Cindy peered over his shoulder. She had slipped into her robe.

"Craig, I need you to come with me."

"Again?" He blinked the sleep from his eyes. "Why?"

"I need your help with something."

"Sorry, babe, but I'm taken."

"Grow up, would you?" I snapped. "This is serious."

Cindy patted her lover's arm. "I think you had better go, honey bear. Otherwise, we'll never get any rest."

"But I'm exhausted," Craig complained.

"I'll rub your back when you're done," Cindy promised. "You always like that."

"Listen to her, 'honey bear.'"

Craig sighed heavily and knotted the belt of his robe. "Okay. Let's make this quick."

As Craig followed me down the main staircase, I asked, "You didn't happen to put back the table and tapestry, did you?"

"What table and tapestry?" He sounded unhappy and short-tempered.

"The ones hiding the door to the root cellar."

"Outside?"

"No, in the hall."

"I don't know what you are talking about." Craig's impatience was plain. "Where are we going? What is this all about?"

We stopped on the main floor. "We're going to the root cellar."

Craig cursed. "You really are crazy, you know that? I can't believe I didn't leave you sooner."

"You didn't leave me," I corrected. "I left you." I led him down the hall toward the cellar entrance. We didn't see or hear anyone else on the way.

Craig eyed the table shoved into the doorway curiously. "What is this?"

"I told you. It's the root cellar. Hold this." I handed Craig the candle and moved the table to one side. I took back the candle and extended my arm, illuminating the steep staircase. "Kim?"

"Right here, Amy." Kim sounded frightened and lonely. How could she have been anything else?

Craig peered through the doorway. "Kim's down there?"

"Yes." I gave him a nudge. "Down you go."

"You want me to go down there?" He looked uncertainly at the rough, wooden steps.

"Yes. Hurry. Dan Sutton is down here, and he's hurt."

"Drat." He looked forlornly at his bare feet. "I should have worn slippers. Who is Dan Sutton?"

"Never mind that." I was losing patience with him. "Hurry."

Craig stumbled down the stairs cursing every step of the way. "It's a freaking dirt floor."

"Stop being such a whiny baby." I pushed past him. "How is he?"

"Okay, I think. He woke up for a minute." Kim ran her fingers along Dan's forehead. "I think he recognized me."

"That's a good sign," I said.

"Come on, Craig. Help us get him upstairs."

Kim's hand rested on Dan's cheek. "Are you sure it's okay to move him, Amy?"

"I don't think he has any broken bones. Even if he does, with help hours away, the best thing we can do for him is to move him someplace cleaner, drier, and warmer."

"You're right."

Craig stared. "Who is that guy? I think I've seen him around before."

"Dan is my boyfriend," Kim answered. "And he's hurt."

"Save the questions for later, Craig." I squeezed between Dan's comatose body and the wooden bin. "Grab his shoulders. Kim and I will each grab a leg."

That way Kim and I could each still hold a candle. We'd never manage to navigate around the cellar and get him up those steep steps in the dark.

"What's he doing down here?" Craig hissed and groaned as he strained to lift Dan's limp form. Craig had never been the fittest of the male of the species.

"He came down here to see Helen," Kim answered.

"What?"

Kim angled her light over the wooden bin to the left, illuminating Helen's dead body.

Craig froze. "What the—" His eyes flew to me. "What is going on, Amy?"

"I have no idea," I snapped. "Why don't you tell me? You invited all these crazy people up here. Not me."

We glared at one another.

Dan groaned.

"Can you two please stop fighting? We need to get Dan upstairs," Kim said.

"Sorry," I replied.

"Yeah. Let's do this."

It was awkward, but the three of us managed to get Dan up to the first-floor hallway without doing him any further harm.

We were all winded, though. Once there, Kim and I ran our hands over his arms and legs. We were relieved to see that the only visible injury was the one to the back of his head.

"What are we going to do with him?" Craig pressed his hand against the wall for support.

"Let's take him to our room," Kim suggested.

"Good idea," I said.

"All the way up another set of stairs? Why don't we carry him to the study?"

"Because he'll be more comfortable in a bed. Plus, the bathroom is there, and I can wash his wound." Kim's fingers moved gently through Dan's hair.

"Then let me call Jackson and Robert."

"No."

"No, Amy? Why no?"

"Because I said so."

"Well, that isn't good enough—"

Kim laid a hand on each of us. "Let's get Dan upstairs to bed. After that, the two of you can spar all you like."

Properly chastised, we set aside our differences—for the moment—and slowly but surely carried Dan up to our room. We laid him gently on Kim's bed.

Craig leaned over, hands on his knees. "I've never worked so hard in all my life."

I fell back on my bed. "That I believe."

Dan's legs twitched.

"How is he, Kim?"

She held the candle overhead. "Dan, can you hear me?"

"Kim? What happened?" Dan's voice came out dry and raspy. His eyelids fluttered. "Kim? Wh—"

Kim gasped.

My body tensed. "Is Dan all right?"

Kim managed a small smile. "His breathing is steady. There's a good-sized knot on the back of his head. The bleeding has stopped."

"I'll go get some damp towels. Maybe I can find some disinfectant." I started to rise.

"I'll go, Amy."

I let her go. Letting her help Dan was the best thing I could do to help her.

Craig loomed over me. "Do you want to tell me what is going on now, Amy?"

19

I pulled the bedcovers up to Dan's chest to keep him warm.

Kim returned with a handful of dampened washcloths and hand towels.

"Let's talk outside." Craig followed me out the door. I stuck my head back inside. "Let me know if you need anything or if Dan's condition changes."

Kim nodded as she applied a damp cloth to Dan's head wound.

"Let's go to the study."

We arrived at the study to find that the flames had gone out.

"Rats." Craig pulled back the fire screen and jabbed at the remaining bits of logs. They fell apart as he did, sending gray ash into the air.

Craig grabbed several fresh pieces of split oak. He set them clumsily on the grate and tossed in a handful of kindling. Using a long-stemmed match, he lit the kindling and blew on the tiny flame.

It was the wrong way to go about building a fire, but I wasn't in the mood to correct him.

Craig set the fire screen back on the hearth. "You want a drink?"

"No thanks."

Craig fashioned himself a scotch and soda and carried to the fireplace. "What happened to Helen? Did she fall or something?"

I took the chair beside the fireplace and pulled my legs to my chest. "No. I think she was strangled."

"You mean murdered?" Craig's hand tightened around his glass.

I leaned my head against the back of the chair. "Three people are dead, Craig. Who would want to kill them?"

Craig's lips contorted. "You think I know? What? You think one of my friends is responsible for all this?" He slammed back his drink. "If you ask me, it's some psycho."

"Need I remind you? We are in the middle of nowhere, Craig. Whoever is responsible is right here with us."

Craig set his drink on the mantel and grabbed the bellows. He pumped air madly at the small flame. Rather than helping the burn, the flame went out.

Craig swore, wrenched the fire screen away from the hearth, and rebuilt the logs—no better than the first time.

"I think you have to put the kindling on the bottom then make a sort of pyramid out of the logs." I motioned with my finger.

Craig glared at me. Nonetheless, he rebuilt the logs in the fireplace as I had instructed, and lit it once again. The fire started small and sluggish but built slowly to a steady flame. He picked up his glass, carried it to the bar, and refilled it.

"Should you really be drinking so much?"

"There's little else to do in this accursed house." He drilled his eyes into mine as he drank. "Besides drink and get yourself killed."

I pressed my elbows into my knees and steepled my fingers. "I've never seen you looking so nervous. What's bothering you more? The fact that people are dying like flies all around us or the fact that your precious business deal has blown up in your face?"

"I may not be out of the woods yet but, believe me, the deal isn't dead. If it was, there would be another murder." Craig snorted as he polished off his second drink in a matter of minutes.

"What do you mean?"

He slammed the glass on the bar and left it there, running his hands through his hair. "If you must know, Cindy would kill me."

"Cindy?"

"Yeah." Craig sat at the edge of the hearth. "She's invested a bit of money in the deal."

"Really? She told me about some big deal you were trying to put together. I hadn't realized she was also an investor in this latest scheme of yours." I gnawed at my lower lip. This put Cindy Pym in a whole new perspective. "Define *a bit*."

"Two-fifty."

"Two hundred and fifty thousand dollars?" My impression of Cindy just went up and down at the same time. Up because she had a quarter of a million dollars to spare. Down because she had lent it to Craig.

"Yes. And her investment is fine. In fact, I expect to double it for her, just like I promised her I would."

"I'm impressed." I squeezed my knees together.

Craig swung his head toward me. "You should be. I'm a good businessman. I know what I'm doing. Besides, Robert assured me that I'd get my money from the group."

"The Holberg Group?"

"That's right."

"Helen told me that her husband had backed out of the deal."

Craig swatted his hand at me. "That was just Mike being Mike. He got off on getting people to kiss up to him. That's what this trip was all about. I knew once I plied him with some food and drink that he'd come around."

"And if he didn't? What then?"

The corner of Craig's mouth turned down. "If you are suggesting I would murder him if he refused to give me some money, you are way out of line, Amy." Craig jumped to his feet.

"Relax. I am not accusing you of anything, Craig. I only want to make sense of what's going on. Mike *and* Helen Holberg are dead. Doesn't that mean something?"

Craig shrugged. "One of the caretakers is dead, too. Unless Stanley Usher has come back from the grave, it means there's a nut on the loose. Can we be sure Augusta didn't kill them both and then herself?"

"Helen was alive long after Augusta, remember?"

Craig cursed. "Right. So that means it has to be Jackson, her husband."

My brow rose slowly. "Why do you say that?"

"Because there's only me, you, Kim, Robert, Rosalie, and Cindy left." He gripped the ends of his belt and tugged. "I guarantee none of us are killers."

Craig loomed over me. "That leaves only Jackson Canning."

"What do you know about him?"

"Next to nothing. He came with the house. Until yesterday, he and Augusta kept to themselves except for basic housekeeping jobs.

"I wish I'd never taken this place. It is in the middle of nowhere. At least if we were in town, we'd be able to get out. Up here, it takes an hour to get anywhere. And that's without freaking snowstorms adding to the trouble."

"You have no one to blame but yourself, Craig. You were the one who picked this remote house."

"Hardly."

"Hardly? I thought you said you found this place online?"

"I did. I mean, Mike told me about it—said he heard it was nice and available—and then I looked it up."

"Mike Holberg told you about the Usher House? How did he hear of it? Had he stayed here before?" That could change things.

"I don't know. We were talking on the phone. I told him that I had to come down to a town called Ruby Lake. He mentioned that he'd heard of a house for rent in the area and gave me the name. I invited Mike and his wife and Robert and his girlfriend to come. Cindy thought it was a great idea, a real getaway from city living." He sniffed. "It sure is that."

"But had Mike rented the house previously?"

Craig shook his head as he paced. "I don't know." He stopped in the middle of the rug. "No. I'm sure not. I mean, I got the impression from the way he talked that he was seeing the place for the first time when he arrived."

I pressed my head against the back of the chair and shut my eyes.

"How did Kim's boyfriend get here? Has he got some kind of super four-by-four that he can get us out of here in?"

"Dan Sutton is an officer with the Ruby Lake Police Department. He drove part of the way, then took a snowmobile, and finally snowshoed up to the house."

Craig whistled. "Wow, he really wanted to see Kim."

"He wanted to be sure we were okay." And see Kim.

"I know. I know." Craig massaged his hands. "What about this snowmobile? Since Dan is injured, do you think he'd mind if I borrowed it to drive into town?"

"You?"

"Yeah."

"Drive a snowmobile? In the middle of the night? Down a mountain?" Craig snapped his chin in response to my every question. "Forget it. Even if you wanted to do something that foolhardy, it wouldn't work."

"Why not?" Craig was clearly insulted by my doubting his ability to play the role of superhero. Apparently, he'd conveniently forgotten about the recent tractor off the bridge into the ditch incident already.

"The snowmobile is out of gas." Which, in this particular case, was probably a good thing. Craig would probably run it off a cliff or into a ditch. That was Dan's personal snowmobile.

"What was he doing in the root cellar? Come to think of it, what was Helen doing there?" Craig demanded.

"I have no idea how Helen ended up there. Maybe she was killed someplace else and then the killer left her body there, hoping it might never be found.

"Maybe the killer figured they'd hide her there until they could dispose of the body permanently later. Your guess is as good as mine."

"So, what happened exactly?"

"What happened is that Kim and I searched the house looking for Helen. Nobody else seemed too concerned about her disappearance—"

"I wish you wouldn't put it like that. You make me sound insensitive. I have feelings, Amy."

I kept my mouth shut. Now was not the time.

"It isn't that I wasn't concerned. I didn't think she had disappeared. I only figured that she was keeping out of sight because she didn't want to face the rest of us. We all did."

"In any case, we searched this house top to bottom. At least, I thought we had. We even checked to see if she'd gone out."

"You mean left the house? That would be nuts."

"I agree. People crazy with grief sometimes do crazy things."

"I suppose." The way he'd said that, I wondered if he would ever be that upset over the loss of someone in his life.

"Then I found the door to the root cellar."

"Behind that tapestry in the hall." Craig frowned. "I had no idea that door was there, and I must have walked past it a couple dozen times or more."

I was inclined to believe him.

"That's right. We went down and found Helen Holberg lying dead in one of the bins."

"Just like I saw her."

"Just like you saw her." I yawned. "Not long after, Dan arrived. We told him about Helen, and he went down to investigate."

"And what? He fell and hit his head?"

"Come on, Craig. Seriously? Don't you think it more likely that someone knocked him out? Maybe even meant to kill him?"

"I suppose," Craig muttered. His bare feet did a shuffle on the hardwood floor. "Still, going down in that dark cellar is dangerous. A person could get hurt."

"A person did get hurt. Two people got hurt." One mortally.

Craig's eyes bulged. "Hey, you don't think this Dan guy would sue me, do you?"

"Why would he sue you?"

"For getting hurt in my house."

"This isn't your house. You're only renting."

Craig smiled with relief. "Yeah. He's the owner's problem. And the rental agency's."

"Lucky you," I said drily.

"You know, they ought to have some sort of backup power system for this dump. When this is over, I'm going to write a strongly worded complaint. Maybe I can get a refund."

"Even if they give you all your money back for the rental," I informed him as I counted the items off on my fingers, "you'll be lucky if you break even after paying for the damages to the side of the house, the bridge, and the tractor."

Craig balled up his hands and cursed. I could picture the dollar signs adding up in his head. "What happens next?"

I thought a moment. "Do you trust Cindy?"

"Of course. I'd trust her with my life."

I slapped my knees and rose. "Then go back to bed and lock your door." Hopefully, he wouldn't be locking himself in his bedroom with our killer. "I'm going to go check on Kim and Dan."

I picked up a lit candle and Craig followed me to the study entrance.

"In the morning, the police will come. And our nightmare will be over."

"It had better be," groused Craig. "All this murder stuff is bad for business."

"If I were you, I'd worry about my health."

Craig stopped dead in his tracks. "You don't think somebody would try to kill me, do you, Amy?"

I pushed him forward up the first step. "You never know." That would give him something to think about.

And Kim wouldn't have to worry about any more unwanted noises coming from the room next door that night.

As Craig opened his bedroom door and disappeared inside, I found myself thinking dark thoughts. Craig and Cindy had taken out million-dollar life insurance policies on each other. Cindy had loaned Craig a quarter of a million dollars.

If Cindy were to die, Craig would find his debt wiped clean and end up with a million extra bucks in his pocket.

Would he kill to make that happen?

Could Cindy be the next one of us in danger?

Or was I having Craig issues?

20

When I returned to the bedroom, I found Kim seated at the edge of the bed.

"Hi, Amy," whispered Kim. A steaming cup of tea sat on the night table within Dan's reach. She had also brought up a plate of cookies.

"How is he?" I whispered.

"He's asleep."

"No." Dan wriggled. "I'm awake." His face was drawn and pale. He looked overwhelmingly tired. He managed a small smile as he looked at Kim. "What did you hit me with this time?"

"Very funny." Kim tucked the quilt under Dan's stubbled chin.

I blew out my candle. Kim already had two tapers burning, one on the dresser, the other on the night table. I moved closer to the bed. "What happened down there in the cellar, Dan? Do you feel up to talking?"

Dan nodded and opened and closed his mouth several times. Kim reached for the tea, braced her hand behind his neck, and helped him to drink.

"Thanks." He slowly lowered himself, wincing as the back of his head touched the pillow. "Somebody hit me."

Kim folded a fresh, moist hand towel and draped it over Dan's forehead.

"Did you see who it was?"

"No." Dan coughed.

"Drink." Kim brought the warm tea to his lips and he took another small sip. "Not too fast."

"I thought I heard something, but before I could begin to turn around…"

I sat on my bed, helping myself to a cookie. "Did you get a chance to look at Helen?"

"Yeah." Dan squeezed his eyes shut for a moment. He looked like he was having trouble concentrating, maybe even staying awake.

"Maybe we should let you rest." Kim shot me a look that read: stop asking questions and let the poor man sleep.

"Yeah," Dan said again. "She was definitely dead. Poisoned, I'd say."

I straightened. "Poisoned?"

"I-I think so."

Kim forced Dan to nibble on a cookie, then wash it down with tea. When I was old and feeble, hopefully she'd provide me the same service.

"I thought she was strangled."

"I don't believe so, Amy."

"But those marks on her throat…" My right hand went to my own throat.

"She might have been clawing at her neck."

Kim frowned. "Why would Helen do that?"

"Cyanide is nasty stuff. The poison prevents the body from absorbing oxygen. You can breathe, but you're still suffocating."

"That's horrible."

"A victim might thrash about, scream, claw at their throat…" Dan turned his head toward me. "It's practically like being strangled."

From the way Dan described it, I wondered if it might not be the more painful of the two ways to go.

"How awful!" Kim's hand flew to her mouth.

"I only saw Helen's face briefly before something hit me from behind. Her face was bright red. They say that's a sign."

"But cyanide?" It was almost unbelievable. "Doesn't cyanide smell like almonds? Or is that some other poison, like arsenic?"

Kim supplied the answer for him and it was as plausible as any. "Are you kidding, Amy? It smelled so bad down there, how could you tell?"

"You're right." Traces of rotten vegetables remained under my fingernails no matter how hard I scrubbed. The foul odor of the root cellar still lingered everywhere I went. "How would somebody even get their hands on something like that?"

Dan's eyelids fluttered. "I don't know. The killer could have brought it. Or maybe there's some in the house."

I leaned closer. Dan's voice was growing faint.

Dan closed his eyes and licked his lip. "The chief will check in the morning…sorry, can't hardly keep my eyes open."

Kim took his hand and squeezed. "You get some sleep, Dan. I'll be right here if you need me."

I smothered a yawn and stood.

"Where are you going?" Kim whispered.

"If there is any cyanide in this house, I am going to find it."

I pulled open the door.

Kim hurried to my side. "What for? You heard Dan," she whispered. "Let the police look for it in the morning." She tugged my sleeve. "Stay here. Get some rest."

"Number one," I said softly, "the police may get here tomorrow, like Dan says, but they may not get here in the morning. I, for one, would rather not wait that long."

And I was certain I wouldn't be able to rest. I wasn't closing my eyes for a minute even if I had to spend a fortnight in the Usher House.

"Is there a number two?"

"Number two," I answered. "If there's cyanide in this house and somebody who is willing to use it, I want to know about it. Otherwise..."

"Otherwise what?"

"One of us could end up like Helen."

Kim released her grip on my arm. "Fine. But check in with me before too long. Otherwise I'm going to be worrying to death about you, too." She looked over her shoulder. Dan was sleeping peacefully. "I'd rather not have another patient."

"Trust me. I remember how you took care of that injured sparrow we found when we were ten. I don't want to be your patient."

Kim crossed her arms over her chest. "That sparrow did just fine."

"Yeah, after I came by your house and made you stop feeding it grilled cheese, carrots, and chocolate milk."

Kim lowered her chin like a boxer protecting himself. "That's what my mother gave me to eat when I was under the weather. And it worked." Kim giggled despite herself. "How was I to know sparrows were any different?"

"Birds are different," I said with a grin. "Birds have feathers. You, on the other hand"—I tousled her hair—"can be a featherbrain."

"Ha-ha." Kim hugged me. "Be careful."

"I will. Take care of Dan." I pulled open the door and found myself searching the hall for sign of killers. "Keep your door locked."

"You don't have to tell me twice."

I heard the door shut and lock behind me, and I crept down the dark hallway.

Downstairs, I set the candle on a small table and opened the front door. I dug around in the snow. There was still no sign of Dan's flashlight.

Then I remembered someone had said something about a lantern being in the barn. If that was true, why hadn't Jackson mentioned it? A lantern would be helpful. And where there was one lantern, there might be more.

The more I thought, the more I wondered. Except for the house and, briefly, the shed, I had no idea what was in the other buildings around the house. That included the barn, the caretaker cottage and a couple of smaller buildings that looked to be sheds as well.

Who knew what secrets they held?

I retrieved my candle and went to the study. The fire burned quietly. The fireplace poker stuck off the edge of the hearth where Craig had left it.

The room was empty. I put the poker back on the rack and noticed for the first time that one of the fireplace tools was missing, although I didn't know what it might be. Only that there was an empty hook. The other hooks held the poker, a brush, and the bellows.

I inspected the gun case. The lock was in place. I gave it a tug. It appeared secure. None of the guns were missing.

"What about the gun Cindy and Craig had used for their puerile prank?" I whispered to the hideous paintings of Stanley and Shirley Usher on the wall on either side of the fireplace. The paintings provided no answers— just plenty of chills— neither did the duck decoys.

I moved quietly to the library. The pistol wasn't in sight but after digging, I found it in a desk drawer. It was unloaded. I rummaged around some more but could find no ammunition for it.

That was a good thing.

I wasn't about to use a gun except under the direst of circumstances. Even then, I wasn't certain I would have had the nerve to fire it, let alone in the direction of anyone.

But no bullets meant that the pistol would be useless in the hands of the killer, too.

Unless they had ammunition or knew where some might be. I picked up the cold gun by the barrel. I carried it to the front door and hurled it as far as I could out into the snow.

It disappeared from sight.

Next, I went back to the cellar. The table and tapestry sat just as we had left them when we carried Dan upstairs. I wedged the table into the doorway behind me and crept down slowly.

The candle was growing smaller by the minute. I wasn't sure how much time I had before it would go out completely. "Hello?" I whispered, praying fervently that I would not get any answer.

I didn't. My feet hit bottom. I had no desire to see Helen once again. In fact, I would have done nearly anything to avoid it, but I was curious as to whether there might be some evidence of who might have struck Dan.

A careful examination of the ground revealed nothing but scattered, shallow footprints in the earth. The prints were smudged and could have belonged to any of us.

Shining the light in the wood bin next to the one holding Helen's body, I caught sight of an iron handle reminiscent of the handles on the fireplace tools. Someone had thrust it deep into the rotting pile.

My breath caught in my throat. This could be the missing fireplace tool. I wished I could remember whether all the tools had been on the rack the night we arrived. But I could not.

Not wanting to disturb it because it might be evidence— there might even be fingerprints on the handle—I left it there. I would tell Dan and the police about it. It could be what the killer had used to strike him down.

Turning back toward the stairs, I moved the candle along the uneven shelves, taking a closer look. There were old implements and products, most of which were unidentifiable.

One of the upper shelves of the middle unit appeared to have been touched recently. There were dusty marks and several of the tins and Mason jars appeared to have been moved.

I read the almost indiscernible paper labels on the jars and packages and the rusted words on several tins of varying sizes and shapes.

One item caught my eye. I moved aside two jars that looked like pickled brains—okay, so my imagination was running away from me again—and held the wick of the candle closer. It was a small rectangular carton with the top flap slightly ajar. The red writing on the box was barely legible but there was no doubting what it held. The box was decorated with a sketch of a dead, upside-down rat, its feet in the air and whiskers waving. A smiling skull-and-crossbones was hovering above the dead rat.

The product was called Rats-No-More. It sold for the princely sum of fifteen cents per can.

Its main ingredient was cyanide.

I pulled a glove from my pocket and put it on. Gingerly, I lifted the box by the upper edges. I wasn't going to leave this behind. I would deliver it to Dan.

With the candle shrunken to less than an inch in height, I fled the basement with my prize. I breathed a sigh of relief that no one had moved the table on me.

In the kitchen, I lit a fresh taper and searched under the sink. I had seen a box of plastic storage bags there earlier. I put the rat poison in the bag and zipped it shut.

Hearing footsteps approaching, I hid the poison on the shelf of an upper cabinet over the refrigerator, shoving it behind some Bakelite cookware.

A ball of moving light appeared in the hallway.

"Oh, it's you, Amy." Robert blinked and pressed the screen of his cell phone, turning off his flashlight. "I thought I heard some rattling around."

I shut the cabinet quickly. "Hi, Robert."

"What are you up to?"

"Nothing. I mean, I couldn't sleep." I moved away from the cabinetry. "I guess you are having the same problem? You and Rosalie."

"Rosalie?" Robert's brow furrowed.

"Yes. She was downstairs a little while ago." The table sat in shadows, but I could see the empty sausage can where Robert's girlfriend had sat earlier munching on salty sausages and bourbon. "She couldn't sleep, either."

"Of course." Robert's eyes went to the cabinet above the fridge. "Find anything good?"

"Excuse me." I took a step back.

"To eat."

"Not much. I had prepared a plate earlier for Helen. I put it in the oven, but it's gone now."

"Too bad. I'm famished." He pulled open the fridge and shined his light inside. "This place isn't exactly the Ritz, is it?"

He hadn't reacted at all, not so much as a blink or a flinch when I had said Helen's name aloud. "Would you have come had you known?"

"I didn't have much choice in the matter. What Mike wanted, Mike got."

"Right. It doesn't sound like the two of you ever got along."

"Our feelings for one another were no secret."

"So, why stay partners?"

"I told you before. I was buying him out. Mike was planning to retire."

"Had he told anyone else about those plans?"

Robert folded his hands over his chest. "Mike wanted to keep it secret for the time being. He didn't want any of our investors getting nervous. After I bought him out, we were going to make the announcement."

"What happens now?"

The beginnings of a smile formed on his face. "Life goes on."

"For some of us. Our numbers seem to be dwindling."

"What is that supposed to mean?"

I moved our dirty cups from the kitchen table to the sink, giving myself time to think before replying. "Robert, have you been up long?"

"A little while," he said nonchalantly. "Why do you ask?"

"I was only curious."

"About my sleeping habits?"

"About a lot of things." I pressed my spine against the kitchen counter. The cold tile cut like a dull knife across my back. "Have you seen or heard anything…unusual?"

Robert appeared amused. "Unusual?" He came close and draped an arm possessively over my shoulder. "Don't tell me you're afraid of ghosts, Amy?" His voice was husky and warm.

I slipped from his grasp. "I think I should go."

"Stay," Robert urged. "Have a drink with me. We can sit by the fire."

"Don't you think Rosalie might mind?"

He looked down his nose at me. "We aren't married, Amy."

"Would it matter if you were?" I found myself saying.

Robert shrugged. "Yeah, I suppose so. Not that every guy feels that way about marriage. Mike sure didn't."

"Oh?" For the first time since he'd shown up in the kitchen, I was interested in what Robert had to say. "What's that supposed to mean?"

"I'm not speaking ill of the dead. Even when the dead is a bastard like Mike."

"Mike cheated on Helen?"

Robert's smile was chilly. "You'd have to ask Mike that. Oh wait," he added, wryly, "you can't. He's dead."

"Isn't that convenient," I quipped.

"Hey, believe what you want. All I know is that they were planning to divorce."

"Mike and Helen?" They seemed like such a lovely couple. Could Helen have murdered her husband and then committed suicide?

"Ask Rosalie, if you don't believe me."

"I just might do that." Although the woman was not high on my list of reliable sources. "At dinner, Rosalie told me she wanted a word with me. Do you know what about?" She hadn't mentioned anything when we were in the kitchen earlier. Was it because she didn't want to talk with Kim in the room?

"Not a clue. You'll have to ask her that," he said a little too quickly for my taste. "Maybe she wanted to compliment your cooking."

I've tasted my cooking, so I knew that was not the reason.

"I was sleeping. I borrowed sleeping pills. The trouble is, every time I use the things, I fall dead asleep for a couple hours. Then I pop completely awake, feeling lousy and regretting it." Robert smiled sheepishly although there was no mistaking the wolf underneath. "You'd think I'd learn, wouldn't you?"

"Who did you borrow the pills from, Rosalie?"

"Nah. She doesn't go in for anything like that. Alcohol is her sleeping medicine of choice. I got them from the bottle in Helen's room."

"Helen gave them to you? When did you see her?"

"No. She wasn't there so I helped myself. I'm sure she won't mind." He flashed that sheepish, or should I say wolfish, grin once more. "Why, what's up?"

"Helen is dead."

Robert planted his hands on the kitchen counter. "What happened? Suicide or did her heart give out?"

"Someone poisoned her."

"Poisoned her?" Robert sounded skeptical. "Who would want to do a thing like that?" He grinned. "Besides Mike, of course, and he's dead."

He seemed to relish repeating those words.

Robert glanced out the kitchen window. "Are you sure about this, Amy?"

"I found her body myself. Me and Kim."

"Where? She wasn't in her room last time I checked."

I hesitated before answering but, in the end, couldn't see what harm telling him might do. "In the root cellar. Her body is still down there."

"Interesting. Remind me not to go to the cellar." Robert's hands slapped a beat on the counter. "In fact, first thing in the morning, Rosalie and I are going to pack our bags and get out of this house. I don't care if we have to walk down the mountain. I am not going to risk staying here another night. In fact…"

Robert strutted from the room, taking a lit candle with him. I hurried after him.

"Rosalie was in the kitchen, drinking, after Kim and I found Helen dead in the root cellar," I said from behind.

"And you think Rosalie is a suspect?" Robert shook his head. "You're barking up the wrong tree. Rosalie is more the 'make love, not war' type."

"So, she has been with you in your room all night? She's there now?"

"Of course. I can't vouch for every minute of her life any more than I can yours."

"What are you doing?" I watched as he shook the lock on the gun cabinet in the study.

Robert cursed. He turned and scanned the room. His eyes fell on the fireplace tools. He picked up the tongs, waved it in his hand as if testing it, then strode to the cabinet once again.

"Robert, what do—"

Robert raised his hand to me. "Stay back." He tested the tool once more. He pulled back his arm and savagely struck the glass case hard with the tip of the iron tongs.

I flinched as the glass shattered and fell in jagged pieces to the floor. Craig wouldn't like it—more damages that he would be responsible for.

Robert smiled and tossed the tongs on the floor. He removed an antique single-shot shotgun with silver filigree and a box of shells from the gun case. "This will keep us safe." He broke the shotgun open and slid a shell into the chamber. "It's only birdshot, but it will do."

"Are you sure you want to do that? Do you even know how to work that thing?"

Robert grinned confidently. "Oh yeah. I've been a hunter for years. I grew up hunting deer, pheasant, duck. You name it, I probably shot it. My dad taught me."

Robert stepped over the broken glass, carrying the shotgun in one hand, its muzzle aimed at the ceiling. In the other hand, he clutched the box of shells. "Now, I am going to make a pot of coffee, then I intend to lock myself in our room with the barrel of this bad boy aiming at the door."

I stepped aside as he and the weapon moved past me. "Care to join me?"

"No."

"Okay," Robert said. "If you change your mind, make sure you knock first."

I winced as he carelessly waved the gun at me and strode away using the beam of his cellphone to light his way, with the shells tucked under his arm.

21

I picked up the candle he'd left behind. As I tiptoed upstairs, I could hear Robert in the kitchen. I went to Helen's room.

I wanted another look, thinking maybe there would be some evidence of her murder. What I found instead, tucked inside her suitcase were two travel vouchers for a trip to Saint Croix. Helen and Mike Holberg were booked a few days from now on a flight from Charlotte to Miami. From there, they were scheduled for a ten-day Caribbean cruise. That didn't sound like a couple on the verge of divorce to me.

"Searching a dead woman's belongings," a voice said, rather jovially. "That's low even for you."

I about jumped out of my skin. The candle I was holding flew from my hand, hit the floor, and went out.

A moment later, the beam of a cell phone flashlight was aimed at my face. "Hello, Amy."

"Hello, Craig." I cursed and picked up the fallen candle. I fumbled in my coat for the matches I had taken from the kitchen and relit the wick. "What are you doing here?"

"I was looking for you." Craig came into the room and closed the door behind him. "I saw the glow of the light. I ran into Robert downstairs. He told me you were wandering around. So, here I am."

I scrambled to my feet. "What do you want?"

"I wanted to talk to you."

"About what?"

"Why are you looking through Mike and Helen's things?"

"I don't know." I wiped my hands against my sweats trying to remove the hot, melted wax that had landed on my fingers in my fright. "I was curious. Did you know they were planning a cruise next week?"

Craig sat on the corner of the Holbergs' bed. "Sure, Mike told me all about it. It was a second honeymoon. They've been married thirty years."

"A second honeymoon?"

"That's right. They were spending a few days here and then leaving from Charlotte. Why?"

"Robert told me that Mike and Helen weren't getting along." I took a seat at the head of the bed.

"I suppose they had their ups and downs. Everybody does. Mind if I shut this off?" He held up his phone. I shook my head in the negative. "My battery is getting low."

We sat in the dim glow of the single candle. It was almost romantic—except that I was in a room belonging to two recently deceased guests—who had both died of foul play—in a haunted house, with a killer on the loose, sitting beside my cheating ex-boyfriend.

Well, the candle was romantic…all that was missing was Derek.

"Why were you looking for me?" I asked.

"Because of those things you said."

"What things?"

Craig let out a long, hard sigh. "I was lying in bed, next to Cindy, you know?"

"And?"

"I got to wondering. Maybe Cindy murdered Mike. Maybe she murdered Helen, too."

My heart skipped a beat or three. "Can you think of some reason that she might have done that?"

Craig was silent a moment. "No, not really. I mean, I don't know. She knew Mike before I did."

"Cindy knew Mike?"

"She was his shrink. He went to her office in Chapel Hill for a spell."

"I didn't know."

"It's no big deal. Anyhow, that's how I met Mike. Since then, we've done a few deals together and me and Cindy, well, you know."

I knew.

"When Mike told me he was backing out of our deal, Cindy was furious. I've never seen her madder."

"I can't blame her, can you? If the deal fell through, she stood to lose a great deal of money."

Craig nodded. “Her entire life savings.”

“That does not make her a murderer.”

“She said she’d kill him if he didn’t keep his word and put up the rest of the money.”

“People say a lot of things, Craig.” Like the way he said he loved me while fooling around with other women. Like Cindy. “It does not make them murderers.”

“It was a quarter of a million bucks, Amy. People have killed for less.”

That they had.

I slid nearer and placed my hand on Craig’s arm. “Look, Craig. I’m sure that Cindy is a lovely girl. She’s smart, she’s beautiful.” I slapped his shoulder. “And she’s no killer.”

“I hope not.”

“I am curious, though. Where did Cindy get the money to invest with you?”

“Her mom left her a small inheritance.”

A quarter of a million dollars was Craig’s idea of a small inheritance?

“Listen, I’ll tell you what.” I removed my hand and stood, crossing to the curtained window. “If I’m wrong and she strangles you in your sleep tonight, tomorrow you can tell me ‘I told you so.’” I peeked out. I could see a sky full of stars. Hopefully, the worst of the snowstorm was past us.

Craig slid off the bed with a sigh. “Great.” He walked to the door. “How’s Kim’s boyfriend?”

“Okay, I guess. I was just going to check on them.”

“Is Helen still…”

“Yes. In the root cellar. Dan said to leave her there until morning when the police come.” If they could get here. “One compromised crime scene is already going to be enough to make our chief of police blow a fuse. I don’t know how he’d handle a second one.”

Craig opened the door. “Robert said you told him that Helen had been poisoned. Is that true?”

“That’s what Dan thinks.”

Craig scratched behind his ear. “You know, the day we arrived, there were signs of rats or mice under the kitchen sink. Somebody said something about rat poison. Could that be something?”

“It could. Do you remember who mentioned the poison?”

Craig shook his head. “Sorry.”

“Let me know if you remember.”

Craig nodded thoughtfully. “See you in the morning.”

I followed Craig out into the hallway and watched him disappear into the darkness.

The door to Jackson's room was slightly ajar, no more than an inch. I was going to shut it for him but thought I heard a sound. I put my ear to the crack and listened. I heard nothing.

I quietly pushed open the door, not wanting to wake Jackson. The man had been through so much already. Sleep was the best antidote for him now.

The candle cast moving shadows on the walls. The ducks in the room appeared to be lazily swimming. The bed was empty. A cup and saucer sat on the night table.

"Jackson?" I whispered.

A cold draught ran across my cheeks and nose. I imagined a ghost brushing past me and shivered.

I turned toward the red-curtained cubby. The draught seemed to be coming from that direction. I set the candle holder on the nightstand and drew back the curtain. The few items of clothing hanging from the wooden rod had been pushed to the left side.

The two halves of a darkly-stained pine bifold door were propped open on the left and right side of the closet with duck decoys. A black curtain covered the backside. The cold draught came from around its edge. I pulled it aside slowly, making barely a sound.

Retrieving my candle from the night table, I stepped into the closet and shined the feeble light. A narrow, wooden set of stairs, not much more than a rough ladder really, led downward. I held the candle over the space.

I couldn't make out the bottom. Feeling like Alice about to go through the looking-glass, I turned around and started down.

I had to grip the steps with one hand while holding the candle with the other. It was slow, hard going. After half a dozen steps, the candle blew out.

I gasped and clung to the ladder in the blackness. Fear and claustrophobia washed over me. I didn't like dark spaces. I particularly did not like cold, dark, unknown tight spaces.

I fumbled for the matchbook in my pocket. It slipped from my fingers and fell.

I cursed as I hung there, my fingers tight on the wobbly steps. My fear of what was down below fought with my curiosity.

Finally, with my fingers weakening and my legs shaking, I urged myself downward. Another half-dozen steps and I was on the ground and standing in what appeared to be a deep black hole that sloped slightly downhill.

There was no light.

It was a narrow space. My head brushed the dirt ceiling, the walls barely wider apart than my shoulders.

I bent my knees and scoured the ground for the matchbook. I came up empty and cursed again.

I took a step and immediately felt something underfoot. I knelt down. My matches!

I lit one quickly and the draft snuffed it out. I turned my back to the light breeze and lit another. This time, I quickly held the match to the candle. The wick caught, and I was relieved that I could see once more.

Unfortunately, there was little to see besides an endless seeming dark tunnel.

I knew in my heart that I should go back, get a stronger light and even a companion but the mysterious passage had a grip on me, pulling me onward. I took a couple of shallow breaths and let gravity lead me down the gentle slope into the black unknown.

The candle went out yet again. I only had one match left. I decided to continue in the dark rather than risk using up my last match. I might have a greater need for it later.

I moved on.

Despite the coldness, sweat rose along the back of my neck as I felt my way tentatively with hands and feet across the uneven ground. I followed the passage for what seemed an eternity.

At one point, something crunched underfoot, and I was convinced it was bones.

Human bones.

I shook it off and continued blindly on. After several more steps, my left hand reached to the side and felt nothing rather than the hard-packed earthen tunnel wall I was expecting.

I stopped. There was a second branch to the tunnel. I debated whether to continue straight on or turn.

My brow was bathed in perspiration. I wiped my hand across my forehead and unzipped my coat.

In the end, I decided to continue straight on. Distance had become unmeasurable, but several steps further my hands hit dirt. I had reached the termination of the tunnel.

Another narrow set of stairs led upward. My eyes had adjusted to the inky blackness and through a crack at the top of the steps, I saw a faint light.

22

I set my unlit candle on the ground, took a deep breath to steady myself, and started upward. I pushed open a wooden hatch with one hand. It moved with the tiniest of squeaks.

I peeked my eyes and nose out and blinked. Where was I? It was too dark to be certain but, wherever I was, I didn't appear to be in any danger from above.

I clambered up the remaining steps and dusted myself off. A dim light coming from beyond a pair of shutters provided some detail. I was standing in a small room. The air was stale. I crossed to the window hoping to let more light inside.

The shutters were fixed to the outside of the building. I could not open them. Squinting, I could make out the shape of the Usher house across the way and the stars sparkling in the night sky.

I was in the barn. More specifically, in some cold, dark room of the barn.

"Hello?" I whispered.

Only the wind blowing outside answered with a rattle of the shutters. I climbed back down into the passageway, retrieved my candle and hurried back up.

I pulled out the matchbook and lit the wick with my last remaining match. As my eyes adjusted, I saw that I was in a narrow workroom. Long, sturdy worktables and shelves filled the space.

Woodworking tools, covered in dust, lay neatly arranged on the workbenches. There was a pile of duck decoys gathered on an oilcloth in the corner. The assortment included pintail drakes, a pair of bluebills, loons, canvasbacks and mallards. A dozen other species were also represented.

Stanley Usher had been an avid duck decoy carver and collector. He had little chance to use this room, but he had clearly built it as a studio where he could practice his art.

He might have ordered the construction of the underground passageway so he wouldn't have to brave the elements when the weather was inhospitable.

I circled the room. The floor was wide-board pine and dirty with age, dust and rodent droppings.

There was a lantern on the end of one of the worktables near a collection of knives and saws. The vintage hurricane-style lantern was red with a clear glass globe. I opened the fuel reservoir and moved my nose over the opening. I smelled kerosene.

The wick was charred. I touched the tip and found that it was damp. I pressed the candle flame against the wick of the lantern. I was rewarded with a quick, strong little flame.

I blew out the candle and set it on the bench. I took the lantern by the handle and moved to the door on the opposite side of the room. It was held in place with a simple latch.

I opened it and found myself in the main section of the barn. All was quiet. The expansive space smelled damp. A ladder ran to the hayloft. I walked the length of the barn slowly, holding the lantern in front of me. My heart skipped a beat each time I heard, or thought I heard, a sound.

But there was nothing much to see.

The old Jeep that Jackson had mentioned sat in the far corner of the barn. There was a small metal gas can beside the back tire.

I noticed a couple more lanterns hanging from nails on thick support posts. I made a mental note to tell the others about them in the morning.

Not that we'd likely need them.

I set the lantern on the ground and pulled on one of the barn doors. It moved sideways grudgingly. I could see the Usher House standing dark and quiet.

Which was as it should be.

I knew that the toolshed and Mike Holberg's body were right around the corner on the other side of the wall to my right.

The caretaker's cottage, too, sat dark and quiet, squatting like a giant slumbering black bear in the snow. I thought I saw a glint of light from one of the cottage's side windows. I stared at the cottage for a moment and saw nothing more. It could have been my imagination, already highly overactive, or my eyes playing tricks on me.

Cold and tired, I slid the barn door shut and returned to the workroom. Gripping the lantern carefully in my left hand, I started down into the underground passageway once again. This time I had a nice, steady light to guide my way.

I walked quickly and confidently. It was time to check on Kim and Dan. If he was awake, I would tell him what I had found. This secret tunnel raised all kinds of questions.

As I approached the second branch of the passageway, which was now on my right side, a hand shot out and grabbed my wrist.

"You should not have come down here."

It was Jackson Canning. He was bundled in a green-and-black flannel coat and heavy denim trousers.

"Jackson!" My blood was pounding to escape from my ears. "What are you doing here? You scared me."

"You don't belong here."

The back of my neck bristled with fear.

I fought down my fright and gulped. "I was looking for you," I said with as much composure as I could muster. I forced a small smile. "This is quite a setup. You can get to and from the house and the barn without ever stepping foot outdoors."

Jackson stared woodenly at me. His eyes were heavy, puffy from lack of sleep, and his face was unshaved.

"Funny you didn't mention it earlier," I stupidly added.

Jackson was stooped forward, too tall to stand erect in the close quarters of the tunnel. The long, strong fingers of his left hand flexed and unflexed nervously. His right hand gripped an unlit flashlight. He must have heard me coming, switched off his own light, and been lying in wait for me.

Was that Dan's flashlight he was gripping?

"Where does that other branch lead? To your cottage?" I tugged, and he released his grip on my wrist.

Jackson's eyes narrowed. I pictured a snake getting ready to strike.

And this snake was deadly poisonous.

When he refused to answer, I continued. Against my better judgment, I admit. "This is how you managed everything, isn't it?"

I inched nearly imperceptibly away, my back pressing against the packed dirt wall behind me. "You used the tunnels. You were able to appear and reappear whenever you wanted to. Very slick."

The lantern shook in my hand. I was unable to control my nerves. Unfortunately, I was also unable to control my mouth. "And you almost got away with three murders," I said. And, unless I was able to think of something and quick, I was about to be his fourth victim.

"Three?"

"That's right. Augusta might have thrown herself or fallen off that cliff, but her blood is on your hands. You killed her just as surely as you killed the others!"

"That's sick!" Jackson's face filled with anger and anguish.

"Is it, Jackson? Augusta was cheating on you with Mike Holberg, or at least you assumed they were. You found them together in the study and stabbed him to death with a kitchen knife.

"Augusta probably saw you kill him. She must have been mad with rage and grief. She ran out into the snow, blind with sorrow and fear. Your wife fell or jumped to her death. But you may as well have pushed her over the precipice yourself," I said harshly.

"You're crazy." Jackson chopped his hand through the air. "Cheat on me? Augusta was my sister."

"Your sister?" I felt as if I were falling down an elevator shaft.

"That's right. My only family, as a matter of fact. There's nobody left but us. I would never harm her."

The funny thing was, for a cold-blooded killer, he seemed sincere. "But—" My suddenly constructed theory was coming apart before my eyes.

Jackson took a step closer. "I'm afraid I can't let you go back," Jackson said. Again, I had to admit, he actually sounded a little sad as he said it. "Not now."

I did what any self-respecting hero would do in my position.

I swung the lantern at him. He raised his arm to defend himself. The lantern slammed into the flashlight and I heard the sound of broken glass mingled with his curses as the light winked out and we were thrust into darkness.

Jackson barked and cursed some more. His fingers clutched at me, pulling viciously at my sleeves. I ripped off my coat and let him have it.

Then I ran for my life!

23

I had gotten turned around. I did not know if I was heading back to the Usher house or out to the barn, maybe even to the caretaker's cottage.

I really didn't care where I was going. I just wanted to go and go and go!

I bounced off the earthen walls as I scurried through the dark tunnel. The dull thud of Jackson's footsteps hounded me.

My nose ached, and my eyes filled with dirt as I slammed into the wall yet again. I fell to the ground.

I heard Jackson's panting breath and knew he was closing in on me. I screamed and scrambled to my feet even as his fingers grabbed at my boot.

I kicked. My boot came loose from my foot. Jackson cursed, and I ran. I felt a hard, sudden impact. I had hit the steep stairs at the end of the tunnel. My hands clawed for grip. By the growing sounds of heavy breathing and pounding steps, Jackson wasn't far behind.

Digging my fingers into the rough wood, I hauled myself up the steps, coming out in the closet of Jackson's room. My first instinct was to run to the room I shared with Kim for help. Dan was there. Dan was a police officer. Dan could save me.

Then again, Dan was an injured police officer. Maybe even a sleeping or unconscious one.

If I led Jackson to our room, rather than saving myself, I might be placing Kim and Dan at risk.

My arms tangled in the clothing and drapery. I yelped in frustration. Jackson was on his way up the steps, moving fast. He was far more used to going through that passage and up and down that impossible staircase than I was.

He was also bigger and stronger.

And, somehow, I needed to stop him.

If not stop him, at least prevent him from catching and killing me.

Once again, I decided to do the only thing a self-respecting hero could do. Well, either self-respecting hero or blithering idiot. Sometimes, the two were indistinguishable.

I half-ran, half-tripped my way through Jackson and Augusta's bedroom. I threw open the door and raced down the murky hall.

Jackson howled, low and deep, never giving up the chase.

I was out of breath, which might have been a good thing because I had forgotten to breathe about two minutes earlier—which was just about the same instant that my heart had frozen in my chest cavity and my brain had turned to mush.

My goal was Robert and Rosalie's room. Robert had a shotgun. Robert had a loaded shotgun. He said he knew how to use it and, judging by the way he acted, I believed him.

He'd also said he was going to drink a pot of coffee and sit up all night staring at the door. He had given me the impression that he was going to shoot the first thing in sight and fill whoever dared open that door with birdshot.

I was hoping that most of that was true.

However, if he was going to shoot anything, I was praying it would be the *second* thing in sight!

I pounded along the hall runner and stopped outside Robert and Rosalie's door. I made the mistake of looking over my shoulder. A dark blur was coming in long strides towards me.

I reached out and placed my hand on the doorknob. I bit my lip and my fingers hesitated over the knob.

Was I going to get strangled or beaten to death or filled with birdshot at close range?

Choices, choices, choices. This modern world was filled with too many of them.

Jackson loomed nearer, his arms reaching.

With an anguished cry, I made my choice. I threw my hand over the knob. I could only pray the door wasn't locked.

I turned my wrist and the knob rotated. I flung open the bedroom door and threw myself at the floor.

"Huh? What the—" a sleepy, puzzled male voice said from the darkness.

Jackson was right behind me.

"Robert! It's me!" My hands hit the ground hard, buckling my wrists. My knees struck the rug and I tumbled sideways, striking the bottom of the bedframe.

Jackson hurled himself into the doorway with a shout.

A deafening explosion filled the air.

"Oops!" That was Robert. I heard something hit the ground and the sound of rolling objects scattering around the floor. My palm fell over a hard cylinder and I recognized it as a shotgun shell.

Robert cursed. "Impossible to reload this damn thing in the dark!" He fiddled noisily with the shotgun.

Jackson leapt on me. I fought him off, kicking and punching as hard as I could.

I heard a steady, high-pitched screaming sound and it finally registered that it was Rosalie shrieking from the bed.

"Let her up." That was Robert again and he sounded serious. So, did the cocking of the shotgun.

Jackson's fingers dug ruthlessly into my neck. I gasped for breath. Another moment and I would succumb.

"Rosalie," Robert commanded. "Stop screaming to wake the dead and light a candle for Pete's sake!"

"Oh!" A moment later, soft light filled the room. Rosalie leaned over the edge of the bed gripping her lighter. She was bundled in a thick robe and pajamas with a knit cap on her head.

Robert stood beside us, fully dressed. A heavy quilt lay on the floor next to a rocking chair facing the bedroom door. The muzzle of the shotgun was aimed at Jackson's head.

Jackson's eyes grew wide as he looked at the death delivering black hole of the shotgun inches from his nose. He released his grip and I gulped savagely for air. I thrashed and knocked him off my chest.

There was a mad look of desperation on Jackson's face. He looked more like a trapped animal than a human being in that moment. I wondered what he would do next. Would he renew his attack on me? Would he lunge for Robert, hell-bent on self-destruction?

Finally, he curled up onto his knees and buried his face in his hands.

And cried.

"What the devil is going on?" Craig came running in, clutching his cellphone, its flashlight app darting from me and Jackson to Rosalie, who was now lighting a bedside candle. Then he turned to Robert, still clutching the shotgun and holding its barrel menacingly at Jackson's head.

I did not think for a second that he would hesitate to use it—hopefully, Jackson Canning was thinking the same thing.

A bit of plaster fell from overhead. Craig looked up. "What the devil, Robert. Look what you did to the ceiling!"

Cindy came up next, followed by Kim.

"Never mind the ceiling, Craig. Jackson here attacked Amy."

"What for?" demanded Craig.

"Ask him." Rosalie pointed to Jackson.

Jackson's shoulders shook as he sobbed.

"Amy!" Kim cried. "Are you okay? What happened?" Her eyes flew around the room for answers.

I nodded. Kim helped me to my feet. "I'm fine." A glance at the ceiling told me that Craig's property damages were rising. Any security deposit he'd made, shy of several thousand dollars, would be gone.

I moved away as far as I could from Jackson. There was an open suitcase beside the bed. A weathered duck decoy lay among an assortment of women's lacy underwear and rolled up pairs of socks.

"Jackson is our murderer. He murdered the Holbergs and is responsible for his sister's death too." I rubbed my throat. The pain of Jackson's unrelenting fingers gouging into my neck, as he tried to silence me, lingered.

"His sister?" Cindy asked, breathily.

"Augusta was Jackson's sister, not his wife."

"Well, well…" Rosalie said from the edge of the bed.

"I'll be damned." Robert tapped Jackson on the shoulder with the tip of the muzzle. "Got anything to say for yourself, pal?"

Jackson remained stubbornly silent.

Robert shrugged. "I'm sure the police won't have much trouble getting you to talk."

"Speaking of police," I said, turning to Kim, "how is Dan?"

"He's weak but better." Kim smiled. "He was sleeping until all the commotion started." She turned to leave. "I'll go check on him and tell him what's going on."

"What are we going to do with Jackson?" Craig asked.

"It will be light soon. Maybe we should all stay together," I suggested. "Until help arrives."

"And if it doesn't?" Cindy asked.

"It will." Eventually. "But I noticed a gas can in the barn."

"You were in the barn?" Craig asked.

"Yes. There's a tunnel leading from the house to the barn."

Everybody started remarking and asking questions at once.

I raised my hands in the air for them to stop. "I'll explain later. The point is, there is a gas can out there. And"—I waited for Craig and Cindy to shut up—"there is a snowmobile down the road a piece. All it needs is gasoline. If the can in the barn is empty, we can siphon some from one of our vehicles."

Voices rose excitedly once more. We were all sick of being trapped it the Usher House.

"Thank goodness." Rosalie rolled off the bed, her wary eyes on Jackson as he kneeled on the floor, hands still hiding his face.

"Yes," I said. "If help doesn't arrive soon after daylight, one of us can ride into town."

"Me!" Robert and Craig said as one. The two men glared at one another.

"This is my responsibility," Craig huffed.

"Yeah," cracked Robert, "but I've seen the way you drive. If you handle a snowmobile the way you handle a tractor, we are all in trouble. I'd rather one of us actually make it down this freaking mountain alive."

Craig frowned.

"Enough. We'll flip a coin," I said. "If it comes to that."

"Fine." Craig wrapped his arm around Cindy's waist. "I'll make us some coffee. Let's get Jackson down to the study where we can keep an eye on him."

"Good idea, honey bear. I'll help."

"I'll be right behind you." Rosalie snatched the brandy bottle from the bedside and poured herself a stiff drink. "I didn't know you had it in you, Jackson." She raised her glass and drank.

Robert nodded and gave Jackson a nudge with the tip of the shotgun. "Come on, pal. Let's go." Jackson flinched and swatted at the gun with his hand.

Robert jumped back and stiffened. "Uh-uh." He held the gun tight to his side. "Don't make me use this. A shotgun at close range can make quite the mess."

Blood spatter would be the death knell for any remaining security deposit Craig might have hopes of recouping.

Rosalie turned to her husband and gave him a peck on the cheek. "If you must shoot him, please try not to get bloodstains on my things, dear." She departed.

Apparently, she and I were on the same wavelength.

Jackson lowered his hands and pushed himself to his feet.

With Robert training the gun on him, he followed us docilely down the stairs to the study.

I relit the fire. Rosalie made herself comfortable behind the bar. Robert dragged a wingback chair to the entrance, putting himself between the study and the hallway in case Jackson decided to make a run for it.

Robert settled back with the shotgun over his knees. He looked like he was itching to use it.

Rosalie brought him a drink that he refused.

Jackson sat on the floor beside the chess set. I saw his eyes go to the broken glass of the gun cabinet. I wondered for a minute if he would try to grab one of the other guns. In the end, he remained seated, shoulders slumped, staring at the rug.

Craig and Cindy appeared with coffee, doughnuts and cookies.

Under the circumstances, it was as good a breakfast as any. I helped myself then grabbed a throw pillow and took a seat on the rug in front of the fire.

A little later, with the sugar and caffeine rushing through me and the heat of the flames washing over me, my eyelids drooped.

When I woke up, somebody was kicking me.

24

"Leave it to you to sleep through a murder, Simms!"

I painfully lifted an eyelid then, thinking I was hallucinating, opened the other. "Jerry?" I lifted myself up on one elbow.

Chief Jerry Kennedy loomed over me, kicking my left thigh with his square-toed boot. "Wake up, woman."

"You can stop kicking me now, Jerry." I twisted my stiff neck side to side. "I'm awake." My mouth was dry and tasted like I'd eaten a sack of sunflower seed shells.

I sat up and pulled my knees to my chest.

"Good. My leg was getting tired," he said with a grin. A blue knitted wool cap with the police insignia on the front covered Jerry's blond crew cut. He and I were the same age, although he still looked as boyish now as he had back in the day. Maybe it was the fleshy, squat nose, freckles, and goofy dark jade eyes.

"Very funny." I rubbed my eyes. "Where is everybody?"

"Most everyone is in the dining room. Except for that Jackson Canning fella. He's locked up outside."

"Alone?"

"No. Al is keeping an eye on him."

Al was Albert Pratt, a recent police department hire from New Orleans.

"How did you get here?"

"We borrowed a Range Rover from Robert LaChance," Chief Kennedy said loudly. "He had it on his lot. That thing is impressive. I'm thinking of requesting that the town buy it for the department." Among other ventures, Robert LaChance owned a used car lot in town. "That's where we've sequestered Canning, out in the Rover."

"Good idea," I stood. "Are we free to leave?"

Jerry unzipped his navy-blue parka and fell into the chair by the fireplace. He plucked the cap from atop his skull and scratched his hair rapidly. "In a little bit. There isn't room for everybody in one trip. I want to get Jackson and Dan into town. Kim is going to ride with him."

"How is Dan?"

Jerry grinned. "Dan's fine. He's got a thick skull. He showed me where he got hit. Down in the cellar, I mean."

"Is Helen Holberg still down there?"

"Yeah." Jerry extended his legs and I heard his knees crack. "We'll be hauling her up soon. Nasty business, that. Greeley is down there now with Larry."

Greeley was Andrew Greeley, the septuagenarian town coroner whose daytime gig was owner of the local mortuary. Larry was Larry Reynolds, another police officer.

"What about Augusta Canning?"

"The woman you say is down in the ravine?" Chief Kennedy smothered a yawn with his hand. "I haven't been out to check on her body yet. I want to interview everyone first. The dead can wait. We've got Mike Holberg in the back of the Range Rover already."

I shivered. I had nearly forgotten about him. I examined my empty coffee cup. "I need some coffee."

Jerry clamped his hands over his knees then rose. "Fine. We'll get some coffee in the kitchen while you give me your take on what went on out here the past couple of days."

I couldn't help grinning as I led the way to the kitchen. "You want my insight, eh?" Even as I teased Jerry, something about the affair bugged me but I didn't know what.

"Don't get too big for your panties, Simms. I want your witness statement, that's all." Jerry's heavy boots shook the floor as he walked.

I crossed to the stove, grabbed the kettle and filled it under the kitchen faucet.

Jerry drew his brows together. "What are you doing that for?"

"I'm boiling water for instant coffee."

"Instant coffee?" Jerry rocked back on his heels. "Who wants that swill when you've got a percolator right there?" He pointed at the device at the corner of the counter.

"No electricity. The power's been out since—"

Jerry rolled his eyes at me and flipped the kitchen light switch on and off, on and off.

"Hey, you fixed it?"

"There was nothing wrong with it. Canning turned off the gas supply."

"Figures." I sighed and cleaned the coffee grounds from the percolator filter, then refilled it to the brim with fresh coffee.

Jerry asked me a lot of questions, some of which I knew the answers to. Other questions, I told him that his guesses were as good as mine.

"What does Jackson have to say for himself?" I asked.

Jerry groaned a lot. "Jackson Canning hasn't said a single word. He hasn't even asked for a lawyer."

Satisfied with my answers for what had happened and what I had seen and heard, Jerry sent me to the dining room.

Jerry looked at his notebook. "Tell Robert Flud I want a word him next." The chief wanted all of our statements before we were allowed to leave the mountain. "And I'm going to need you to show me where this other body is."

I nodded and left the room.

It wasn't until nearly two excruciating hours later that Jerry Kennedy summoned me once again.

"Let's go take a look at Jackson's sister's body," Jerry said as he stuck his head in the dining room. I was the only one remaining. Everybody else had gone into town, even Craig and Cindy, who were paying to rent the house, had opted to go to town. Craig said he had a line on a place the two of them could stay.

I wished him luck but was happy to have him out of my sight. A little ex-boyfriend goes a long way.

Jerry pushed open the front door. I was immediately hit by a wall of heat and light.

I threw my arms wide and aimed my face at the sky. "It must be fifty degrees out here!"

"Yeah, the forecast calls for a couple days of unseasonably warm weather. The roads ought to be completely clear soon."

Melting snow dripped from my minivan and Craig's car. Melting footprints littered the driveway. The Range Rover sat on the other side of the busted bridge.

"Come on," Jerry beckoned with his hand. "You can work on your tan later. Show me this body of yours."

"It isn't *my* body, Jerry." I hurried after him. "None of any of this was my fault or my doing," I felt compelled to say. "My only mistake was agreeing to have dinner with my ex-boyfriend."

Jerry turned and smirked. “Yeah, I heard he was the guy who dumped you.” He chuckled.

“He didn’t dump me.” I planted my fists on my hips. “*I* dumped *him*.”

Jerry shrugged. “His girlfriend sure is cute.”

I narrowed my eyes at him. “What’s that supposed to mean?” I pushed past him and tromped toward the ravine without waiting for an answer. I wasn’t going to like it, no matter what he said.

“Down there.” I pointed as we reached the end of the trail. Augusta’s footprints, and the prints that we had made afterward, had all but melted away.

Jerry moved carefully to the edge.

“Afraid of heights, Jerry?”

Jerry looked nervously at me then back to his feet. “I’m trying not to ruin my new boots, that’s all.”

“Yeah, right.” I inched closer. I wasn’t too fond of heights myself. Especially when they ended in sudden drops. “She’s right down there.” I moved my eyes among the rocks. “Somewhere.”

The area below looked different now with much of the snow melted away.

Jerry rubbed up against me and dug his fingers into my shoulder. “I don’t see anybody.”

“I’m telling you. She was right there.” I scanned the rocks to the right and to the left. “Maybe she was further up this way.” I stepped away from the precipice and moved right after taking my bearings off the tarn and the house. I looked down into the ravine once more. “Right there! That’s her by—”

Jerry caught up to me. “Where?”

“Never mind. I thought I saw a scrap of clothing.” I huffed. “I should have brought the binoculars and spotting scope. Maybe we should go back and get them.”

“Never mind,” Jerry replied. “I’ve seen enough for now. We’ll send some men down to find her and bring her up once they do. With all this snow melting, her body might have washed downstream.”

“I suppose you’re right.”

“It’s not going to be an easy up and down. We might need some climbing equipment.”

“Craig tells me there is a path of sorts further up that way.” I waved to my right.

“I’ll tell Larry and Al to check it out as soon as they can.” Jerry’s radio squawked, and he answered. The coroner was packing up.

We worked our way back to the house. The waterfowl were out in force now, mallards and wood ducks drifted lazily on the glassy surface, enjoying the unseasonably warm weather as much as I was.

I was given a ride back into town in the Range Rover with Officers Pratt and Reynolds. Chief Kennedy drove. I could tell he really loved that black Range Rover. Would the Town of Ruby Lake let him keep it?

Robert LaChance had a lot of pull with the mayor and the town council so they just might.

Fortunately, there were no dead bodies making the trip down the mountain with us.

25

I was greeted with a hero's and lover's welcome on my arrival at Birds & Bees. Mom and Esther were waiting inside the door. Derek was there, too.

"Dirk!" I cried, leaping into his arms. I felt tears well up in the corners of my eyes.

Derek twitched. "What did you call me?"

"Derek." I blushed. "I mean, what else would I call you?" I silently cursed Craig for the umpteenth time that week.

Derek smothered me in his arms and his warm lips covered mine. "Welcome home. I'm glad you are safe."

I held on to his shoulders. "Were you worried about me?"

"We all were." My mother opened her arms. I reluctantly let go of Derek and gave her a hug.

"It was uncomfortable," I said. "But I was never in any real danger."

"That's not what Kim told us," Esther snapped. "She said some guy chased you through a secret passage and that you came this close to either being strangled by a crazed killer or having your head blown off by one of Craig's houseguests." She pinched her index finger and thumb nearly together.

I brushed aside her remark with a flick of the wrist. "It wasn't as bad as all that."

It was but I had been hoping to avoid my mother finding out. No matter how old I got, there were still some things, like near death experiences, that it was better she didn't learn about.

"No?" Derek rolled his eyes. "Craig and Cindy also told us you nearly got your head blown off by one of their shotgun wielding houseguests."

"You talked to Craig and Cindy?" I started to pull off my coat.

Derek stopped me. "Leave it on. We're all going to the diner for lunch to celebrate your return."

"Great. I'm famished."

"I'll mind the store," Esther said. She moved behind the sales counter.

"Are you sure?" I asked.

"Yeah, yeah. Go before I change my mind."

Mom, Derek and I walked across the street to the Ruby's Diner. Tiffany LaChance, Robert LaChance's ex-wife, waitressed at the diner. "Hi, Amy." Tiffany squeezed my arm. "I'm glad to see you back and in one piece." Tiff is a buxom, green-eyed blonde several years my senior.

"You heard about my little adventure?" I unzipped my jacket and hung it on the coatrack next to the door.

"Robert told me all about it. Is it true that the police commandeered one of his vehicles to rescue you?"

"Yes, I'm afraid so."

"Well, I'm glad you're safe."

"Thanks."

Tiffany's face darkened. "Though I heard there was a death at the Usher house?"

Mom nodded briskly. "Three deaths." She held up three fingers as if to back up her claim.

Tiffany sucked in a breath through her teeth.

"Don't worry," I said. "They caught the killer." I felt a niggling in my head even as I spoke. What was it that was wrong?

"That's a relief." Tiffany led us to a booth in front and took our drink orders. Mom and Derek were going with coffee. I opted for a large strawberry milkshake with whipped cream and a cherry on top. After what I had been through, I deserved it.

Over cheeseburgers and onion rings, I felt the weight of the last few days catching up with me. I yawned repeatedly and drank black coffee from Derek's cup. Mom sat across from us.

Derek chuckled and kissed my ear. "You could use a good night's rest."

"I could use a good week's hibernation." I took another gulp of his coffee. It wasn't settling well on top of the milkshake in my gut, but I wasn't going to let that stop me. "Unfortunately, I have to go back to the Usher house."

"Whatever for?" Mom sounded incredulous. "You wouldn't catch me going back there after what happened."

"Believe me, I'd rather not. The whole point of going out there in the first place was to check on the waterfowl. I never got the chance."

"Can't somebody else do it?" asked my mom.

"Who?"

"Amy to the rescue." Derek chuckled. "I'm sure it will be fine, Barbara. The house is empty, and the culprit is behind bars."

"I suppose." Mom knotted up her napkin and tossed it on her empty plate. "But I don't have to like it."

"Neither do I," I said. "Did I tell you that weird house is chock full of trophy ducks and duck decoys?"

"No." Derek slid the check closer and laid some money atop it. "I'll have to mention that to my dad."

"Your dad?"

"Yeah, he was a duck hunter."

"A duck hunter!"

"*Was* a duck hunter. Dad is a reformed duck hunter," Derek explained. "He still has a few old decoys himself. In fact, he collects them."

"Now that you mention it," Mom said, "I've seen them up at his cottage." Mom and Ben Harlan casually dated.

"Right," Derek said. "Wait until Dad hears there's a cache of them out at the Usher house. I wonder if the owners would be interested in selling any. I know Dad would love to add to his collection."

"I'll see if I can find out," I replied. "I wonder if Ben would like to loan us a few to put on display in Birds and Bees."

"I'll ask him." Derek folded his hands on the table. "He will probably be delighted. The duck decoys have been a hobby of his for a very long time. He'll be flattered that you are interested."

"Tell him we'll take good care of them," I said.

"I'll be sure to. I don't know about the carvings in Dad's collection, but some of those decoys can be worth big money."

I tilted my head and looked at him. "Really? How big?"

Derek shrugged. "Thousands of dollars. Maybe more. I remember Dad telling me about one that sold at auction for thirty grand."

"That's an expensive hobby," quipped Mom.

"That's funny, I mean, what you say about the decoys." I gave Derek back his empty coffee cup. "You're out of coffee."

"Gee, thanks." Derek shook his head. "What's so funny about the decoys?"

"Nothing, maybe." I thought a moment before continuing. "Like I said, the Usher house is full of them. And after Jackson attacked me in Robert and Rosalie's room, I noticed that Rosalie had an old duck decoy in her open suitcase."

"You think she brought it with her?" asked Mom. "Maybe she intended to go duck hunting."

"Not a chance," I replied. "Rosalie doesn't strike me as the duck hunting type. Plus, the whole idea of using decoys is to have a flock of them in the hopes of attracting live ducks. Not one. Although…" I tapped my fingers on the table.

"Yes?" Mom urged.

"From what Robert mentioned to me, he is."

"Did you ask Rosalie about it?" Derek asked.

"I never got the chance."

"Where are Robert and Rosalie now?" Mom looked across the street toward Birds & Bees. A pair of customers were heading up the walk.

"Probably at the Ruby Lake Motor Inn. Unless they've returned to Raleigh already."

"So soon?" Mom asked.

"Can you blame them after everything that's happened?"

"I suppose not."

"If she took it from the house, technically, that's theft," Derek pointed out.

"I'll mention it to Craig. I guess I'll let him worry about that. It's his rental and they're his friends." I turned and eyed the glass case beside the cash register. It was filled with pies, other pastries and dark chocolate brownies.

"Dessert?" Derek draped his arm over my shoulder and rubbed my neck muscles.

"No. I wouldn't want you to get the wrong impression." Besides, all I really wanted was to get home.

"What impression is that?" Derek asked with a smile. "The impression that you like good food?"

"Ha-ha. Is that peach shortcake?" I pointed at the distant glass.

Mom leaned forward, squinting. "No. I believe it is apple. Shall we share a piece?"

"Peach shortcake."

Mom and Derek exchanged a troubled look.

"Are you all right, dear?" asked Mom.

I ran my teeth over my lower lip. "I'm not sure. There's something about peach shortcake, though…"

Derek gave me a push. "Come on, Amy. Let's get you home."

"Good idea." Mom slid from the booth. "Esther and I can manage the rest of the day. You should try to get some rest."

I let them drag me across the street. Something was nagging at my brain, but I couldn't quite figure out what it was.

Derek kissed me good-bye on the front porch and headed back to his office, promising to call me again in the evening to see how I was doing.

"Upstairs you go!" Mom said, taking my coat and hanging it.

Esther was ringing up a customer's seed order.

"Okay, okay. I'm going." I stopped on the first step. "You mentioned Craig and Cindy. Do you know where they're staying?"

I wanted to probe Craig some more about his houseguests. And mention the possibly purloined duck decoy.

"Why, upstairs, of course."

I frowned and glanced upward. "Upstairs?"

"They're staying in Paul's apartment."

I felt my mouth go dry. "For how long?"

"For the rest of their stay, dear. They didn't want to go back to that house. I can't blame them, can you?"

I shut my eyes for a moment to steady myself. "No. But when Craig arrived, I specifically told him that he couldn't stay in Paul's apartment. I'll go talk to him." I started moving.

Mom rushed over. "I wouldn't do that, Amy."

"Why not?"

"Because Barbara told Craig and Cindy they could stay in Paul's apartment for as long as they like!" shouted Esther from the front of the store.

"Mom!"

My mother colored and wrung her hands.

"Mom?"

"Look at the bright side," Mom stammered.

"Bright side?"

Mom nodded rapidly. "Cindy told me that the two of you were practically best friends now, sharing clothes and everything!"

Craig and Cindy would be here nearly three more weeks. Three long, long weeks.

The Usher house truly was cursed.

I started slowly up the steps. "I am going to get some sleep. Wake me up in—" I sighed. "Scratch that. I'll be down to work in the morning." I stopped once again on the second-floor landing. "Is Princess upstairs?"

"Craig and Cindy are keeping the dog with them. They felt she would be more comfortable in her own apartment."

"Right."

"Speaking of dogs, have you had a chance to consider that cat policy of yours?" Esther planted her hands on the counter and glared up at me.

"Yes." I climbed the next step. "My policy is that cats are cute and fluffy and that I am still allergic to them."

"Uh, dear..." Mom craned her neck.

"Yes?" I said wearily, as I peered over the railing.

"Never mind. It can keep."

I managed a small smile, gave an even bigger yawn, and dragged myself upstairs to bed. What this building needed was an elevator, I thought as I opened the front door to our apartment. I kicked off my shoes and went to my bedroom. I pulled the drapes shut, closed the bedroom door and fell into bed.

As I shut my eyes waiting for the sandman to overtake me, I heard strange noises, squeaks and grunts, coming from below. I couldn't quite make out what those noises were, and I didn't want to know—because Paul's apartment was down there.

* * * *

Early the next day, I was on my way back to the Usher House. While I would have preferred never setting foot in the house again, I was going to check on the ducks.

Cousin Riley was at the wheel of his pickup truck. Jane Buchman, a local veterinarian who shared an office with her father, was at the passenger side window. I was squeezed between the two of them.

"Wow." Jane pressed her nose against the glass. "This is the first time I've seen the Usher House. Dad has talked about it." Jane had generously agreed to take time away from her practice and come with me to examine the ducks to make sure they were healthy.

"He was familiar with the Ushers?" I asked as Riley pulled his truck up off the road and brought it to a stop beside the broken bridge leading to the house. The tractor, evidence of Craig's failed attempt at going for help, remained on its side in the ditch.

Jane shook her head. Her honey-blond ponytail was flicking from side to side. "His grandfather told him the story." Jane was several years younger than me.

The temperature had dipped once more, and I pulled the collar of my coat tight to my neck as I slid out of the pickup after Jane. Riley shook his head, while making *tsk-tsk*ing noises as he inspected the busted bridge. "Just like you said, Amy. Good thing I brought these planks."

Riley moved to the back of the pickup. He lowered the tailgate and began removing two-by-ten-foot pine boards from the truck bed.

"Let me give you a hand." Jane and I carried several lengths of lumber to the edge of the ditch.

"Thanks." Riley dropped a couple of boards on the ground next to the damaged bridge.

Working together, the three of us laid out a temporary but relatively sturdy-looking bridge beside the old one.

"That should do it." Riley rubbed his leather-gloved hands together. "Why don't the two of you wait on the other side while I get the truck across?"

"Good idea," I said. If the bridge collapsed, there was no point in all three of us going down with the proverbial ship. Somebody had to stay on solid ground, if only to rescue Riley.

"Yes," said Jane. "We'll guide you."

Riley climbed behind the wheel, started the engine, and ever so slowly inched his way across the makeshift bridge.

Jane and I waved our hands about, called out encouragement, and sometimes shrieked in fear as Riley drove across.

"Perfect!" I shouted as his rear wheels cleared the planks on our side.

Riley jumped out and inspected his work. "Only a couple of boards shifted." He kicked them back in place with his boot. "I'll nail a couple of braces to the underside. It ought to hold up well enough to get your van out of here, Amy."

"Thank goodness." I felt helpless without my wheels. "What about Craig's Porsche?"

"He said he wasn't in any hurry." Riley told us to climb back inside. We did, and he drove up to the house, parking behind my minivan.

Riley grabbed the twenty-pound sack of balanced diet waterfowl kibble that I'd brought from Birds & Bees out of the bed of the pickup.

Jane slung a canvas satchel over her shoulder, which contained her medical kit.

"Why don't the two of you get started?" I pulled a set of house keys from my purse. "I promised Craig I would check to make sure everything was locked up tight and that all was in order."

Craig was afraid the police might have left the water running or the stove on or the door wide open for the deer to make themselves at home.

I had heard that Jackson Canning was in the Ruby Lake Police Department jail and still not talking. His sister, Augusta, was still missing.

I was still puzzled. By what, I didn't know. I was hoping another look around the Usher House would give me closure, if not the answers that Jackson was not providing.

The police were due back out later that day to conduct a more thorough search for Augusta Canning's remains. I'd heard through Kim, who had heard through Dan, that the owners of the house were also on their way back, wanting to get a look at the damage done by Craig & Company for themselves, no doubt.

Craig had hired Cousin Riley to begin immediate repairs to the bridge, the bedroom ceiling, the outside corner of the house, and anything else that had been damaged over the course of the past few days. A glass company had been hired to repair the gun case.

Riley was our de facto town handyman, but I wasn't sure that even he could complete all the necessary repairs before the Usher House's owners arrived and began counting up their losses.

As for the Cannings personally, it wasn't the missing Augusta that bothered me so much.

It was the peach shortcake.

26

The interior of the Usher House was cool and dark.

And spooky.

"I never thought being alone in this house would be worse than spending the night in it with Craig and company," I muttered to no one but the ghosts as I wandered from room to room.

I stared at the strange portrait of Stanley Usher in the study. He didn't look happy to see me.

I avoided the root cellar and went upstairs. The hole in the ceiling of Robert and Rosalie's room didn't look too bad in the light of day.

I was confident that Riley would be able to repair it to its former glory. A little Sheetrock, a bit of spackle, and a can of paint and the ceiling would be as good as new.

If Robert's wild shot had struck me, though, all the spackle and paint in the world couldn't have put me right.

I pulled aside the curtain and looked out the window. Pressing my nose up to the glass, I spotted Riley and Jane down by the tarn, standing close to the shore. Several ducks scooted near them, no doubt attracted by the food we'd brought.

My eyes fell on the caretaker cottage. I'd never been inside. I jiggled the key ring dangling from my finger.

My curiosity got the better of me, and I decided to take a look. I had no doubt that the police had already been there and searched it thoroughly. But that peach shortcake still stuck in my mind.

The first night, when we had been served the peach shortcake, Mike Holberg had blurted out that it was better than the peach shortcake in the diner.

How had he known? When had he ever eaten the Ruby Diner's peach shortcake?

Everybody said he had never been to Ruby Lake before this trip. The peach shortcake at the diner was a seasonal dish. There was no peach shortcake at the diner this time of year. Only in the fall. Everybody in town knew that.

Had Mike Holberg lied? Had he been to Ruby Lake prior to this visit? Craig had told me that it was Mike who had told him about the Usher House.

All of that had to mean something. I just didn't know what.

The only thing I was certain of was that there were still unanswered questions regarding the murders of the Holbergs.

Although Chief Kennedy seemed content that the case was completely wrapped up, Jackson Canning's refusal to talk wasn't helping my sleep. I had awakened that morning feeling like I'd spent the night in a spinning washing machine.

I moved downstairs and went outside through the kitchen.

I crossed the muddy ground to the cottage and tried the door. It was locked.

I tried key after key in the slot, but none fit. Frustrated, I proceeded to the barn. There had to be a way into the cottage via the tunnel. As much as I loathed the idea of going back down there, it was my only hope.

Besides, Jackson was locked up. What could go wrong?

I slid open the barn door and stepped inside. The Cannings' rugged navy-blue Jeep sat in the far corner.

I went to the small workshop I had first entered the barn through the other night. I flipped on the light switch and slowly moved my eyes around the space. The pile of duck decoys that had been lying on a tarp in the corner were missing; so was the tarp.

Why?

Had the police removed them?

I moved closer and stared at the empty space, my mind searching for answers. Those decoys could have been very valuable. I had spent an hour before leaving that morning scouring the Internet. Derek had been right. The duck decoy collectors market was far larger than I would ever have imagined. The owners of the Usher House were sitting on a possible fortune in decoys.

Jackson could not have taken them. He hadn't had the time. He had chased me in the tunnel after I'd found them. And now he was in a jail cell. Could it have been Rosalie and Robert?

Had that been their goal all along? To steal the decoys, knowing that they were worth a small fortune? If Robert had been having money troubles, those decoys could have been quite a temptation.

Rosalie and Robert could have murdered his partner, Mike Holberg, erasing his debt to the man. Maybe Helen had figured out their scheme, so they'd killed her, too.

I wasn't certain. But it made sense. I needed to collect Riley and Jane, make sure the waterfowl were all right, then get back to town. Chief Kennedy needed to know about the missing decoys and their potential value.

Jackson might be behind bars, but I had a feeling there could be another killer or two on the loose.

I turned to go, but as I did, I felt a pair of strong hands tighten around my neck.

"Don't scream." The fingers pushed hard into my throat. "Not a sound or I finish you now."

The hands tightened once again, and I gagged.

"Understood?"

I nodded as best I could under the circumstances. The hands slowly slipped from my throat.

"Hello, Augusta," I said, rubbing my neck. "It's nice to see you back from the dead." I struggled to sound calm and collected. I was anything but. Fear raced through me and would not stop.

I had recognized her commanding voice as she hissed in my ear. Looking at her now, her hair stuffed up under a knit cap, bundled in a heavy black coat and corduroys with boots on her feet, I saw the danger in her green and gold eyes.

The look she gave me told me that she wasn't afraid to kill me.

"You should have stuck to your ducks, Amy. But now that you're here, you'll be my insurance policy."

"Tell me"—I inched back—"who killed Helen and Mike Holberg? Was it you or your brother? Or did each of you murder one?"

I shivered at the thought and the idea that I might be next.

Augusta tossed her head and snorted. "That idiot wouldn't hurt a fly."

"Could have fooled me." I could practically feel Jackson's hot fingers around my neck, squeezing the life out of me.

It all made sense now. When I had confronted Jackson about his sister, he had spoken of her in the present tense. "Your brother was hiding you, protecting you. You do realize he's been charged with the murders of Mike and Helen?"

Augusta moved to the workbench and picked up a long saw with wooden handle and jagged, sharklike teeth. “My brother always wanted us to go away someplace, like Alaska. Looks like he’s going to get his chance. Only he’ll spend his life in prison, if he’s lucky, and I’ll be far away.” She smiled. “Maybe I’ll send him a postcard from Juneau.”

Augusta stepped closer and waved the saw at me. “Let’s go.”

I started for the workbench. There were other tools, and all I needed was one that could fend her off until I could call for help.

Augusta darted between me and the bench. The saw slashed the air between us, barely missing my nose. “Do I have to ask you again?”

She jabbed the saw at my midsection and urged me to move.

“Where are we going?” I asked as we reached the muddy Jeep.

“None of your business.”

There were a couple of suitcases tossed in the back of the SUV, along with camping gear and a tarp. “Are all the decoys you’ve stolen under there?”

“Just shut up and get inside.”

I did as I was told. Riley and Jane were probably too far away to hear me scream, and I didn’t doubt for a second that Augusta would slit my throat given the least provocation.

She threw the saw out the window. My hands flew to the door handle.

“Uh-uh.” Augusta whipped a long-handled knife that had been stuffed against the seat cushion and jabbed it at my face.

I pulled the door closed. It’s hard to argue with a knife and win.

Augusta turned the key in the ignition, and the Jeep’s engine sprang to life.

“Tell me,” I said, “how are you planning to get out of here? The bridge is broken.”

“Nice try. I saw that guy that came with you out there laying down some boards. Nice of him. Saves me the trouble.”

“The police will catch you, Augusta. Why not turn yourself in?”

She laughed a wicked laugh. “The police think I’m dead. I plan to be long gone before they even figure out that I’m alive.”

“How did you work that out?” It didn’t sound like Augusta Canning was planning on releasing me anytime soon—not alive, at least. I decided it was best not to dwell on the thought.

“Easy. I had a change of clothes. I climbed down, left the clothes where they could be seen, knowing that anybody who saw them would assume I had fallen to my death.

“I took the path further down and went back to the cottage.”

“And from the cottage you could pass unseen into the house.”

"Usher may not have lived to enjoy his designs, but my brother and I found them useful."

"Like the duck decoys. You found out they were valuable, didn't you?"

"Yeah." Augusta smiled. "That's one thing I have to give my brother credit for. He was surfing the Internet one afternoon, killing time, and discovered a website devoted to the things.

"I couldn't believe it when he showed me how much some of the old ones were worth. I always thought the things were hideous. It turns out people will pay big bucks for them!"

"So, you stabbed Mike, left a trail to show you had fled, knowing that we would all assume you had killed yourself. Then you planned to empty the house of the decoys and disappear." I nodded as missing pieces of the puzzle fell into place. "Clever."

"I thought so."

"That seems awfully foolhardy. You might have actually died going down that cliff."

"That was nothing," Augusta boasted. "I've made trickier ascents and descents. I climb all the time. I ran a CrossFit studio for years."

"You were still taking a big risk."

"It bought me some time."

"Why kill Mike Holberg? What did he ever do to you? Did he catch you stealing the decoys?"

Augusta put the Jeep in gear and rolled slowly to the rear barn door. "Do you always talk so much? Don't move." She jumped out, rolled the door open, and climbed back inside the SUV.

I suddenly realized this was not about money and ducks. Augusta's anger came from betrayal. "Was it because he ended the affair?" I pressed. "The affair he was having with you?"

Augusta's face turned dark red. "I met Mike at my gym in Chapel Hill. After a couple of weeks, he told me he loved me." She stabbed the dashboard with the knife, leaving a deep, jagged gash in the vinyl.

I gasped.

"Yes! He promised me he was going to leave his wife." She shook her head. Spittle foamed from her lips. "Jackson was right. Men lie." She stabbed the dash once more.

I felt every muscle in my body tense.

"Jackson warned me that it was a bad idea to ask Mike to come here. I thought it would be our chance finally to spend some time together. Then he brought his stupid wife. And"—her voice rose higher in pitch—"he told me they had reconciled and were going on a second honeymoon as soon as they left here!"

"So, you decided that if you couldn't have him, nobody could, either."

Augusta sneered. "Jackson panicked. I told him to leave everything to me. You know what my brother's problem is?" She didn't wait for an answer. "He's too skittish. Always has been. Always will be."

Her mouth turned down. "Mike was rich. He said he'd take care of me. Of both of us. Me and Jackson. My brother's never been much good at anything."

"But Mike changed his mind."

"He lied. But now I'll have enough money to take care of myself." Augusta blew out an angry breath through her nostrils. "They always lie!" She slashed again and again.

My mouth went dry, and my heart was practically bursting out of my chest. "I know how you feel. Craig is my ex-boyfriend. He cheated on me. He lied to me, too," I managed to say.

"Did he go back to his wife?"

"No," I admitted. "But I understand what it feels like to be betrayed." I spoke softly, forcing myself to speak in a steady, even tone. "Tell me about it."

"There's nothing to tell!" she snarled and stepped on the accelerator. The knife slipped from her fingers and clattered to the floorboard. We surged forward. My spine pressed against the hard back of the seat.

The Jeep arced around the corner of the house, bouncing wildly across the uneven ground. I clutched the armrest with one hand and the dashboard with the other.

"Why kill Helen, too?" I shouted as we passed the front of the house and started quickly down the gravel drive. Small piles of dirty snow lay melting along the edges. "With Mike dead there was no reason to be jealous of her."

"She was pathetic. I don't know what he ever saw in that woman."

"How did you get her down to the cellar with no one noticing?"

"That was easy. I snuck into her room when the rest of you were busy downstairs." Augusta giggled madly. "Boy, was she surprised to see me. She thought I was a ghost!"

"I'll bet." I felt my arms grow cold at the image Augusta painted.

"I told Helen I had been hiding because the real killer was on the loose. I told her there was evidence in the cellar that would prove who really killed her husband."

"And once you had her down there, you forced her to drink the poisoned tea."

"She put up a fight, but nothing I couldn't handle."

"You murdered her out of nothing more than spite. You've lost everything now. Mike, your brother. Give up, Augusta. It's over."

"It's never over!" Augusta's hands tightened on the wheel, and her eyes bulged. I was making her crazy mad.

But that was the idea.

I wanted her to do something stupid.

As long as that something stupid did not involve stabbing me.

"You can't run from the police, and there's no escaping what you've done. Stop the truck."

"SHUT UP!" She stomped on the gas.

"Stop!" I screamed. "You're going to run over Riley!"

"Who cares?"

I leaned across the seat and pressed on the horn. I twisted the steering wheel, and Augusta fought with me for control.

I lost.

Riley, who had been reassembling the makeshift bridge, looked up.

"Riley! Look out!" I hollered out the window and waved my arms frantically.

Riley looked up and his mouth fell open. He held up his arms and yelled for us to stop. But Augusta was not listening. She raced on.

"The boards, Riley! The boards!" I shouted and pointed at the lumber spanning the ditch.

We were only a few seconds from Riley's temporary bridge now. I saw understanding come to Riley's face. He kicked at the boards, scattering several of them.

Augusta did not stop.

"Stop, Augusta!" I pleaded. "We aren't going to make it!"

She wasn't listening. The Jeep's tires hit the boards on the right side, but the left side found only air.

In a blur, we went tumbling over into the ditch. My teeth rattled, and my arms, legs, and head bounced around the compartment. When I could see clearly, I was lying sideways atop Augusta.

Augusta wasn't moving any more than the Jeep was, although the front wheels were still spinning madly.

Riley rushed to the beached SUV and stared at me through the cracked windshield. "You okay, Amy?"

I closed my eyes and sighed.

Riley pulled me out as Jane raced over. I tottered dizzily. The earth seemed to be spinning under my feet. Duck decoys had spilled from the rear of the Jeep and were scattered all over the ditch. Riley braced his left arm under my shoulder to keep me from falling back down. With his right hand, he picked up a wooden mallard lying at his feet.

"Amy! Are you hurt?" Jane asked breathlessly. Her hands went to my face. Fingers poked my flesh. I hardly noticed. "What happened, Riley?"

"I think Cousin Amy's run *afoul* of another murderer," Riley answered with a grin.

My brow shot up like a busted window shade. "Riley made a funny," I said.

And then I fainted.

27

I felt a warm pair of lips on my forehead and opened my eyes. "Derek."

He grinned. "You must be okay. You didn't call me Dirk."

I blushed and forced myself up on my elbows. "I'm in the hospital?" I was in a small, sterile room with two beds. The second bed was empty.

"Riley said you fainted," said my mother, rising from a chair near the window. "We were worried about you."

"It is standard procedure," Esther explained. She hovered next to the bed holding a white plastic water pitcher. "You can leave as soon as the doctor checks you out." She pushed the pitcher toward me. "You want some ice water?"

"No, thank you, Esther." I clutched Derek's hand.

"Where is Cousin Riley?"

"He went back up to the Usher House with the police. Jerry's up there now gathering evidence. Riley's making repairs."

"What about Augusta, is she…"

"No." Derek squeezed my fingers. "She's a little busted up. She's a couple doors down."

I tensed.

"Don't worry. Jerry's got his men keeping an eye on her."

"It had better be a close eye. That woman is smart. And strong."

I explained how she had managed to climb down the cliff, leaving bright clothing exposed in the rocks, fooling us all into thinking she was dead.

"She will have to be more than clever to get out of the mess she's gotten herself into now." Mom pulled open the curtains. The sun was shining.

"Chief Kennedy is still holding Jackson. He might not have murdered the Holbergs, but he is an accessory."

"Not to mention he tried to kill me."

"Trust me, I'll never forget that." Derek sat on the edge of the bed and took my hand in his. "Augusta switched the license plate on the Jeep with that on Craig's Porsche just to confuse matters. I guess she figured she'd be long gone, probably to Canada, before anyone realized she was alive and on the run."

"I thought Augusta and Jackson seemed a little creepy when we met them," Kim said. "Don't you remember me telling you so, Amy?"

I remembered her saying no such thing. In fact, I remembered her telling me that she thought they made a cute couple. But there was no point in putting her on the spot.

"I guess. How long was I asleep?" I remembered waking up in the truck as Riley drove like a bat out of hell for town, but I couldn't remember anything about being brought into the ER.

"A couple of hours," Mom answered, flying into the room. "Your vital signs were stable, and you've only got a couple of minor gashes and bruises."

"How is Dan?" I asked, gladly accepting the chocolate bar my mother had brought me from the vending machine in the waiting room.

"You can ask him yourself," Kim said. "He's on guard duty down the hall."

"So, he's as good as new?"

"Yep, never better." Kim's eyes fell. "I was worried, though, when we first found him in the cellar."

I smiled. "What about the waterfowl out at the tarn?"

"Jane Buchman said to tell you that the ducks are going to be fine." Esther supplied the answer. "She has agreed to look in on the waterfowl up at the Usher House every couple of days for the next week.

"She also said to tell you that she agreed with your theory about them merely being fed a lot of junk by Craig and Cindy." Mom peeled back the candy bar wrapper for me, and I took a nibble. "She went to the biergarten and set the two of them straight in no uncertain terms."

Derek stood. "Since you seem to be doing fine now, I'll go look for the doctor and see about checking you out." He leaned over and kissed me on the lips.

"Thanks." I watched him go with a pang in my heart. I'd missed him the past couple of days.

Esther poured herself a glass of water and thumped down in a chair that she had pushed up next to my bed. "Since we're all here—"

I furrowed my brow. "'All' who?"

"All us investors in Birds and Bees."

I blinked. “Aunt Betty isn’t here.”

“Your Aunt Betty is a flake, if you don’t mind my saying.”

Married three times, scads of pets, two goofy but lovable children…I shrugged. Esther wasn’t wholly wrong.

“Besides, she’s your mom’s sister, she’ll go along with whatever she votes.”

I looked at my mother and Kim for an explanation as to what Esther the Pester was blabbering about but got no answers. “Votes on what?”

Kim went to the window and found something apparently fascinating to look at outdoors. Mom began rearranging a vase holding a colorful bouquet of flowers that had Derek’s name on it as the sender.

Esther took a big gulp of water and slammed the glass back down on the built-in bedside table. “An investor should not have to pay rent any longer.”

My mouth fell open as I stared at Esther. “Are you joking?”

Esther stared back, her hands folded in the lap of her flower print dress.

“Mom, is she joking?”

“Sorry, dear.” Mom carried the vase to the bathroom. I heard the sound of running water.

“Esther,” I began, forcing myself to remain calm. I was already in a hospital, so having a stroke or a heart attack or bursting a blood vessel might not have proven fatal, but still… “Esther,” I began again, “you are an investor in Birds and Bees. And I am very, very grateful for your investment and your work. But,” I said firmly, “you are not an investor in my house. You must pay rent.”

Esther thrust her chin out. “Let’s put it to a vote.”

“A vote!” I shrilled. The chocolate bar slid under the covers. “We most definitely are not putting it to a vote.” The machinery at my bedside squawked.

“I vote yes.” Esther raised her right hand. “Barbara?”

Mom looked like she’d been caught in a vise. Her lips moved from side to side. Slowly, her hand went up.

“Mom!”

“Sorry, dear,” she mumbled, eyes on the linoleum floor, not daring to look me in the eye.

“Me, too,” Kim replied, her back to me.

“What?” I gasped. I looked from my mother, to Kim to Esther.

The Pester smiled victoriously.

“What is it, blackmail?” I narrowed my eyes at her. “You’ve got something on them, don’t you?”

Esther tilted her head, and the shadow of a smile crossed her face. "I don't know what you are talking about."

"Well." I turned on my side and winced in pain. "It isn't going to work. Vote or no vote, you have to pay rent."

"Oh, come on, Amy," Kim wheedled. "Let Esther stay for free. What's it gonna hurt?"

"What's it going to hurt?" I stared at my best friend in disbelief. "It is going to hurt my ability to meet my mortgage, that's what it's going to hurt."

Esther tapped me on the shoulder, her sharp nail digging into my skin through the thin pale blue hospital gown. "And I'd like a cat."

"You've got a cat," I snarled. The complicated machine I was hooked to begin beeping more shrilly.

"If a tree falls in the forest…" was Esther's vague reply. I smelled peppermint candy on her breath.

"Watch your blood pressure, dear," Mom cautioned.

A primly dressed nurse poked her head in the room and scolded me. She hit some buttons, stopping the horrible noise.

I pulled the covers up to my chest. Where was Derek? When could I get out of this hospital? Where had they stuck me? In the loony bin?

"You know I'm allergic to cats, Esther."

Was I overmedicated? On some psychedelic drug?

Esther cackled. "Ha!"

I looked down my nose at her. Maybe I was still unconscious, having a dream. A nightmare. Either that or the world had gone mad.

"Tell her, Barbara." Esther looked at my mother.

"Well…" Mom worried her fingers. "Actually, dear…" Her voice faded.

"You are not allergic to cats!" Esther pointed her finger at me and wagged it from side to side. She had a big grin on her face.

A chill crept over my skin, and a companion coldness encompassed my heart. "What do you mean, I am not allergic to cats? Of course I'm allergic to cats!" I laughed and shook my head. "Now I know I'm dreaming."

"I'm afraid Esther's right, Amy." That was Kim, hovering near the window.

I turned to my mom for support and answers. "Mom?"

"Yes?"

"Would you mind setting these two clowns straight?"

Mom sighed. "Amy, you are not allergic to cats."

"You see, I told you I—" I froze. "Wait. What?"

"You aren't allergic to pussycats," Esther replied.

Mom nodded.

"I've always been allergic to cats. Big cats, little cats, furry cats, Siamese cats! Come on, guys. Enough with the jokes."

Mom took my hand. "You were never allergic, dear. You only thought you were."

"I had allergies. I remember. I would sneeze and sneeze and sneeze until my nose and throat hurt and my head pounded."

"But not to cats," Mom answered crisply.

"What was I allergic to?'

"Goldenrod," explained Mom.

"What? We didn't have goldenrod."

"Yes, we did. I tried to tell you it was the goldenrod outside your bedroom window. I pulled it from the flower beds due to your allergy."

"I thought Goldenrod was the name of the cat," I mumbled, tucking my chin into my neck.

"What, dear?"

"I said I thought Goldenrod was the name of that orange tabby the neighbors had."

Kim and Esther hooted.

"It wasn't the cat?" My face felt hot and clammy. My palms were sweating profusely.

Mom shook her head from side to side. "It wasn't the cat."

"Why didn't you tell me, Mom?"

"Believe me, your father and I tried. Many, many times." She started to smile. "You were a willful child."

"You mean stubborn." Esther had to put her two cents in.

My mother shrugged a shoulder.

"So, I'm not allergic to cats…"

"No, dear."

I scratched the side of my head. "How about that."

"Yeah." Esther grinned with satisfaction. "How about that."

I leaned my head against my pillow, feeling dizzy. Reality seemed to have pulled the rug out from under me.

Again.

"How are you feeling?" Mom asked. "You look pale."

"Every muscle in my body is stiff and sore." I pressed my fingers into my lower back. "I feel like I've gone through the heavy-duty cycle of the washing machine."

Not to mention that my head was now spinning with this latest revelation.

"I've got just what you need." Kim dove into her big purse and pulled out a tube of cream. "Try this. It's perfect for aches and pains."

"Are you sure? What is it?" There was no label on the squeeze tube.

"An all-natural product I get made up at a lotions and potions boutique at the mall in Charlotte."

"Fine." I squirted some into my hand and rubbed it on my arms.

"Here, let me help you." Kim snatched the tube and began applying a generous amount to my arms.

"Thanks." I squeezed my eyes shut as she smeared some over my face.

"All done." Kim wiped her hands on the towel. "Here." She tossed me the tube. "You can keep this."

"Thanks again." I took a whiff. "Smells good." I sniffed my forearm. "Smells like coconut."

"Yeah, right?" Kim giggled. "Kind of *juicy* even."

"I guess so. How long does it take to work?"

"Oh, I shouldn't imagine it will take too long." Kim smiled enigmatically, waved, and departed.

"What's with her?" I asked Mom.

Esther lifted up on her toes, put her hand to my mother's ear, and whispered. "Is it me or is Amy turning orange?"

"What's that?" I leaned closer. "What did you say?"

Mom nodded once and shot Esther a warning look. "Nothing, dear."

I threw back the covers and leapt from the bed, ignoring the protesting monitoring devices. My bare feet slapped the cold tile as I raced to the tiny, windowless bathroom. I hit the light switch. Blinded but only momentarily.

Too bad it hadn't been permanently.

Because staring back at me from the plain mirror above the stainless-steel sink was a grimacing orange monstrosity.

That's right.

Pumpkinhead Simms was back.

About the Author

In addition to writing the Bird Lover's mystery series, **J.R. Ripley** is the critically acclaimed author of the Maggie Miller mysteries and the Kitty Karlyle mysteries (written as Marie Celine) among other works. J.R. is a member of the American Birding Association, the American Bird Conservancy, and is an Audubon Ambassador with the National Audubon Society. Before becoming a full-time author, J.R. worked at a multitude of jobs including: archaeologist, cook, factory worker, copywriter, technical writer, editor, musician, entrepreneur and window washer. You may visit jrripley.net. for more information or visit J.R. on Facebook at facebook.com/jrripley.

How The Finch
Stole Christmas
A Bird Lover's
Mystery
LYRICAL
UNDERGROUND
J.R. RIPLEY

CHICKADEE
CHICKADEE
BANG
BANG
A Bird Lover's
Mystery
J.R. RIPLEY

Printed in the United States
by Baker & Taylor Publisher Services